UNDERWATER

Also by Julia McDermott

Make That Deux

JULIA McDERMOTT

UNDERWATER

fTHOMAS & MERCER

Published by Thomas & Mercer, Seattle

www.apub.com

Amazon, the Amazon logo, and Thomas & Mercer are trademarks of Amazon.com, Inc., or its affiliates.

ISBN-13: 9781477826201
ISBN-10: 1477826203

Cover design by Scott Barrie

Library of Congress Control Number: 2014941532

Printed in the United States of America

For my mother,
Sally

Table of Contents

Her first memory was of being underwater, of moving her arms and legs and struggling to push herself up to the surface. Her eyes were open and she could see the world above her, blurry and unreachable. The force of the water kept her down and away from the dry world. Panicking, she kicked and pulled and held her breath. Then she felt her legs going limp, her arms getting tired, and her resolve fading. Her strength was gone. The world and its comforts were close. Yet she couldn't break through the cold, transparent ceiling of water.

She couldn't breathe.

Full of terror, she saw a solitary figure staring down at her, smiling. Her mother? She couldn't tell. It was a woman with blonde hair and colorless eyes. The woman motioned to her, encouraging her.

She felt her lungs burning and saw a trail of blood floating up next to her. Then she felt the water force her body farther and farther down.

1

The Bluff

Candace Morgan's mind wouldn't stop racing.

Eyes closed and head resting on a spa pillow, she exhaled, trying to focus on her senses as the therapist finished peeling off her mask. The dim lighting, soft music, and faint citrus fragrance were intended to soothe, but Candace found the odor annoying and the atmosphere distracting. She wiggled her fingers as the woman smoothed her forehead and temples with a light, practiced touch.

"I hope you enjoyed your facial. Take your time and I'll see you out front when you're ready," the therapist said, exiting the room and closing the door quietly behind her.

Candace dressed and checked her cell phone for messages, hoping to see no more from her brother, Monty. There were none—good. She certainly wasn't going to return his earlier call, and she would wait before sending him yet another email. She studied herself in the mirror, then shook her honey-blonde, shoulder-length hair and checked the roots. It was almost time for a coloring appointment with her stylist.

Emerging from the treatment room a few minutes later, Candace paid for her service, left the day spa, and unlocked her Mercedes. Just as she was fastening her seat belt, her phone buzzed. She glanced at the screen. It was Monty.

Staring straight ahead, she gripped the steering wheel. What could he want now? She'd just signed another check for twenty thousand dollars, and she was getting fed up. This pattern was one she needed to halt once and for all. But how?

She let the phone go to voicemail, wondering if he'd leave her another message or just hang up and expect her to call back. She needed to talk to David, her personal financial counselor. Her money man. She and David talked several times a week about how her investments were doing. David also handled her credit cards and other obligations and, when asked, offered his financial advice. He had warned her repeatedly about investing in her brother's real estate venture. For some reason, she hadn't listened to him, and she had let Monty suck her into his mess.

At the time, the real estate market was hot, and prices had been increasing for a decade. Candace was still reveling in the success of the company she'd founded before her twenty-ninth birthday, back in 1999. How had her life become what it was now, despite the fortune that she had worked so hard to build? No one except David knew exactly how much money she had or what her assets were worth. Monty would probably love to know, and his guess of eighty million wasn't too far off. He thought that she had more money than she could ever spend. But Candace knew better. She didn't think it was all that much, not compared with her friends: the beautiful and super-wealthy, some of them minor celebrities.

Her iPhone vibrated, signaling an email message. Candace looked down and saw it was from David. Stopping for a red light a few seconds later, she clicked on the message, scrolling down to read the one he had forwarded to her first:

From: Monty Carawan <monty.carawan86@me.com>
Sent: Tuesday, March 9, 2010 9:34 AM EST
To: David Shepherd <david.shepherd@efp.com>
Subject: Question

David,
I thought I had been clear with you at our recent meeting. We have nothing to talk about until you answer my question. What amount will your client settle for upon the sale of the property?

Rest assured that if I do not get a satisfactory answer within the week, I will take steps that will be both devastating to your client, and public.

Monty Carawan

Alarmed, Candace read David's message:

From: David Shepherd <david.shepherd@efp.com>
Sent: Tuesday, March 9, 2010 9:58 AM EST
To: Candace Morgan <candace.morgan@slimz.org>
Subject: FW: Question

Candace:
See below. I don't know how to assess it, other than he seems to be very confused. You have no risk on the $845,000 you've invested so far, as I believe there is sufficient equity to cover it upon eventual sale of the

property. Though it's not fully drawn yet, the $500,000 home equity loan you cosigned is another matter.

My take is that he is trying to bully you into prematurely writing off your investment and the monies owed.

Let me know your thoughts.

David K. Shepherd
Elite Financial Planning
4900 Capstone Road
Atlanta, GA 30305
www.efp.com

Candace dialed David's number.

"David Shep—"

"David. *What the fuck?*"

"Candace, calm—"

"I am calm, David. What in the *fuck* is Monty doing? 'Devastating' and 'public?'"

"This isn't the first—"

"I know it isn't the first time he's threatened me, David, but I'm starting to worry. What the hell happened during your meeting with him on Friday?"

"Well, he went nuts," said David. "I brought up all of your concerns, but he wouldn't answer any of my questions. Then he got belligerent and demanded to know what amount you would take to erase everything."

"What do you mean, 'belligerent?'"

"He spouted profanities and threatened me physically. I had to call security."

"Are you *kidding* me?"

"I wish. He insisted that I give him an amount to settle all his debts to you, since he knows he won't get anywhere near his asking price."

"David, you know I'm not about to agree to that."

"I know, and I wouldn't counsel you to. Before the meeting, I sent him a list of issues, copying you. He wrote me back Thursday night. I forwarded it to you. I also left you a voicemail—"

"I didn't listen to it. I saw your email to him, but I didn't have time to look at his response. Read it to me now."

"Let me pull it up." After a short pause, David continued, "Okay, here it is: 'Monty: Six weeks ago, you agreed to provide Candace with your complete personal financial information, an updated overall construction budget, past vendor receipts on the renovation, and ongoing monthly progress reports. You have not complied with this as of yet, so—'"

"Skip to the list," ordered Candace.

"'Number One: You did not earn any income during the past three years—'"

"What else is new? Sorry, David, go on."

"'During the past three years, so I don't understand your basis for this year's projected income.' He answered, and I quote: 'It is true that I did not claim any income for 2007, 2008, and 2009. My projected income for this year is based on my plan to get a job with an Internet company that is about to launch on the West Coast. I will of course be working from my home.'"

"*What* fucking Internet company?"

"I don't know. He didn't mention it at the meeting."

"Find out. And google it. I want verification, for once."

"'Number Two: In addition to Candace's investment of six hundred thousand dollars, you owe her another two hundred and forty-five thousand dollars—'"

"I know this, David."

"'You should have one hundred thousand dollars available to draw on the home equity line, so why are you asking her for another one-hundred-thousand-dollar loan?'"

"*What?*"

"Just wait," said David. "Here's his response: 'We have closer to eighty-five thousand dollars available to draw, but we will not do so or move forward with the renovation until we receive an additional hundred from Candace. The eighty-five thousand is a cushion, a safeguard which we will not use.'"

Candace gritted her teeth. "Go on."

"'Number Three: Based on your lack of repayment so far, I cannot recommend that she make an additional loan. Given your unstable financial position and unreliable track record, you have put her investment in the property at risk.'"

"And he said?"

"'I disagree about her investment being at risk. We do not plan to get behind on payments to the bank, so we are not in danger of losing the home. Based on comparable sales, listings in the neighborhood will sell for over two and a half million. As you know, our plan is to sell the house, pay all creditors including Candace—'"

"Damn right."

"'—and buy another home with the profit we will make.'"

"He's delusional. I don't know why I ever subscribed to such fantasy."

"'Number Four: Whether Candace agrees to an additional loan or not, we need an updated construction budget, monthly progress reports on the project, and all vendor receipts through today and in the future.'"

"Good."

"And he responded: 'If you think that I am going to provide any such documentation or receipts, you are dreaming. This is my project and I will carry it out with no further harassment from you or your client.'"

Candace's stomach dropped. Her voice rose. "David, what can I *do*?"

"Here's a solution. You take it over and get the renovation done yourself. He and Helen move to a rental they can afford on her salary. You get a new general contractor, complete the work, and sell the place yourself."

"I don't want to do that. You know I can't throw them out. What about the baby?"

"She'll survive, Candace. They all will. Helen, at least, will see to that."

"But I don't want to take it over. I just want my money."

"Well, you should get it back, ultimately. It just depends on how long you're willing to wait. If they can't sell it, or won't, and if they don't keep up with the all the payments—"

"Which they won't be able to, on her salary."

"If they don't," continued David, "then we'll buy the note from the bank, foreclose on the property, sell it, and recoup your investment."

"Foreclosure? I can't do that to them."

"It's not the ideal solution, but effectively the result would be the same for you. And with the epidemic of foreclosures now, the stigma's not the same as it's been in the past."

"But their credit will be ruined. For years."

"Yes, but then they'll be forced to live on only what they can afford, without the benefit of credit. Live within their means, as you've said they ought to do. I don't mean to be harsh about it, but it may be the best thing for them. It would be the best thing for you. You know if this were anyone else, purely a business deal, you wouldn't hesitate—"

"You're right. I wouldn't. But I let myself get sucked to this deal at a weak moment. Back when they bought the house, my portfolio was up, and I just let Monty talk me into it, damn it." *No—guilt me into it.*

"That was then, though. Your stocks are lower now, and more important, the real estate market is way down. Especially the high-end segment."

Candace grimaced. "Even before it crashed, Monty was an idiot to think he could ever sell the house for over three times what he paid. I knew that then, and so did you. But I didn't listen."

"That's in the past. You've been extremely generous to him, I'd say, going deep into your pocket to allow him to get into it, with only a two-hundred-thousand-dollar mortgage. Gifting them twelve thousand apiece, every year since. Cosigning the home equity loan last fall, then making the additional loans."

"I didn't feel I had much choice, after things got so out of control."

"Well, you've gotten in deep, but I don't really understand why. I know he's your brother, and with your parents gone, you've tried to help him. But in all truth, at least in this case, he's made some very bad choices."

"He's a master manipulator. If he would just work half as hard at some job—any job—as he has at getting other people to support him, he'd be fine. I don't see how Helen has any respect for him. I hate to think what their marriage is like."

"In any case, we need to make a decision going forward, and I'm counseling you to decline this last hundred thousand. Let them draw down the eighty-five they have left, if they must."

"I certainly don't want to shell out another hundred. But let's go back to today's email from him. That threat."

"Candace, I think he's bluffing. He's just being a bully. Besides, what can he really do to you?"

She paused. "I don't know. I hate to imagine what he could do online."

"Well, I have no idea how his brain works, but I do believe it's all bluster, bravado, and more manipulation. If he did put anything online, who's going to see it? No one that's important to you would take any rumor on the Internet or on social media seriously. Anything he said would reflect badly only on him. You're a well-known CEO and a public persona. A decades-old story or reference would be quickly discarded and buried under new scandals."

"Coming from my own brother, though, it could bubble up into a major embarrassment, especially during a slow news cycle. What could something like that do to my stock price?"

"Candace, relax. I really don't think it's going to happen. He's just trying to scare you, I promise."

"Logically, I agree with you. But I'm worried. Don't send him any more emails. I'm not going to contact him, either. He'll figure out he's not getting the money."

"Got it. Anything else?"

"No. Thanks for your thoughts, David. We'll talk later."

Candace clicked off the phone and let out a deep breath. At the next red light, she checked her appearance in the rearview mirror. She shook her head slightly, inspected her teeth, and flinched at a short honk when the light changed. Accelerating, she glanced at the dashboard clock. She was going to be late to the luncheon at the museum in Midtown.

Without warning, her mind switched to an image of herself as an overweight teenager of twenty-plus years ago. Her stomach clenched as she remembered her constant fear of catching her reflection in a mirror. She had graduated high school a year early, but no funds were available for college—her parents' bleak financial situation had been frustrating, at best. In an indirect way, it had been the cause of everything. Stuck at home, she had found a job as a clerk at a travel agency and started saving her money.

But that fall, her Aunt Stella died and left her an inheritance to attend her alma mater up north, the elite Wynnton College. Over the next several months, Candace starved herself down to a size six; ever since, she had maintained her figure through a newfound discipline in eating habits and exercise. At Wynnton, she majored in marketing, and just after graduation, she married her boyfriend, Ted Morgan, and moved to his hometown of Dallas.

There she began her career on the sales floor at the now-defunct women's apparel store A Clothes Mind. She'd never understood the rationale behind the last word—she would have chosen the less objectionable *Mine*. Over the next few years, she was promoted to assistant buyer, then buyer—she was even awarded a bonus for coming up with the new slogan: "A Clothes Mind: Your Wardrobe Gold Mine." No matter her successes, though, her in-laws denigrated her for stooping to work in retail, for hanging up (and marking down) trendy women's fashions. Meanwhile, Ted studied law at SMU on his father's dime.

After seven years, they separated and put their posh Highland Park home on the market. Once the divorce was final, Ted married a willowy six-foot-tall, twenty-something graduate of SMU. While Candace was out busting her butt working retail and developing a business idea that would yield her a fortune, Ted had been cheating on her with that blonde bitch.

What a different life she lived now. She owned a country home in the south of France but spent most of her time in her apartment on the Upper East Side of Manhattan, with occasional visits to Atlanta. She braked quickly to avoid a Lexus SUV that cut her off on Roswell Road. The woman driving it was a thirty-something Buckhead mom, the target customer for the product Candace had invented during a simmering hot Texas summer. The product that had made her a millionaire.

She had thought her idea so obvious that she almost immediately dismissed it. It was an undergarment that provided the benefits of panty hose with none of the drawbacks. It didn't have feet and it didn't roll up, so it stayed in place: it was the first shapewear product. It erased VPL—Visible Panty Line—something previously avoided only by wearing a thong. Candace knew her invention was revolutionary and a potential gold mine. She kept her idea to herself because she didn't want to have to defend it to naysayers. Without telling anyone, she had a prototype made and started pitching it to textile factory owners in North Carolina. After a few months, one of them took a chance on her after his wife convinced him that it was marvelous, and that it would take off.

Of course, it had, but not without Candace's hard work. She patented her invention and studied the psychology of branding. She discovered that the *z* sound connotes pleasure, speed of gratification, and luxury, then selected a one syllable descriptive name using the sound and letter. She sent a batch of prototypes to a popular national talk show host, who loved it and chose it as her favorite product of the year.

Then orders flew in and her company became famous almost overnight. Over a decade later, the brand name SlimZ was as much a part of the English language as Kleenex. The company she founded when she moved back to Atlanta had added several product lines over the years. As CEO, her basic principles guided all of her ninety-nine mostly female employees: trust your instincts, ask for feedback, keep emotion at bay, and be willing to change—principles that Candace applied so well in business, but that she hadn't fully adopted regarding Monty.

Her phone buzzed again. She looked at the screen and clicked it on. "Rob?"

"Hello, darling. How's your day going?"

"Not well. It's Monty again."

"What's he done now?"

"He went crazy last Friday with David, and today he threatened me in an email. I'm going to forward it to you."

"Do. But don't worry. He can't do anything to you—I won't let him."

"David says it's all bluster, that he's just trying to bully me."

"Don't let him succeed. Where are you right now?"

"On the way to Midtown. I'm late for a luncheon."

"Then what?"

"Meeting at the office around three, or when I get there."

"How about we meet for cocktails, then dinner?"

"That could work," Candace said while racing to make it through a yellow light. "Where?"

"Better yet, let's don't meet. I'll pick you up at the condo. Shall we say six?"

"Six thirty. Where are we going?"

"Somewhere lovely. I want to surprise you. Let me."

"If you insist. See you then, Rob."

After dropping off her car with the museum's valet, Candace hurried into the building and found her way to the table reserved for the board. Conversation hummed as waiters hurried to serve entrees and refill beverages. The program hadn't begun yet.

Almost two hours later, her obligation completed, Candace took Peachtree Road to her company's office in Buckhead. She dialed the number of her assistant, Jessica Copeland.

"Yes, Candace?"

"Hello, Jess. Is everything on track for the meeting this afternoon?"

"All except for Darlene. She had to take her son in for an emergency appendectomy this morning."

"Oh my God. Is he going to be all right?"

"We think so—"

"Good. I'm assuming all the other department heads are in?"

"I believe so."

"Well, make sure. Also, have you bought my ticket for New York yet?"

"I'm working on it."

"Don't. I may change the date. I'm not certain yet. Do you know what hospital Darlene's son is in?"

"I think he's at Scottish Rite."

"Find out, then send a bouquet with a get-well wish from me."

"Of course. Anything else?"

"Not at the moment. See you in a bit."

• • •

That evening, wearing a dark blue cocktail dress that bared one sexy shoulder, Candace opened the door of her luxury penthouse condominium at exactly six thirty. She had appreciated Rob's punctuality when their relationship began many years ago, as business associates only. When it developed into friendship, and eventually, romance, she valued it even more.

"My love," he said. He kissed her, running a finger from her bare shoulder down the length of her arm.

"I need a drink, Rob. But I'm eager to find out where you're taking me. You know I'm not fond of surprises."

"You'll be fond of this one. I promise," he said, smiling. "But I like you eager."

Candace laughed. Sometimes she felt a little bewildered that this tall, attentive, and gorgeous man wanted her—she couldn't imagine such a thing when she was young—and that he was in love with her. "And I *expect* you eager. There's a single malt over there waiting for you, *mon amour*." She led the way to the mirrored bar, where French crystal sparkled and an array of spirits beckoned. "I'll get some ice."

"Martini with a twist?" he asked, reaching for a bottle of Grey Goose.

"Perfect," she called from the kitchen.

A few minutes later, the two sat opposite each other, drinks in hand, in the living room. One huge glass wall offered a splendid view of the lighted cityscape below.

"Where are we going? Tell me now."

"It's a new spot. You've not heard of it."

Candace crossed her legs, impatient now. "How do you know?"

"It's just opened. Trust me. You'll approve."

She gave him a look. "So, did you read the emails?"

He nodded. "Not to worry."

"How can you say that, Rob? I think I need to take any threat from him seriously."

"That's just what Monty would like. You can't keep giving him what he wants—"

"We've been over this before, and you know more about him than anyone, even David, probably—"

"Let's just examine it, then. Monty can't do anything public to you. At least, nothing that would have any consequence or hurt you in any way."

"That's what David said. But he could definitely embarrass me—"

"Worst case, he could. But what can he say that's true, that isn't already out there? You know what people see when they google you. The accident—"

"It was so long ago." She shook her head and shuddered.

"Ages. You dealt with it back then, and there's nothing new, legally or otherwise."

"But Monty could say whatever he wants to about it. He could spin it, maybe twist the facts around. Who knows who'll believe him? He won't go get a job, but he'll sit at his computer all day and fabricate lies."

"Hasn't he always been a loose cannon? Not just since the day your mum died, but all his life?"

"Yes, he's always lied. He lies so much that he believes whatever he says to be the truth."

"I know, love." Rob took another sip of Scotch. "Just remember, you've *nothing* to feel guilty over."

Candace sipped her martini, brows furrowed. "It's just . . . I've always wondered what would have happened if I had—if I hadn't—"

"Darling, don't torture yourself. There was nothing you could have done."

However, Candace believed there was, but it had been easier to push away the painful memory than to think about it. She dropped her eyes and took a deep breath. She rarely shed tears, and remembering the event now didn't summon them.

"Life is so unpredictable," Rob continued. "Your world can change in one day. Mine did, the day my father was diagnosed with a brain tumor."

"What a horrible day."

He cocked his head to one side. "But it's what happened, and six months later, he was gone." He put down his rocks glass, drained of liquid. "But enough about the past. Let's focus on the present. On tonight."

"I'm hungry, Rob."

"Then let's not tarry any longer. Finish your drink. The owner is holding our table."

"Okay. Let me go to the 'loo' first, as you call it," said Candace. "I hope I'll like your new restaurant."

"You will, I guarantee it," he said while rising.

2

Lying

As the sky darkened with the threat of a thunderstorm, Helen Carawan pulled her Volvo sedan onto a cracked driveway and parked at the end, in front of the property's small guest cottage. The detached garage that Monty wanted to have constructed next to the cottage was still in the planning stages, ground unbroken. Helen grabbed her purse and briefcase, unbuckled her two-and-a-half-year-old daughter from her car seat, and hastened to the door with the child in her arms as the first fat drops of rain fell.

"Mommy! I getting wet!" exclaimed Adele, laughing.

"It's okay," Helen said, unsmiling and feeling exhausted. Finding the door of the cottage locked, she rapped on it loudly. "Monty!"

A trim, fit man of just under six feet tall with a full head of blond hair unlocked the door and opened it. "You have a key," Monty grumbled, turning away.

"My hands were full! And we were getting rained on," said Helen. She put Adele down and dropped her bag and case. "Thanks."

He gave her a backward glance as if to make sure no sarcasm was intended, then sat down at his desk and laptop in a corner of the small living area.

"Hi, Daddy! What're you doing?"

He let out an irritated sigh. Helen shivered, hoping he would choose to be silent. She looked down at Adele. "Don't bother Daddy, sweetie."

Adele looked up at her mother. "But he's not busy!"

"Yes, he is. Come on, follow Mommy." Helen walked through the room to the cottage's one bedroom with Adele toddling behind. Shutting the door behind her, Helen began to change her clothes as her daughter entertained herself in front of a full-length mirror.

"Why were you so late?" called Monty, a bite to his voice.

"Traffic," answered Helen. She didn't bother to add that she had to work late and had arrived at the day care center right before it closed. She flipped on the small television and turned to an educational channel for Adele, who plopped down on a blanket in front of it. Helen hoped it would distract the little girl until she got her dinner ready.

Helen pulled on a hoodie, then heard her phone vibrating inside her purse. She grabbed it. "Dawn?"

"Hi, sis! Is this a good time?"

"Well, no, actually. I just got home—late—and Adele's probably getting hungry. Unless they gave her a late snack at school."

"Oh. Well, can you call me later?" Dawn lived in Chicago, where the two women had grown up.

"I'll try. I just have to see how things go."

"What do you mean?"

"Well, Monty's in kind of a bad mood—"

"So? Does that mean you can't talk to your sister?"

"Dawn, relax. It's not just that. I want to talk, when I have some time to myself." Helen evaluated herself in the mirror, reflexively pulling one shoulder of the hoodie closer to her neck to cover the scarred skin. "But first I have to feed Adele, give her a bath, and put her to bed." The little girl had been mesmerized by Big Bird until she heard her mother's voice—now she got up and began to pull on Helen's legs and whine softly. "You know how she is. As soon as I start talking on the phone, it's like a bell rings in her head, and she won't let me."

"Fine," said Dawn. "Really. I know you're busy. Just call me later? And if you can't talk at all tonight, text me or something."

"Is something up?"

"No. Everything's great. Just wanted to know how you're doing. With the whole situation down there."

Helen exhaled. "Fine. I'll call you. Don't worry. Bye now."

"Bye."

Helen zipped up her jacket and gave Adele a kiss. "Now, baby, Mommy's off the phone. Watch your show, okay?"

Adele sat back down on the blanket and Helen went into the small bathroom between the bedroom and the tiny L-shaped kitchen.

What had Monty been doing all day? He usually claimed he had been working on the house, but Helen never saw any changes. Whenever she brought up the subject, he either gave her a cold stare and ignored her questions or flew off the handle, sometimes scaring her. She couldn't risk the latter when Adele was in the house. Not that he had ever hurt his daughter, who had seen him go nuts more than once. When he had his rages, he just threw things or pounded on furniture and walls. Last fall he had broken all the china Helen had inherited from her grandmother. Over time, she had learned to read his face, tiptoe around him, and avoid looking directly into his eyes.

How had this become her life? Monty had been so wonderful and so romantic in the beginning, over three years ago. In her twenties, Helen had had a couple of serious boyfriends, but she'd never met anyone like Monty. Able to talk to anyone, he commanded attention whenever he walked into a room. His charm was

20

overpowering, and during those early weeks, it was on for Helen, nonstop. He knew all the hip restaurants, all the fashionable places to go and the best things to buy. He was the *coolest* person she had ever known.

They'd met at a Christmas party, and by the end of the evening, he had seduced her. They began going out, usually ending up at Helen's apartment in Vinings, though some weekends he claimed to be away on business. She had had no idea he was lying and living with his girlfriend, Jeanine, who knew how wealthy his sister was— and whose own baby clock was ticking. Weeks before Helen met him, Jeanine had given Monty an ultimatum: either set a wedding date or she would stop supporting him. Of course, he'd agreed, and Jeanine had bought herself a huge diamond ring.

That spring, Helen discovered she was pregnant. Without mentioning he was engaged—and that his fiancée was planning a November wedding—Monty promised to marry Helen once the baby was born. It was one of the few promises he had kept, though not until he'd demanded proof that he was the father. Adele was born in September 2007, and in mid-October, her parents got married in a courthouse on a Friday afternoon.

Walking into the kitchen, Helen peeked over at her husband. She didn't dare ask what he was doing on the computer. She opened the fridge and tried to shake the memory of Jeanine's wrath. She had blamed Helen, and looking back, Helen could almost understand. But then Jeanine had moved on and married someone else. Life was so weird.

With her back to Monty, Helen pulled out a hot dog and some leftover macaroni and cheese to warm up for Adele. She glanced over to see if Monty had unwittingly left the day's mail on the counter, something he almost never did. Even though it was her paycheck alone that supported them and was automatically deposited into their joint checking account twice a month, he gathered the mail every day and paid the bills. At least, he said he did. Helen had stopped asking about it a long time ago, after a horrible argument about her lack of trust in him and her disrespect of his need for autonomy. When he caught her looking for the bills again the following week, he had broken a chair.

Not wanting things to escalate, she had meekly retreated and strangled her wish to fight back. What might happen if she did was just too frightening.

"That damn bitch," Monty muttered, his eyes glued to the laptop's screen. Helen glanced furtively over at him, then looked back at the plate she was preparing for Adele. After grabbing a pink vinyl place mat, she brought the food into the bedroom. Adele could eat on the blanket in front of the TV.

Helen wasn't hungry herself. She'd had a late lunch at work, and recently she hadn't had much of an appetite. She hoped she wasn't coming down with some kind of stomach bug. The kids at Adele's school—day care center—were constantly passing around germs, and Adele had been home sick a lot. Which meant that Helen either had to call in sick or take a personal day. Her firm didn't allow many of either, and she'd taken several of both. And it was only March.

She looked out the window at the falling rain. It was coming down hard now, the tall pine trees surrounding the cottage swaying with the strong winds. The plan over two years ago had been to take them out when the property was landscaped, after renovating all three levels of the house. The entire project was supposed to take no more than a year, and then they were going to sell for a big profit.

Monty had assured her that he'd learned all about construction and home renovation from his father, Jack, who had made his living in the business. He drew up plans for a large gourmet kitchen and five bathrooms (the original house only had three), complete with imported tile, marble, and granite. The blueprints reflected a major increase in the home's square footage, with an expanded master suite, one additional bedroom, and bigger closets throughout. There would even be built-in electronics and an outdoor Jacuzzi.

But the plans hung on his sister's promise of financial help, which Monty claimed to have in writing. He met with her in late 2007 and said he had sold her on the idea. Why had Helen believed him when he said his wealthy sibling was more than willing to lay out all the necessary funding? That she would make loans to them without any expectation of repayment, and that she would fork over more money as gifts? That Candace *wanted* to give them all the money they might request, without even asking what it was for?

What a huge mistake it had been to go to Candace. They should have just bought a home they could have afforded and saved their money for any future upgrades. Helen was sick of making mistakes, and looking back now over the past few years, she realized she'd made several. Some of them weren't her fault, but just bad luck.

Like when the home's basement flooded in spring 2008, right after they had moved in and the kitchen and upstairs baths had already been demolished. It had rained almost nonstop for two months, and many neighborhoods in the city had flooded. Then a violent thunderstorm hit and took out the power for two days.

Water flowed into the basement, and the bedroom, bathroom, kitchen, and living area were ruined. They'd had to move into the guesthouse—the cottage—with whatever they could salvage. It sat on a hill in the back of the property, and there had been no plan to redo it, thank goodness.

Sitting on the bed, Helen stared at the rain now pelting the windows. She felt so isolated and alone, and so tired. At least the occasional lightning and thunder didn't bother Adele, who had finished her dinner and was still mesmerized by her television show. It was almost eight o'clock and the little girl had to be getting tired. She got up early every day with her mother, and the two got ready for the day while Monty slept.

Helen picked up Adele's plate. "It's almost time for your bath, sweetie."

"Fi'e minutes," said Adele, making a cute begging face. "Please, Mommy?"

Helen smiled. Adele was a precocious child and the joy of her life. Everything she was dealing with, everything she had been through, was all worth it for her sake.

"Okay, but that's all. Then you get to pick out a story for bedtime."

Adele nodded and reached her arm around to hold her mother's ankle. Helen closed her eyes and lay back on the bed to rest for a few minutes.

A loud bang came from the other room—not outside—startling her and the toddler.

"It's all right, Boo," Helen said. She got up and grabbed her daughter's small hand. "Come on."

She closed the door from the bathroom to the living room and ran the bathwater while Adele used the toilet. A few moments later, as the girl played with her toys in the tub, Helen fetched her cell phone from the bedroom and sat down on the bathroom floor.

She typed in a text message. *Adele's in tub & I'm beat. Will call u tmrw from work. All's well. No worries. xoxo*

Maybe Dawn wouldn't realize she was lying.

3

Proposal

Monty banged the small computer desk hard with the side of his fist again and blew out air as he stared at his email inbox. "*Fuck!*"

He ran his fingers through his thick hair and shook his head. What was he going to do if Candace just ignored his request for a hundred grand? That was her pattern. Whenever he asked her for anything, and especially if he threatened her, she ignored him. Perhaps he needed to follow through this time. It would be easy to do.

He looked at the clock—it was almost eight thirty. She was probably out to dinner somewhere with her scumbag-lawyer boyfriend. He dialed her number anyway.

"Hey," he said after the beep, his tone friendly. "I've been wondering why you haven't called me back after I tried you this morning. We need to discuss some specifics as to the property. I'll be available after ten o'clock tomorrow morning."

He'd sleep on it, after a couple more drinks. Acting desperate and sorrowful worked much better than threats, he had found, and in the morning, once he had the place to himself, he'd apologize. Well, not exactly. He wouldn't say he was sorry, but he would send her a semiregretful email. He'd attach a few photos of Adele. Better yet, he'd send a whole bunch of the latest photos of her in a separate email first. Candace was a sucker for that.

His beautiful daughter was looking more like his mother every day. He was glad she resembled his side of the family rather than Helen's and that she looked nothing like Helen's bitchy sister. He gazed at the framed photo on his desk of his mother, taken when he was a boy. He missed her, even after so many years. She'd been his only source of affirmation and encouragement. Assuring him that all good things would happen to him—that he deserved no less— she had treated him like a prince. She had constantly reassured him that he would never have to do menial work like his father did.

Candace probably couldn't even have children by now, her eggs had gotten so old. Not that he was convinced that she wanted a kid. It seemed unlikely. She'd been dating—sleeping with—that asshole for a couple years now, and even though Monty hadn't seen any indication that a legal attachment was imminent, one never knew. A newfound wish to have a baby (due to a midlife crisis?) might be the one and only reason she would consider sharing her millions with a spouse. Her boyfriend was an IPO lawyer and had helped take her company public a few years ago. He'd been extremely lucky in life so far, and so had Candace.

She thought that her obscene wealth was the result of hard work only, and that he was lazy. Ever since Monty could remember, she'd called him a slacker. But she didn't understand that he worked very hard—with his mind. He was smarter than she was and much more intelligent than most people. Especially the schmucks who got up every single day and went to work at some nothing job for pennies. He was better than such idiots, most of whom didn't even know how unhappy they were.

What annoyed him the most was that some of those half-wits made real money. But he was happy to have the freedom to spend his time the way he wanted. He'd go crazy if he had to live his life at the beck and call of someone else.

He stood up, stretched, and looked out the window. Let that paranoid bitch worry some more tonight about what he might do to her reputation. But he had to get that money. He owed three construction vendors about twenty grand, and he had his own plans for the other eighty. He poured himself another glass of vodka, and switching gears, sat back down at his laptop and began writing.

From: Monty Carawan <monty.carawan86@me.com>
Sent: Tuesday, March 9, 2010 8:21 PM EST
To: Adam Langford <Adam.Langford@svpd.net>
Subject: website venture

Adam:
Just wanted to touch base about your interest in personal-assistant.com. As I said during our recent conversation, I have some very strong investors lined up to join you in making this a reality.

Let's meet for drinks at the Ritz downtown when you are visiting next week. Let me know your schedule and I will be happy to meet at your convenience.

Best,
Monty Carawan

He had met Langford last month at a charity event. In a benevolent moment, Candace had invited him to it, saying it was a good opportunity to network and implying that he should mine her business contacts for a crappy position pushing paper for some middle manager. But he had finessed the situation by ingratiating himself with Langford, a hedge fund manager and a big swinging dick in the technology world. The guy lived in San Francisco and didn't know Candace personally—they were acquainted through some women's apparel company's founder.

Monty had a talent for being able to read people, and right away he could tell that Langford was looking for something to invest in. So he pitched his idea for a website that would provide a subscriber with a virtual personal assistant. It would keep track of usernames and passwords, miles/points/rewards, debit and credit cards, buying and travel habits, Internet searches, and even taxes and social security.

It was a great idea—it had the potential to be even bigger than Facebook. Who wouldn't want to use one website to manage all their personal information? Plus it would do away with spam and marketing emails by evaluating and streamlining offers from merchants. Reentering contact information each time a transaction was made would no longer be necessary. Calendar reminders, medical information, even showtimes for movies and concerts would all be in one place. It would revolutionize the Internet, and Monty was the creative genius behind it. It was his ticket to fortune, the one he had been waiting for.

He had picked up the necessary coding knowledge from some nerds he'd sucked up to, and he could figure out the rest. He had already put time into the site, starting with the spam and calendar segments. Adding other components would be simple, but he didn't want to spend any more time on it until Langford pledged some funds and promised a customer base. Hopefully, the guy would seize the opportunity to partner with him and make a killing. When that happened, the world would begin to appreciate Monty Carawan and his talents.

He migrated to the worn camel-colored sofa and turned on the big-screen HD TV on the dresser against the opposite wall. Thank God he'd disconnected it and carried it out to the guesthouse when the basement flooded two years ago. Sipping his cocktail, he settled in and stretched out. He slept on this sofa about half the time now, which suited him fine. Sleeping in the bedroom with his daughter nestled on a toddler mattress next to the bed wasn't ideal. This way he could get eight hours and not be awakened when they stirred in the morning. Tomorrow, he'd go for a run around nine o'clock or so, if the weather was decent.

• • •

A few hours later, naked and exhausted, Candace lay on her side next to Rob under the duvet, her head resting on his broad shoulder.

"How are you, darling?" he asked.

"Lovely." She let out a deep breath.

"My very thought."

Candace smiled and looked into his deep blue eyes. "Are you happy?"

"Ecstatic." He nudged a strand of hair away from her face. "However, I could be happier."

"How? I couldn't." She looked up at the ceiling.

"Couldn't you?"

She turned back toward him and looked in his eyes again. "What do you mean?"

"I mean, we make this relationship legal. 'Marriage' is the term, I believe."

"You're such a lawyer, Rob. Are you proposing? Because if so, that wasn't very romantic."

"Love, *you're* not very romantic."

She raised up on her elbow and gave him a look.

"I'm just being honest," said Rob. "I'm not saying you don't have feelings, or that you're not feminine. I'm just saying that you're not sappy or needy. You're strong, successful, and confident."

She smiled. "Go on."

"And, you're sexy, smart, and charming. Look at all that you've achieved."

Candace raised her eyebrows. "But is that *all* I am? The head of a successful company?"

"No, you're much more than that, and you know it. However, I dare say you've got more testosterone than most men."

"Testosterone? What are you saying?"

"Darling, I mean that as a huge compliment. Of course I don't mean it literally. Everything about you attracts me, and it's been two years. How long do we go on this way? I'm convinced that you're the woman I've been waiting for. And I want to know whether you feel the same."

Candace looked directly into his eyes and traced her finger from his neck down.

"Will you marry me?" he asked.

"Yes," she said, reaching lower. Finding what she was looking for, she added, "Let's seal the deal."

• • •

At seven thirty the next morning, Rob lay between Candace's fifteen-hundred-thread-count Egyptian cotton linens, his long frame stretched out and his head propped on a goose down pillow. Dressed in designer workout attire, Candace emerged from the cavernous mirrored closet. She leaned over, ran her fingers through Rob's dark hair, and tenderly brushed the back of her hand against the stubble on his cheek. This wonderful man wanted to wake up with her for the rest of his life. She smiled to herself, thinking of future mornings when she wouldn't be in a rush and might slumber in his arms.

He caught hold of her hand and drew her toward him.

"No time," she said, pulling away. "I'm going to the gym. Don't pout."

"Love, your body's already perfect."

"Well, I need to keep it that way. Then I'm going to the office. I have to get caught up if I'm to go to New York this Sunday."

Naked, Rob ambled in the direction of the bathroom. "Is that definite?"

"I haven't decided. It depends on whether Jess has lined up a meeting with the swimwear people for Monday morning up there." Candace unplugged her phone from the charger and scanned through the missed calls. "*Damn it.*"

"What is it?"

"Monty called. And left me a voicemail. Which I don't want to hear."

Rob opened the glass shower door and turned on the water. "Then don't listen. Erase it."

"But here's something I do want to see. David copied me on an email he sent to Monty, and sent me another separate email."

Rob stepped under the jets of hot water as steam began to fill the room. "The saga continues."

"Mmm," Candace murmured. She closed the door to the bath, sat down on a leopard-print Italian chair, and clicked on David's email.

From: David Shepherd <david.shepherd@efp.com>
Sent: Wednesday, March 10, 2010 7:21 AM EST
To: Monty Carawan <monty.carawan86@me.com>
cc: Candace Morgan <candace.morgan@slimz.org>
Subject: Internet job

Monty:
Hope this finds you well. Candace has asked me to follow up with you about the Internet job you referred to in your email of last Thursday. Specifically, she would like

to know the name of the company, the principals' names, and what date you are to start.

Best,
David K. Shepherd
Elite Financial Planning

From: David Shepherd <david.shepherd@efp.com>
Sent: Wednesday, March 10, 2010 7:23 AM EST
To: Candace Morgan <candace.morgan@slimz.org>
Subject: Monty

Candace:
Anticipating your questions, I took the liberty of asking for his start date as well as principals' names. Per your instructions, I have not answered his request for any additional funds, nor have I responded to any of his questions.

I will be in the office until Friday at noon, if you would like to meet while you are in town; I believe you said you'd be out next week?

David K. Shepherd
Elite Financial Planning

Candace dialed David's number.

"Hello, Candace."

"Good morning, David. I just read your emails. Thanks for sending that. I don't expect that he'll respond."

"Nor do I. Prompt responses have never been the rule with him."

She laughed. "I suppose I'll have to call him to find out about this purported Internet company job. Which I don't want to do, because I know he'll just lie. Again."

"I'd advise you not to call him. I think he'd try to turn any conversation into an emotional appeal."

"I know. My fucking brother is such a fucking asshole." She lowered her voice a little. "I'm sorry, David. I shouldn't vent. I just want to get my money back—all of it."

"Do we need to meet before Friday?"

"I'll decide, and call you back."

"Okay," said David. "Let me know if there's anything else I can do in the meantime."

Candace tossed the phone into her bag, then grabbed her keys and a bottle of Vitaminwater. Rob had just turned off the shower, and she knew he had a busy day ahead. In a way, she couldn't believe that she'd agreed to marry him. There were some things they would need to discuss. Specifically, money: income, assets, even net worths.

He probably knew her income—it was listed on sec.gov. All he had to do was use Edgar to look up her most recent 10k report. It would reflect how much she made, down to the penny. But she didn't know his income. However, she knew about some of his assets. He owned a three-thousand-square-foot apartment in Manhattan near Central Park, not far from Candace's one-bedroom, and had filled it with expensive works of art, a passion of his. He also owned a place in the Hamptons and kept a Maserati for weekend trips.

Rob had grown up with money. His father was a white-shoe New York attorney who met his wife while studying in England. Nick and Deirdre Chandler had sent their son to school in Britain and then to Harvard and Harvard Law, Nick's alma mater. After graduating with honors, Rob joined a prestigious New York law firm where he worked a relentless schedule; a brief marriage to law school classmate Felicia Turnbull had ended with little fuss. Soon Rob was identified as a rising star in the firm's IPO group and recognized as the natural successor to senior partner Charles Chadwick. Candace was sure that Rob had made at least a hundred million over the last decade. He enjoyed his money and gave his "Mummy" plenty of gifts.

Which brought up one of the issues left unsaid last night. An engagement ring. Candace inspected her manicured fingers as she keyed in the settings on the elliptical trainer at the gym. She'd worn a two-carat flawless diamond throughout her marriage to Ted, but for the last ten years she'd kept her hands and arms free of jewelry. She didn't even wear a wristwatch now that all of her devices displayed the time. She adored earrings, however, and Rob had given her quite a few in recent years. She was very particular about necklaces, seldom wearing them because she found them distracting.

But she was surprised that Rob hadn't presented her with a ring last night, even in bed; it wasn't like him to forget. What had he given Felicia? Unless—had he mentioned this to her in the past?—it was a family heirloom passed down from his grandmother.

Well, Candace wasn't sentimental in that way, or in any way, really. Her heart rate climbed as she worked the machine on a high setting and sweat began to pour. Her phone, sitting on a tray under the TV monitor, vibrated. It was a text message from Rob.

Let's go to Tiffany's next week to choose a ring.

Perfect. Of course he knew that she would want to pick it out. Perhaps she'd do something different from the usual diamond. She loved sapphires. That might work.

Gazing at the screen in front of her, she listened to a playlist on her iPod as she pumped her arms and legs. She knew Rob's mind so well. He knew all about her company, her family, her past—at least, almost all. What other things would they need to discuss?

Family—not hers or his. Theirs. Children, or at least, a child. Did he want one? Did she? Is that what had prompted his proposal? They'd brushed up against the topic a few times in the past, but now it was time to iron this out. Did Rob have a desire to be a father—and did he think that if they didn't try now, the opportunity would be lost?

But—did *she* want a baby? More urgently, did she want to be pregnant? She never had been, and had no idea what it might be like. She had worked hard to sculpt her body for so many years now—and the idea of an enormous belly, even temporarily, was repugnant. It would be difficult to get her body back, but countless other women had done it, so she ought to be able to as well. She tightened her arms and glanced at her thighs. She was getting ahead of herself. Here she was, already worried about recovering from an imagined future pregnancy, and she didn't even know how her new fiancé felt about the idea.

The last song on her playlist began and her hour of cardio was almost over. Candace checked her phone again. She scrolled through business emails that could wait and a couple of missed calls from the office; there were no more texts. She would need some time to think about whether she wanted a child and about how one would affect her life. After all, it was her reproductive window that was important. She was in the best shape of her life at the moment, but she'd be turning forty in November. If she didn't have a baby, would she regret the decision in five years or so? She might. She hated regrets. Her pattern had always been to do, rather than not to do.

She started her cool-down, slowing her strides and toweling off the sweat. She and Rob would speak about this, and when they did, she'd be ready.

4

Images

Helen rose quietly early Wednesday morning and showered, taking care not to wake Monty or Adele. After she was dressed, she would get Adele up and get her ready for school—it was much easier that way. She had laid out an outfit for the little girl last night, and now she stood in front of the closet, its dim light turned on. She surveyed her clothing to figure out what to wear to work.

She picked out her slim, olive-colored dress pants; a V-neck, black rayon top; and a pair of black open-toed heels. She would need to wear her SlimZ underneath, the product that Candace had invented over a decade ago. Monty called it nothing but a thin girdle—just cut-off panty hose. Helen knew it was much more than that, though. It was an essential part of her wardrobe. She needed to look professional at the office, where she was regarded as an experienced graphic designer, and was respected for her work. It was her income that supported the family, and the way that she presented herself at the office mattered, especially with all the layoffs recently.

Monty denigrated her job, however, saying that anyone could do it and that it took no special aptitude or intellect. Back when they met, he had been full of compliments about her artistic ability, but once they were married he only criticized and trivialized it. He said she had chosen an easy career and accused her of adopting a superior attitude toward him because she had a degree. Over time, Helen had learned not to let his cutting words pierce.

Monty also disparaged Candace, saying her success had only been the result of good luck. But Helen knew she had worked very hard to achieve it. She pulled on her SlimZ, which was a little more snug than the last time she had worn it. She never put it in the dryer, so how could that be? She'd been watching what she ate more than usual lately, which hadn't been difficult since her appetite was low. She finished getting dressed and sat down in front of a small magnifying mirror in the bathroom to apply her makeup.

An hour later, after feeding and dressing Adele and dropping her off at school, Helen sat down at her desk in the office. Just as she began checking her email, her cell phone vibrated. It was Dawn.

"Hey," said Helen. "I just got to work. Are you already at the office?"

"No, I'm still getting ready, but I thought I'd try you before you get busy. Can you talk?"

Helen took a deep breath and glanced out of the corner of her eye. "Yeah, I guess. How are you? How's Frank?"

"He's good. He's in Minneapolis on business. How's Monty?"

Helen adjusted the left shoulder of her top, trying to conceal the raised, ropey scar on her collarbone. "He's the same."

"If you don't want to talk—"

"I *do* want to talk. I wish you were here."

"I can be there, as soon as you want me," Dawn said in a soothing tone.

Helen picked up her cup of coffee. "It's just—we don't have room." The tiny cottage was barely big enough for the three of them.

"When will you be able to move back into the house?"

Helen took a sip of the hot liquid. "He keeps saying just a few more weeks. But I never see any progress."

"It's been over two years since you guys started this whole thing, Helen. Why isn't the basement redone by now?"

Helen put her cup down. "Dawn—"

"I'm sorry. I know things are screwed up. They have to be. I'm just worried. Not about the house—about *you*. I don't want to add to your problems, though."

Helen swallowed. Dawn had been an emotional substitute for their mother for so long now, and her concern was grounded in kindness and love. "Well, I'm okay. Although I've been feeling kind of queasy lately."

"I hope you're not getting sick. Just tell me: Do you know everything that's going on, financially? Do you pay the bills?"

Helen paused for a second. "He does," she admitted.

"Damn it, Helen!"

"It's just easier that way," said Helen. "I don't expect you to understand, but we get along better if he handles that."

"What about the money you've gotten from Candace? And the loans to her?"

"That's between her and Monty."

"Helen! Don't be such an idiot! Your name is on those loans, isn't it?"

Helen began to scroll through her email. "That's the only way we could get the money, Dawn."

"Look, Frank and I can come down there. We'll stay at a hotel. Then the four of us can sit down together and talk."

"That's a bad idea. Monty won't do it. He won't answer any of *my* questions, so there's no way he'll answer yours."

"Has he gotten a job?"

Helen put down her cup. "He's working on something, I think. And he's busy with the renovation."

"You just said you never see any progress! You keep making excuses for him, but nothing ever changes!"

Helen glanced around. Most of her coworkers had arrived. "I've got to go. I'll call you this weekend, when I have some time."

"You're not mad at me, are you?"

"Of course not," said Helen. "I love you. I know you're worried about me. But I have to go."

"Okay. But call me, all right? Love you!"

"Me, too. Bye."

Helen took another sip of her coffee. Somehow it didn't taste good today.

• • •

Candace's phone buzzed.

"David," she said, sitting behind the wheel of her Mercedes. "What's up?"

"I just got an email from Monty with two vendor invoices and receipts attached."

"Dated?"

"January and February."

"Well, that's a one-eighty from his response last Friday. I'm amazed. He must really want that hundred grand."

"Right. That's what I'm thinking. I wonder if an overall budget and updated progress reports are on the way, too."

Candace slowed down for a red light ahead as light rain began to fall. She had a lot to do at the office. "I doubt it."

"I can forward this to you—"

"No, don't. I don't want to see them. Just have your assistant look them over, and let me know if you do get anything else. I'm not gonna give him that money, even if he does provide everything we've asked for."

"Agreed."

"And, I've decided you're right about his threat. I'm not worried."

"Good," said David. "Before you leave town, why don't you go over to the place and see it for yourself?"

Candace glanced in the rearview mirror. The car behind her was following too close. "You know, I really don't want to see it. More than that, I don't want to talk to him and ask to see it."

"You're a creditor, Candace. You have every right to see it. He's supposedly working at home. You can just pop over there, unannounced, whenever."

Candace focused on the road ahead again. She hardly remembered the blueprints, and she didn't relish viewing the current reality. She preferred to straight-arm it; seeing it in person just might be too much emotionally. "That would be tacky, David."

"Would you like me to drive over?"

"No, I guess not. I don't want you to have to confront him, especially after the fit he had in your office last Friday."

"Well, think about it. It's a way to check up on this, and I think that doing that is in your best interest. Unfortunately."

"You're probably right. As usual."

"Well, that's all I have."

"Okay. And we don't need to meet this week. Talk to you later."

Candace put down her iPhone and mentally shifted to her day's agenda. She would be meeting with the design department this morning to talk about launching a swimsuit line. It had been in the planning stages for several years and would be a big departure from the company's current product lines that so far included only undergarments. But the new line would fit in well with the SlimZ mission to highlight the positive and increase attractiveness.

Candace believed that, for her target customer, an attractive swimsuit—one that she'd be proud to wear on a cruise, at the pool, or at the beach—was built on structure. The brand name would do a lot to sell the new line, but the product had to be perfect. SlimZ technology was patented, so customers would assume they were buying the same look, feel, and confidence of other SlimZ products. The swimsuit's extra support in the lower abdomen would address that problem area that almost all women over twenty-five had to some degree. The line would compete against the Miracle-Suit and the other better swimsuits on the market.

Swimwear was, for all practical purposes, just underwear. You wore nothing under it and displayed your body in it. When a customer bought a swimsuit, she was buying what she *wasn't* going to be wearing more than what she was. Most of her skin would be exposed to the world. Therefore, every bit of the small amount of material in a swimsuit was important and worth its price point. Every decision made in developing the line had to be right.

She pulled the Mercedes into her reserved space in the parking lot next to her Buckhead offices. After checking in with Jess and directing her to go ahead and book a flight to New York for Sunday, she walked into a meeting room filled with six designers and the department head. Whiteboards with swimsuit drawings were propped on easels, and fabric swatches littered a large table in the center of the room.

"Let's get to it," she said, and dropped her bag on a chair. "What have we got?"

• • •

At eight o'clock, a driver was waiting for Rob at the entrance to Candace's Midtown condo. During the short ride to his firm's Atlanta office, he checked his messages and returned a call to New York. He planned to arrive there Friday and had a busy weekend planned. That night, he'd be at a gallery opening, and the following evening he was expected at a cancer charity event, but in between, he would put in some time at the office and the gym. He needed to get a workout in later today as well—he could stop in at the office fitness center and do some lifting, at least.

He was delighted with the decision he and Candace had made to wed. They'd been seeing each other for a couple of years, and while it had been very convenient to continue their separate lives and get together for frequent lusty interludes, Rob wanted to make their merger complete—and permanent. His short marriage had occurred over fifteen years ago now, and as a single man, he'd certainly had an assortment of sexy blondes. However, they'd all been playthings. None had had any brains.

Which had suited him fine at the time. But now his life was different. He and Candace had celebrated his fortieth birthday three weeks ago, and he had come to a realization. He needed a woman he could talk to, who understood business, who appreciated him and not just his money. A woman who had her own money. A woman like Candace. She was quite lovely, and exciting in bed. She was smart and would be a great companion. If they decided to have a child, her genetic makeup was an ideal match.

Their personalities meshed well, too. He loved making her laugh and pushing her to try new things, and he was thankful for the intimacy they shared. It had taken some time to get her to open up to him and to earn her trust after what happened during her marriage to Ted. Her issues with her brother—financial and otherwise—could be dealt with. In fact, Rob had an abundance of confidence in her ability to do so. He would be there for her if she needed him emotionally, and he suspected she would. For even though Candace was a very strong woman, she had a sensitive side that few had seen.

• • •

Monty returned from his morning run just before ten o'clock and sat down at his computer. He'd cool off for about fifteen minutes before he showered and shaved. He pulled up his email and found another message from the granite vendor saying his past due payment would go to a collection agency if he didn't take care of it by Friday.

He deleted it. *Fuck those bastards.* The kitchen and bathroom counters had been installed over six months ago, but he wouldn't pay them until his sister forked over more money. The money that he had requested last week, when he met with Shepherd, her scumbag accountant. Let the collection people call that fucker. Candace had cosigned the home equity loan, so if she was going to cut off any more funds—funds he had to have yesterday—she could deal with it.

He scrolled through the rest of his email, finished his bottle of Powerade, and stripped off his clothes, heading for the shower. He did some of his best thinking standing naked under a hot stream of water. He had scanned and sent those receipts and invoices earlier this morning. If he did some tweaking to an old construction budget, he could make it look credible. He didn't really want to fuck with it. But it might be all he would need to do to push Candace again.

Toweling off, he quickly finished in the bathroom and then put on a pair of designer jeans and a polo shirt. He needed to get out and do some clothes shopping soon, to update his wardrobe. At the meeting with Langford, he'd have to look sharp. Then, once he got him on board as an investor, funds would flow. Being Candace's brother had its advantages, but sometimes he wondered if they were really worth all the shit he had had to put up with from her.

Grabbing his laptop, he headed for the door. A cup of java was what he needed right now, and he could hang out at a coffee shop until lunch.

• • •

Just before one o'clock, Jess brought Candace a lunch of broiled salmon, cooked medium rare, and an arugula salad with a balsamic vinaigrette dressing on the side. Candace took a bite of the fish and, satisfied that it wasn't overcooked, decided she didn't need to send it back. The president and CEO of SlimZ Inc. ate by herself in her office as she perused the swimwear market report prepared by the sales and marketing department. Her employees ate lunch at their desks—when Candace was in town, one was a fool not to. She was manic about keeping ahead of the competition and expected all her employees to adopt not only her work ethic but her frenzied pace as well. If one didn't keep up, one's career at SlimZ was over before it began. Whenever Candace was in town, the office hummed in very high gear.

At 1:20 p.m., finished with her lunch, Candace called Jess to remove her dish and to summon the design department employees to the conference room. Five minutes later, the head of SlimZ entered the room where a group of seven women were seated in front of her, waiting.

"We're not doing big prints," said Candace. "Small prints, maybe, but only if it looks like a solid. We're not Lands' End—we're not going to make women wear upholstery, and it's not about swimming. We're also not Anne Klein or Ralph Lauren, so no buckles, ropes, or bangles. We're SlimZ, and we're doing one-piece swimsuits—for now. We're doing black, of course, and I'm open to other color suggestions."

"What about nude? And white?" asked Meredith, a twenty-something brunette.

"Let's talk about nude," said Candace. "First, if we do it, it won't be nude. It'll be beige. But do we do it? Why would we?"

"Well, if done well, it blends with skin tone and makes a sexy body sexier," said a blonde named Heather.

"True," said Candace, "but that means we won't offer it—or white—in double-digit sizes. If we do white." She studied the group's reaction—no one's eyes met her own. "Does anyone disagree?"

"Can we do that?" asked Meredith.

"We can do whatever we like," said Candace. "Let me explain. Some of you know this, but in the past, I've worn a much larger size than I do now. I noticed something then when I shopped for clothes: the typical designer creates the same patterns, in the same colors, in all sizes—just making them wider—and the stores buy these items."

Everyone waited as Candace paused and surveyed the room.

"Which is a big mistake," she said. "I don't know why it's been so hard for them to figure this out: what works in size two does not often work in size ten, twelve, or fourteen. Women—most women—know this. It's a big reason for markdowns in these larger sizes." Candace cleared her throat. "Our target customer is smart. She wants to look great and *feel* great in her clothes—in her swimsuit—whatever her size. She pays attention to color, and like most people, she believes that black is slimming. So black, we'll do in every size. Now, what other colors? What do you think, Paula?"

Paula, the department head, had been with Candace for six years. "Dark blue—navy, not royal blue. Eggplant, or dark violet. Dark brown—chocolate. Possibly bronze. Dark green—an olive green."

"Good, so far," said Candace, looking around. "Anyone else?"

"How about red?" asked Lucy, also a SlimZ veteran.

"I'm not against red," said Candace. "Not orangey-red, though. Fire-engine red. Small sizes only. Remember: our swimsuit equals the little black dress. Which doesn't have to be black." She walked over to one of the whiteboards, looking at the various drawings, her back to the group. "I like the simpler designs. But they have to be elegant. This one-shoulder piece is sexy. Good job, Meredith. Not everyone can wear it, though." Candace turned around. "It's not just about color or pattern. The SlimZ foundation is our structure—that's a given. It's about matching body type with attractiveness. What flatters a particular body type. Tall, short, or medium height; slender, average, or large frame; pear shape, apple, hourglass, or stick; broad shoulders or narrow; big, small, or average bust; every conceivable neckline."

Paula shifted in her chair and crossed her legs at the ankles. "Allowing the customer to look her absolute best."

"Exactly," said Candace. "We don't just create swimsuits and undergarments. All of our customers are valued, whatever their size and shape. Our mission is to help them look their absolute best. We design and customize our products with this in mind, always." Candace looked around the room. "Now, in New York, I'll be talking about how we're going to incorporate our designs in an interactive tab on our website."

"So a woman can narrow her choices to the most attractive ones online," said Heather.

"But," said Candace, "as I'm sure you know, Lands' End does this, at least their version of it. We're going to do it better. How can we do that?" Her eyes swept the room.

"Lands' End only sells online and via catalogue," said Lucy. "If our customer doesn't want to order online, she can make an appointment to have her choices ready to try on at the nearest Saks, Neiman's, or Nordstrom."

"I like it," said Candace. "Paula, get with Amanda to discuss the idea, not just at those three retailers, but at all of our stores."

"Done," said Paula.

"So here's what I need from the rest of you," said Candace. "All possible body types and sizes. Design matches for each. Drawings, in color. Front and back. Accessible on our internal system for my review."

The group sat motionless.

"Now," said Candace.

In ten seconds, she was alone in the room. Half an hour from now, she had a meeting scheduled with the company's IT group, led by Erin. Ginger, the company's chief operating officer (COO), would also attend. The agenda included a discussion of the new website capabilities and a review of an update to the internal system.

Candace checked her email and opened a message sent this morning from Monty with photos of Adele attached, but no text. He had no shame. Candace clicked through the fifteen shots of Adele taken last month at a friend's birthday party. That little girl was incredibly photogenic—it was as if she had been created to be photographed. Her blonde ringlet curls framed a doll-like face with sparkling blue eyes and an irresistible smile. In the few photos taken with Helen, it was unmistakable: Adele looked nothing like her mother. Her coloring, even her little turned-up nose resembled the Carawans, not the Pipers. Specifically, Adele looked like her grandmother, Susannah Carawan.

Candace closed her eyes. What would her mother look like if she were alive today? She'd be in her early sixties and probably still very attractive. Dying so violently at age forty-one, two years older than Candace was now, Susannah's life had been cut way too short. Three months before her nineteenth birthday, Candace's world had changed forever.

She had been driving the car that rainy August afternoon, speeding along a divided road somewhere in north Georgia. Susannah was next to her, in the passenger seat, and Monty, a senior in high school, was sprawled in the back. Remembering those few seconds over two decades later, Candace shuddered, then exhaled. The air-like feeling as the vehicle hydroplaned when Candace swerved while turning left. The sudden hard splash of water slapping the windshield. The incredible force of a pickup truck ramming the car and propelling it toward a tree. Glass shattering and peppering Susannah's face. Her blood splattering everywhere. Her skull cracking, bits of her brain oozing through. The crunch of her bones against Candace's right side.

With no seat belt on, Monty had been thrown against the opposite side of the backseat, banging his head but not losing consciousness. Candace hadn't been injured, just bruised; in those moments right after the crash, she had gone crazy. Her heart beat a thousand times a minute as she held her mother against her, trying to stop the blood, talking to her, crying, the rain coming down in buckets outside. Monty lay motionless behind them, in shock. The few minutes before help arrived had seemed like hours. Unhurt, the other driver had hurried over to Candace's side, standing outside the door in the pounding rain, trying in vain to reassure her that her mother would be all right.

Why am I reliving it? It won't solve anything. There will never be a way to fix it. It was why Candace always kept mind and body busy, why she worked so hard and kept her pace going, no matter what. So she wouldn't have time for her emotions.

She scanned through more email messages, deleting some, then opened and skimmed through a document from Ginger about the system update. Ginger had been with SlimZ for four years and was hardworking and very good at her job. Like Helen, she had grown up in Chicago.

Candace couldn't fathom her brother's marriage. She didn't know Helen very well, having only seen her a few times. Now things between her and Helen were strained at best. She had tried to reach out to her sister-in-law a few years ago, just after Helen and Monty were married and Adele was a baby. But Helen had always been distant and somewhat aloof. She was a real Midwesterner, focused within her own box and very buttoned-up. Her own parents had divorced when she was a child, and she never mentioned her absent father; her mother had remarried and lived in California.

Helen had moved to Atlanta to work at an investment firm, and she made decent money. Which was imperative, since she was the family's breadwinner. How was she able to deal with their current situation? Was she just in denial? She was equally liable with Monty on the mortgage, the notes to Candace, and the home equity loan from the bank that Candace had foolishly cosigned.

Candace stretched both arms back behind her, releasing tension. Her phone vibrated. It was Rob.

"Darling," he said. "Having a productive day?"

"Fairly. Are you leaving for New York tonight or tomorrow?"

"In the morning, early."

"Marvelous." Candace focused on the screen in front of her, wading through company email. "I think the cleaning lady came today. I should be home around seven."

"I can't wait to unmake the bed."

Candace smiled. "There's another reason I'm glad you're here another night. We need to talk about this decision to marry. There are things we need to discuss."

"Whatever you like," he said. "I'm open to negotiation. I presume we'll be doing a lot of that in the coming years. I'll bring champagne."

Candace loved champagne. "You're so thoughtful, Rob. But you worry me a bit."

He laughed. "You worry *me* a *lot*. However, it's one of your charms."

5

Due

Five weeks later, on a brisk Thursday morning, Monty refilled his coffee mug and headed back to his computer desk. Relishing the solitude, he sat down and pulled up Adam Langford's last email. Initially, Langford had responded positively to Monty's invitation to meet for a drink and talk about investing in personalassistant.com. At the last minute, however, he had reneged, claiming urgent family business.

Monty judged that more than enough time had passed to reestablish contact. He would have to take his time composing an email; it had to be specific, but succinct. Rather than just a reminder of what they had discussed previously, the wording had to be that of the presumptive sale, as though it was a given that Langford was fully on board.

Monty stretched his arms behind him, then began to type up a response. He reread it over and over, tweaking the wording. Twenty minutes later, he felt satisfied with the message and sent it. He'd give the guy until Monday to respond before he would call him. Meanwhile, he would work on developing his brainchild of an idea, using the time to put his creative genius and sharp intellect to work. Let inspiration flow. Monty needed the distraction, anyway, in part to block out the very unwelcome news Helen had given him last night.

Although they had screwed only a handful of times during the last few months, she was pregnant. He remembered at least once or twice when Adele had fallen asleep in front of the big TV and they'd locked the bedroom door. Helen used a diaphragm, and until now it had worked fine. A few years back, when they had conceived Adele, he'd thought (and told her) that he was sterile. He'd had chlamydia back when he was in his twenties, and though he had been treated for it, the doctor had advised him that since he hadn't had symptoms for a long time—typical for men—his fertility was likely permanently impaired.

However, last night after Adele was fast asleep in the bedroom, Helen blurted out that her period was a few weeks late. Then she disappeared into the bathroom to do a pregnancy test. When he heard her gasp, he knew. Apparently this kid was scheduled to arrive in late November, around Thanksgiving. Once Helen got in to see her obgyn and had a sonogram, they'd know the actual due date and could find out the sex.

They didn't need another kid right now, but Monty wasn't too worried about the added expense. Helen would have to figure out how to pay double for day care and all the other costs. But that meant less money would be available to him. Still, there was a potential silver lining. Knowing she was going to have another niece or a nephew could weaken Candace enough to gift them some money again. Maybe she'd even consider forgiving all their debts and paying off the bank loans, like she ought to do. Monty needed more funds to finish the house, to do it right.

Afterward, they needed to live in the house indefinitely, rather than trying to sell it in a crumbling market. He would soon be the head of a family of four, and his family ought to live in a choice neighborhood. Arcadia Lane was located in such a neighborhood. It was in the heart of one of the city's most exclusive areas, where kids went to private schools and families vacationed regularly in Europe. It was the neighborhood where Monty *should* live, where his family belonged.

His sister was a multimillionaire and she thought nothing of dropping ten thousand or more over a weekend—this, he had witnessed in the past. He decided to waste no more time before calling to tell her a new baby was on the way. He dialed her number, got her voicemail, and cursed under his breath. Why couldn't that bitch ever answer his phone calls? He cleared his throat before speaking.

"Hey, Candace," he said after the beep. "Wanted you to be the first to know our big news! Helen's pregnant! We're looking at late November. Give me a call."

If she didn't call back today, she really *was* a bitch, and if she did call and mentioned the house, money, or a job, he'd hang up. His life and his decisions were none of her business.

His laptop dinged, signaling a new email in his inbox.

From: Adam Langford <Adam.Langford@svpd.net>
Sent: Thursday, April 15, 2010 8:57 AM EST
To: Monty Carawan <monty.carawan86@me.com>
Subject: website venture

Monty,
Thanks for your proposal regarding funding for personal-assistant.com. Unfortunately, I don't believe it would be a fit for me. Have you examined all the security ramifications and implications of such an idea? I dare say that if this type of all-inclusive website could have been done, it would have been by now.

Good luck on any future endeavors and give your sister my best.

Adam Langford

Monty slammed his fist against the wall, jarring the shaky table. *"I dare say"? What a fucking jackass.*

Of course it wouldn't have already been done—no one else had come up with it. Of course he had thought of security issues, and knew how to deal with all of them. How could this jerk cut him down so smugly? Apparently, the guy had skimmed Monty's email and written right back without giving it any thought. He was an arrogant asshole and didn't deserve any more of Monty's time, at least not right now.

Monty stood and grabbed his keys. He needed to get out of here and clear his mind.

• • •

Helen Carawan examined her reflection in the ladies' room as she reapplied her lipstick. Leaning close to the mirror, she noticed that her eyes were red, her brows needed attention, and her cheeks looked hollow. She fluffed up her hair, then stepped back and turned to the side to regard her profile and sighed. Thank God she wasn't showing yet. Her waistline had thickened a little, though, and a baby bump would start to protrude soon, probably sooner than it had with Adele. Three years ago, she hadn't had any morning sickness, but this time she felt queasy almost nonstop. At least none of her coworkers had been in the bathroom to hear her vomit. She wanted no one at Vreden Management to know she was pregnant, not yet.

The only person Helen had told so far was her husband. After their terse conversation last night, she had wanted to call Dawn, but had been so depressed that she just couldn't—especially since Dawn and Frank had been going through infertility for some time. Dawn was thirty-six, two years older than Helen, and had been married to Frank for ten years. Soon after tying the knot, they'd started trying to have a baby, but a year later, Dawn was diagnosed with endometriosis. When Helen found herself pregnant so fast after she and

Monty began seeing each other, it had been a little awkward. Dawn was supportive as ever, though, no matter what was going on in her own life. But she wouldn't allow Helen to feel sorry for herself.

Strength—that was what Dawn was for her younger sister, particularly during these last few years. While Dawn had suffered physically and emotionally with infertility, she had continued to be there for Helen, coming down from Chicago when Adele was born. Dawn had never liked Monty—she'd seen right through him when Helen could not. Frank and Dawn were still very much in love and had a fantastic marriage, and Helen envied their relationship. She dialed her sister's number.

"Helen," said Dawn. "How are you?"

Helen swallowed the lump in her throat and spoke in a low tone. "Pregnant."

A second or two passed. "That's great. Really it is—"

"I found out late last night—I think I'm about eight weeks. I'm going to call my doctor this morning to make an appointment."

"Okay, I know you weren't planning this. But it's going to work out."

Helen felt her eyes welling up. "I guess it'll have to."

"How are you feeling?"

"Crappy. Throwing up—every day. Tired. Cranky. Upset."

"So, I guess you told Monty."

"Of course."

"Have you told Adele? Or anyone else?"

"No. I've got to process this first."

"I understand. I won't tell Frank. But you'll tell me when I can?"

Helen glanced around to make sure no one was looking at her and then leaned on her desk. "Oh, Dawn! What am I gonna do? I have hardly any sick days left this year, and this fall I'll be out on maternity. Plus, I've heard rumors of layoffs around here for weeks."

Vreden was a real estate investment trust company, one of several REITs forced to contract in the collapsing market.

"Rumors are just rumors. I know they're hard to deal with. You're a good worker, though, and you've been at the company for years."

"I'm not indispensable. What I do doesn't contribute to the bottom line. All I do is make brochures and write copy for the website. A bunch of people have already quit and found new jobs."

"Okay, look. I know from what I see every day, things are tough. Companies are downsizing. CEOs and top management employees are worried about their investments," said Dawn. She was a private wealth advisor at a financial services company. "But you're the most experienced and the most talented in your area. You're the kind of person they'll keep. You're going to survive, I know you are. Instead of worrying about your job, what you have to focus on is the baby. And yourself."

"I know."

"You're strong, Helen. The thing is, and I know you don't want to hear this, but Monty has to get a job. Any job."

"But he works on the house every day—"

"Fuck the house. He needs to bring in some income, and you need to see his paycheck. Things have changed now, Helen, and you've got to talk to him about it. Confront him."

Helen shifted in her chair. "I know I do. No matter how angry he gets or what he does."

"You're not afraid of him, are you? Please tell me you have no reason to be."

"Dawn. I'm not. But when he loses his temper, that ends any discussion. He walks away." *After breaking something.*

"You cannot let him walk away. You have to deal with this. He has to make some money—he has to help you support your family. This thing with the house is an excuse. You said yourself that even when Candace lends you guys more money, nothing ever changes on the house. You need to find out what he's doing with that money—money that you owe her, too."

Helen leaned farther down and rested her elbows on her desk. "I don't know how I'm going to do that. He'll accuse me of not trusting him—of doubting him."

"Let him accuse you. You shouldn't trust him—you can't anymore, and I wish you never had. You cannot let him keep on bullying you. You're the one with the job—you make a good salary. You have the power. Use it. Open a bank account in your own name. Give him an ultimatum. Tell him he's off your dime unless A, he brings you in on all the financials on the house immediately, and B, he gets a fucking job."

"You make it sound easy. First of all, no one would even hire him. His work record is spotty."

"He can find a job. He can deliver pizzas. Work at the goddamn grocery store, a hardware store. Anything."

"He'll never do it."

"He has to. Listen, I know you're in shock that you're pregnant. You're upset and you feel horrible. But you need to take control of your marriage. If Monty gets off his ass and gets a job, you guys will have more money. And if you take over that renovation, get it done and get the house sold—even at a loss—your world changes."

"If, Dawn. If. Those are big ifs."

"Demand it, Helen. When Candace finds about the baby—"

"I'm not telling her. Not yet," said Helen.

"Well, when she does, and she will, she needs to demand it, too. That he work, not 'on the house,' but at a paying job. Not because she's his sister, but because she's a creditor. She's got a ton of money invested in that house, and I'm sure she requires specifics from him on that renovation—a regular report of where the money's going.

At least I hope she does. I think you need to call her today and tell her you're pregnant."

"I know, but—"

"Before *he* does."

"He may have told her already," said Helen. "He doesn't tell me when they talk."

"Well, I think you need to call her yourself. I know you two aren't close. But she's a businesswoman, and she's your sister-in-law. Both of you have a vested interest in accountability."

"I don't know if I'll call her." *I won't even call Mom. She'd be absolutely no help, as usual—she'd be the opposite.*

"I love you so much. I hate to stand by and watch what you're going through."

Helen saw her boss walk out of his office. "I love you, too. Listen, I gotta go. I'll call you later."

She put the phone down and stared at the computer screen in front of her. She couldn't talk to anyone else right now. Her mind was too focused on her baby forming within her body, and on her altered future.

She had to think of the positives—the negatives were too upsetting. Her situation was far from ideal, but she was already a mother, and thankful for Adele. Maybe this baby was a boy, and if so, maybe that would make a difference to Monty. No matter what it was, maybe just having two children would make him a more of a partner. Maybe it could bring them together as a couple.

Whatever happened, though, she had to deal with it. She had to chase away her initial feelings of panic and despair and replace them with optimism and hope.

• • •

Candace stepped into the conference room at her Atlanta office in Buckhead where all eleven members of the marketing team awaited her, laptops open.

"SwimZ. That's the name," Candace said to the group. "Not SwimZuit, or SwimZ-suit. Five letters, just like SlimZ. Only one letter changes." She glanced from one face to the next. "This will be the label—the change in logo for swimwear. The tall, skinny girl that's the *l* in SlimZ is going to be the *w* in SwimZ, but wearing a black SwimZ and relaxing on a chaise lounge. You'll be getting the proofs in a few days."

Candace's phone buzzed. Checking it, she saw a text message from Rob. She turned to the head of sales and marketing, who led this group as well as the nine-member sales team. "Amanda, I'm leaving you to conduct this meeting. Everyone has received an email of the agenda. Make sure we know where we are on all social media, including our new Twitter account. I want a report on the internal action plan on my desk by five o'clock."

Candace left the room, read Rob's message, and called her twenty-four-year-old assistant into her office.

"Jess, shut the door," she said. "I want you to know that I'm grateful that you've kept knowledge of my engagement to yourself these past few weeks. Where are we on the plans?"

"Oh, not a problem. I've got calls into all the New York City hotels that you and Mr. Chandler wanted me to look into."

"Call him Rob."

Jess smiled. "Rob. And I'm working on the guest list."

Candace reached into an interior compartment of her black leather Fendi Peekaboo bag and took out a small turquoise felt envelope. Opening it, she slid on the engagement ring that she and Rob had selected: a five-carat sapphire surrounded by several large, round diamonds set in platinum. Jess gasped.

"Oh my God! It's gorgeous!"

Candace smiled. "I think so, too. Not too big, is it?"

"Oh, no. Does this mean—are you gonna wear it, now? Let everyone know?"

"Well, Rob finally got a chance to tell his mother in person, so we decided it's time. PR needs to know now anyway, since it's going to happen a few weeks after Fashion Week in September."

"So, do you want me to help get the word out in the office today?"

"I'll decide and let you know. For now, please email me a short summary of where you are on the plans. Your to-do list, showing what's done and what's not done, and look for my response."

"Right away." Jess retreated a step, then turned to exit the office and go back to her desk.

Candace picked up her phone and contemplated listening to Monty's voicemail. He had called this morning while she was getting her nails done. Ever since David had received those copies of vendor invoices from him a few weeks ago, neither she nor her money manager had heard from her brother. Thank God David had been absolutely right when he said Monty's threats in that angry email last month were bluffs. There was nothing Monty could really do to her.

Pretty soon, like the rest of the world, he would know about her decision to marry Rob later this year. She didn't feel the need to tell him herself. When he found out, she knew he would turn the news of her engagement into another petition for cash. She studied her ring. Why shouldn't she and Rob spend their money on a lavish New York wedding—money that both of them had worked very hard to earn? Her brother would never understand it, she was certain. His only mission, what he spent all of his time and energy on, was to guilt her into forking over small chunks of her fortune.

This he did, while judging her for her success. He had no idea what it was like to put in the hours to build a career, much less a business. Candace was sure that any one of her employees here at SlimZ, down to the youngest and last hired, had more work experience than her thirty-seven-year-old brother. It was true that he'd had various jobs over the last two decades, but he'd always either quit or been fired after a few months. Each time, he claimed that he was much smarter than his boss, that his intelligence and talent had been undervalued.

He talked continually about "the next big thing" he was going to produce, the great idea he was going to propose and the mint he would make on it. When Candace had come up with her own invention and founded her company, he'd been extremely critical, insanely jealous, and infuriated. He'd gotten over it, though, and had maintained his pattern of avoiding work, supported by a string of live-in girlfriends and not getting close to the altar until Jeanine.

Then one day he called and said he was the father of a baby girl and was about to marry her mother. The next week, Candace came to meet Adele and Helen. After they got married, she gave the three of them twelve thousand dollars apiece. Then Monty had gotten her alone and made her listen to his appeal. With teary eyes and remorseful about his past mistakes, he fed Candace a sob story about wanting to finally make something of himself, and begged her to give him the chance. He said he'd found the perfect house to renovate. He would do much of the work himself and oversee the rest. It would be a great opportunity, he claimed, to develop his skills and get experience for a career in the business. Invoking the memory of their father and not forgetting to mention their mother's death, he pleaded with Candace to back him financially.

With little rational analysis and overmuch emotion, Candace had caved. Once Monty and Helen bought a house they couldn't afford without Candace's help, Monty had begun his constant pleas for cash. She was glad she had stood her ground in March and refused to supply him with another hundred grand. David hadn't received the rest of the documents he'd requested, but since Candace wasn't out any more money, she had put that fact out of her mind. She'd been very busy.

She listened to Monty's message. Another baby? What was the *matter* with them? She sat back in her chair and exhaled, closing her eyes. After a deep breath, she dialed her brother's number.

He picked up on the first ring. "Candace! Are you in town?"

She cleared her throat. "Congratulations on the pregnancy, Monty. How's Helen?"

"She's terrific. Just found out," he said in a cheery tone. "As happy about it as I am."

"How old will Adele be by then—three, I guess?"

"Right. Listen, Candace—"

Candace leaned back; her grip on the phone tightened. "No, you listen, Monty. I assume that this was planned. Whether it was or wasn't is none of my business."

"*That's* for damn sure," he snapped.

"However, it does underscore your financial situation—"

"Which is also none of your business."

"To the contrary, that is very much my business, and you know it. David hasn't heard anything more from you—"

"Correction, Candace. I haven't heard any more from *you*. For weeks. You don't answer my calls, you don't reply to my emails—"

"Let's just cut to the chase, shall we? What *is* the situation with the house? You need to update me. A year ago, you showed me a list of everything that remained to be done. Here we are today, and I've no idea what's been completed. I don't know what's happened to the funds I loaned you or to the draws you've taken on the home equity loan that I cosigned."

"I sent your little bean counter the invoices last month. Don't tell me he didn't mention them. Perhaps you've been distracted lately."

"David has received exactly two invoices. I presume there have been many more. You know that wasn't all that was required, either. I expect you to comply with the *all* the terms we agreed upon."

"I *have* complied," said Monty, his voice rising. "You're the one who isn't holding up your end of the bargain."

"What are you talking about? Last April, you said all the work would be finished by the end of the summer, and you'd get the certificate of occupancy. That didn't happen. Then you got the home equity loan and said the renovation would be complete by January. You said you'd take photos and get it on the market, and you haven't done it. What's the story on that?"

"We've had several cost overruns that have caused a delay. They were unavoidable."

"Where's the *evidence* of these 'cost overruns'? Explain them to me, Monty. Where's the transparency?"

"I cannot even believe that I'm related to you," he said. "We must have different fathers."

"You're an asshole."

"*You* are a crazy, paranoid, insecure, calculating bitch with a germ phobia and a weight obsession. You won't succeed in manipulating me—"

"Me manipulate *you*? Monty, you're projecting," she said and gave a harsh laugh. "It's you who've been manipulating me. For years."

"Fuck you, Candace. That's complete bullshit. Your narcissism is incredible. I told you I needed more money last month and you ignored me. Do you realize that we're still living in the guesthouse?"

"Are you telling me the house isn't livable? That you still don't have the C.O.?"

"Here's what I'm saying. Listen carefully. We have another baby on the way. You've refused to provide the funds I need to finish the renovation. You know the market has been spiraling downward. You invested in the property, and if you keep on withholding money, if I have to walk away from that house, *you're* the one who's going to be fucked. Not me."

"What in the hell are you talking about?"

"Ask David."

"I will. Look, Monty. You've allowed this project to run massively over budget. If you need more money to complete it, go get a job and make the money."

"I don't have *time* for a job, Candace."

She closed her eyes and clenched her teeth. Then she exhaled. "Why not? What is so hard about getting up off your ass and going to work every day?"

Monty huffed. "I *am* working—seven days a week—as the unpaid general contractor on this property. Every bit of *Helen's* salary is already out the door before she brings it in. I'm not being compensated for what I do, and because of that, we have no extra money."

"Are you saying you want funds from me to pay yourself a salary? Good God, Monty. The ongoing financial issues you and Helen have are not my fault, nor is the state of the real estate market."

"I am saying that I'm acting as general contractor. I'm working. I'm doing everything that needs to be done, and I get no credit for it, no money, and no respect."

"I don't believe for a *second* that you're 'working' every day. If you are, let's see the proof. What's more, I didn't have to do *anything* for you financially."

"Then why did you? As I recall, you said you believed in me, and in this project. That Dad would have loved doing one like it, that he would have *wanted* me to do it—"

"*You* said that, Monty."

"Do you think he would want his grandchildren to be living in a crappy little cottage while you keep us from finishing the house?"

"Look. It's not me who's responsible for this situation. Here's the reality: as a huge favor, I agreed to loan you a considerable sum to buy the place, renovate it, and sell it. You insisted that when you were finished, you'd be able to get three times what you paid for it. You've put my money at risk and your own credit in jeopardy. You've dragged your feet, lied to me, and refused to provide the documentation that you agreed to."

"You must be hallucinating from lack of calories."

"Monty, join the real world. Live up to your commitments and stop being delusional. Your behavior is absolutely inexcusable. You should be expressing only gratitude toward me, not any kind of animosity."

"You're a fucking *lunatic*," he screamed. "You've treated me like shit, not the other way around. As always."

Candace spoke slowly. "I know it's difficult, but you need to understand this. If you don't comply with the terms of our agreement, if you aren't forthright with me and David, I'll take over the whole damn thing and get it sold myself. Immediately. You and your family can find another place to live."

"I'll tell Helen you were *thrilled* to hear about her pregnancy, Candace."

"Do that, Monty. Tell her I wish her the best," she said. Despite her earlier resolve, she continued, "And tell her something else for me: Rob Chandler and I are getting married this fall in New York. She can email me your new address this summer for your invitation to my wedding."

"I don't think so. She'll be eight months pregnant by then. None of your *family* will be able to attend."

"Good-bye, Monty." She hung up and dropped the phone into her bag.

• • •

David Shepherd finished his lunch at the Best Spot Bakery and began to walk the short distance back to his office in the Jefferson-Sloan Building. It was a beautiful April day, with the sun shining high in a cloudless sky at the end of the noon hour. Manicured rows of flowers bloomed along both sides of Peachtree Street, lining the sidewalk and filling every possible space surrounding the downtown hotels, storefronts, and skyscrapers. Spring in Atlanta was lovely, but with it came the pollen season, and David suffered from it every year. He took allergy medication daily beginning in late February and was never without his handkerchief.

His phone vibrated in his pocket. Retrieving it, he saw it was Candace Morgan. He cleared his throat and answered the call.

"Hi, David. I spoke to Monty this morning."

"You took his call?"

"No—I called him back. He'd left me a voicemail earlier saying Helen's pregnant."

"So you offered your congratulations, I presume—"

"Yes, but I didn't leave it at that, unfortunately. I started questioning him about the house and his lack of communication about it. Then he launched into a tirade and attacked me personally. Apparently he still doesn't have the C.O. The three of them are still living in that one-bedroom guesthouse in the back, and the baby is due in November."

David reached Capstone Road and turned the corner. "Did you ask him if he's found a job?"

"After he accused me of not giving him enough funds to complete the project, after he said I'd be 'fucked' if he walks away, I told him to find a job and make the money to finish it."

David entered an elevator and punched in the number fifteen. "And he said?"

"That he *is* working—as general contractor on the place. Then he implied that I should be paying him a salary."

David bit his lip. "How did the conversation end?"

"Badly. I stayed calm, but I said that if he doesn't start complying with the terms we agreed to, I'll take over, sell it for whatever it will fetch, and they'll have to find somewhere else to live."

David exited the elevator. "Did you give him a deadline? A date?"

Candace sighed. "No. Well, I used the word 'immediately.'"

"Okay, look," David said as he entered his private office at Elite Financial Planning. He shut the door and sat down at his desk. "If you like, I'll draft an email to him for your review. I can list the items that we have received from him so far and spell out what we still need, and by what date. Meanwhile, I'll contact Whitney Jamison at the bank and find out the status on the HELOC."

"Yes, do that. But before you call her, before you even write the email, do something else. Go back and figure out how much money I've given him, how much I've lent him directly, and how much I'm liable for on what I cosigned. Then when you talk to Whitney, verify the loan amounts—make sure your information is correct."

"Of course."

"Then send me a list of everything. Can you do it today?"

"Not a problem. Anything else?"

"Not now." Candace's phone signaled a call from Rob. "I've got to take another call. Talk to you later."

David hung up, placed his BlackBerry on his desk, and pulled up Candace's accounts on his computer. Like everyone else's, her stocks had taken a beating, but he was confident that they would recover and perform well over the long term. Her investments in three hedge funds that he had recommended were doing very well. Her overall financial position wasn't bad at all. Even if she had to write off all the funds she had put into her brother's house, her other real estate investments were sound, as long as she chose to hold on to them for a while.

David had managed all of her personal investments since before she had taken her apparel company public five years ago, and his advisory role had gradually morphed into a counselor about private matters. That was what often happened with his array of very wealthy clients: their money and their relationships became interconnected and complicated, especially for those who struggled to define and enforce boundaries. Guilt was usually the cause, and each of them had his or her own unique circumstances. David found satisfaction making his clients' money and investments perform, but he had to admit that he didn't mind the more intimate facets of the job.

Candace's situation puzzled him somewhat, though. Most of his clients who faced similar predicaments were dealing with an adult child, or even an elderly parent—someone they felt a responsibility toward and with whom they had established a pattern of enabling over a period of many years. But Candace had enabled Monty and tolerated his irresponsible behavior even though he was just two years her junior. David wondered what their relationship had been like over the years. He knew she felt guilty about the car wreck that killed her mother, but that was over twenty years ago.

According to Candace, after the tragedy, Monty had briefly enrolled at the University of Georgia. When he flunked out, he had been expected to work construction, but he had shown little interest. He moved in with his girlfriend and found a job as a waiter. A succession of restaurant jobs—and girlfriends—followed. Apparently, the guy had charmed and bedded more women than most men had ever dated. Then Candace's father died of a heart attack. She had been filled with grief and had faulted herself for not being aware of his condition.

Reportedly, Monty had the opposite reaction and focused only on what he had to gain: money. Jack Carawan was a saver with no debt to his name, and left most of his money to his son. However, Monty had been furious that he hadn't received everything. The friction that previously existed between brother and sister turned into extreme animosity. Candace said Monty had developed a permanent sense of entitlement, and David had seen the evidence of it. He felt sorry for his client having such a brother and losing her parents the way she had. The rich had their problems, too, and Candace had had more than her share.

What bewildered David was what Monty had done with all the funds Candace had supplied to him over the last few years. The two invoices from vendors that he had scanned and emailed to David documented only a tiny fraction of the total amount he'd received. Was the man using the money for something else—like gambling? That was possible; his personality seemed indicative of a risk-taker. He was too much of a fitness buff to have a drug problem. Was it women? But paying for sex didn't fit his pattern—he had always had women support him, rather than the reverse.

David wrote a concise email to Monty with bullet points outlining Candace's requirements and saved it as a draft; he'd put together the list of her fund outlays next. He'd call Whitney at Memorial Bank tomorrow, or possibly later today, a Thursday. Yes, that would be better. More work got accomplished on Thursdays than on any other day of the week, and little was decided on Fridays—too many people, especially bankers, took that day off. As he perused the spreadsheet of Candace's loans and gifts to Monty, his inbox indicated a new message. It was from Whitney and marked with a red flag.

From: Whitney.Jamison@MemorialBank.com
Sent: Thursday, April 15, 2010 1:22 PM EST
To: David.Shepherd@efp.com
Subject: Carawan-Morgan loan

David,

Hope you are doing well.

Mr. Monty Carawan has been in touch with me to discuss renewing the Carawan-Morgan home equity loan for another 6 months. He has requested that we refinance the 1st mortgage (balance of $193,148) and $500,000 HELOC (current balance of $479,594), rolling them into a new home equity loan in the amount of $750,000. This will allow over $77,000 in availability to draw on the new HELOC. I will need Ms. Morgan's signature on the new note.

All past due interest on the existing HELOC must be paid, as well as the last 4 months' mortgage payments, currently past due. We also require the next 3 months' interest, the 2010 property taxes, and one year's insurance in escrow.

Shall I FedEx the original new loan document to your office for Ms. Morgan's signature?

Thanks so much.
Whitney Jamison, SVP
Memorial Bank Real Estate Lending

David read the email twice. Candace was going to hit the roof when she saw it and learned what was going on. Only a month ago, Monty declared he had "no plans" to get behind on the bank payments, but didn't say that he was already in arrears. He'd also claimed he had eighty-five thousand left to draw on the HELOC, and here he was with only a little over twenty grand remaining. Candace would be furious that he had contacted the bank to roll the mortgage into it and increase the total liability by another fifty thousand plus. Learning that Monty assumed she would make his back payments and fund interest and insurance fees would further enrage her.

What had begun as a major but ill-planned renovation that Candace had been generous enough to finance had turned into a train wreck.

He dialed Whitney's number at the bank.

6

A Mess

Whitney, this is David Shepherd," he said after the beep. "I've seen your email. Please give me a call as soon as possible." David looked over the numbers on his screen that Candace had requested.

Gifts: $36,000 ($12k each) in 2007, '08, and '09: $108,000
Initial Investment in Home: $600,000
Renovation Loan: $200,000
2 additional loans ($20k + $25k): $45,000

Total: $108,000 + $845,000 = $953,000

HELOC: $500,000, with new request to raise to $750,000

TOTAL: $1,453,000 (with new HELOC, $1,703,000)

The bottom line represented a very small fraction of Candace's net worth. David was sure she didn't expect the $108,000 in gifts to be paid back, so the new number was $1,595,000. However, she had announced back in January that she was wouldn't be gifting any more money to the Carawans. David wondered if she would change her mind now that they had a baby on the way.

Couldn't the Carawans afford the initial $200,000 mortgage and keep it current? Candace would not want to allow them to do away with a mortgage and increase her total exposure in the deal, and David would not advise her to do so. For the bank, a loan of $750,000 guaranteed by one of Atlanta's most successful business-women was as good as gold, even in the depressed housing market.

Several years ago, real estate values in this city—affected by the 1996 Olympics—were sky high and climbing. The property on Arcadia Lane may have fetched two and a half million in those days. But now the home would sell for far less, if it sold at all. Though situated in a prime, high-end location in Buckhead, the unspoken truth was that the pool of buyers in that price range had dwindled severely during the current recession. After the financial crisis of 2008, some said that it would be at least a decade before the prices of these homes returned to their former levels.

David would need to connect with Whitney for the past due mortgage amounts, past due interest, HELOC interest, insurance, and taxes. The home would have to bring well over $1.6 million, and David wasn't sure that it would, especially if—as he feared—much of the renovation work was incomplete.

• • •

Monty opened his laptop and plugged it into an outlet at Starbucks as he waited for the barista to make his grande decaf latte with skim milk. He needed to calm down and wipe his mind clean of his sister's emotionless response to the news of his wife's pregnancy.

Candace was such an unfeeling bitch—almost masculine. Yes, she was a man. Maybe she was gay.

It would make a lot of sense if the two of them didn't have the same father. This wasn't the first time Monty had considered the possibility. Candace favored Jack Carawan, but Monty resembled Susannah. Their mother could have had an affair—or even a tryst— with another man while married to Jack. It was certainly plausible. How could Jack have satisfied her 100 percent of the time, anyway? Susannah had been a strikingly beautiful woman and very charming, with an outgoing personality similar to Monty's. By contrast, Jack had been stoic and cold. Like Candace.

Monty picked up his latte at the counter and sat back down. He shook his head and sipped the hot beverage. He'd never know the truth about his ancestry, but perhaps there was a man out there somewhere, a man other than Jack Carawan, whose genes Monty had inherited. A man who was almost as unique and special as Monty. If that were true, then his surname wouldn't be Carawan, a name with ties to Appalachia. Susannah had chosen the name Candace; his sister had been the fat girl that the other kids called Candy Caravan. Monty had been given Susannah's maiden name, Montgomery. No one had made fun of him.

He scrolled absently through his files—most of the labels were cryptic and obscure. He clicked on roark.xls, a file containing the phony construction budget he had created a while back for his sister's lackey. It would be easy to change the dates, plug in the amounts, rename it, and attach it to an email to Shepherd.

He had named the file after his literary idol, Ayn Rand's Howard Roark. He'd read *The Fountainhead* when he was sixteen and had reread it many times since then, strongly identifying with the novel's protagonist. Like him, Howard Roark had been misunderstood and held back by society. But he had lived by his principles, never caving in to the establishment. An architectural genius, Roark's talent surpassed all others.

When Monty was a teenager, Susannah had told him his IQ was 160, well above the threshold for membership in Mensa. If only he had had the proper training at the right architectural school, Monty could have become a real-life Howard Roark: the world's best architect. He would have built a famous monument, or perhaps whole new city centers. The world would have recognized his genius. But his vision, his creativity, his brilliance, all the qualities that set him apart from the masses had gone unrealized and unappreciated. So far, the world had screwed him, but had rewarded imbeciles like his sister and her boyfriend.

Within a few minutes, Monty completed the changes to the bogus budget, renamed the file, and sent it to Shepherd with no explanation. If that asshole or Candace had any questions, he would just ignore them. Taking a sip of his latte, he checked his watch. In just over an hour, he would go to the gym and do an abbreviated workout before heading over to the practice field later in the afternoon. His old friend Chip Duncan had persuaded him to help coach his son's Little League baseball team. Monty enjoyed being outside with the boys where he was respected and admired. No one controlled him or pressured him there, and it didn't matter if he missed a practice. Though Chip was in charge, he treated Monty like an equal and was grateful to have him.

The two of them had played just about every sport together growing up, including high school baseball and football—Chip was bigger than Monty and had even played for a year at a Division II school. Now he worked in sales, was married to a nurse, and had a son and a baby daughter. Monty would tell Chip today about Helen's pregnancy—maybe she was carrying a boy. Yes, until he received confirmation from the doctor, he would just assume he was going to have a son. Another female in the household might be unbearable.

• • •

Jess looked over the email she had written to Candace listing the tasks completed in planning the wedding. She didn't mind the extra assignment—it would make her job a lot more fun for the next few months. Her boss was demanding, but she wasn't as bad as some people thought, and the list wasn't as long as it could have been. Candace didn't want to bother with a "Save the Date" before sending the formal invitations, for example. Nor did she want a wedding website, as so many couples did. She and Rob already had all the possessions they wanted, so they weren't registering for gifts. Other than the invitation, the tasks centered on the wedding day itself: ceremony, flowers, photographer, music, menu, and cake.

Though this would be the second marriage for both of them, no expense was to be spared. However, Candace had been very clear that the wedding was to be elegant and understated. It would take place at Holy Cross Episcopal Church in Midtown Manhattan, where Rob's mother Deirdre was still a member. Jess had booked the reception at the landmark St. George Hotel on Manhattan's Upper East Side. The guest list included the principals at Rob's firm; a few New York politicians; some of Candace's industry contacts; a few celebrities; and the chairman of the board of SlimZ, Myron Frisch. The only SlimZ employees on the list were Candace's direct reports: Paula in design; Amanda in sales and marketing; COO Ginger; and Courtney, the company's chief financial officer.

Jess glanced at the door to her boss's office, which was shut. She had a feeling that after reviewing the list, Candace would decide to invite the second tier: Shelly, head of product development in design; Darlene, in charge of PR, social media, and marketing; Melinda, head of sales; and Holly (director of fulfillment), Phoebe (product coordinator), and Erin (head of IT). That was what Jess would do—but it wasn't up to her. She exhaled deeply, looked up from her computer screen, and pictured the beautiful sapphire-and-diamond ring Candace had shown her. A faint ding sounded, signaling a new message in her inbox. Jess came back to reality.

It was from her boss, with the subject line "Honeymoon." Candace wanted her to look into a luxury private resort in Bermuda called Kensington Beaches. The wedding was scheduled for Saturday, October 9, and the couple planned to take a two-week honeymoon. Jess replied that she would get on it immediately and included her updated checklist.

Two minutes later, she received a response with an attachment from Rob: his mother's guest list. Jess was supposed to integrate it with Candace's, then send the combined list back. Candace also directed her to include herself and a date. If the only SlimZ employees in attendance were the top tier and herself, it would be pretty awkward. But she suspected—no, she knew—Candace wanted her to be there as her assistant. Even so, it would probably be the most fabulous wedding Jess would ever attend, including her own, someday.

• • •

The list of invited guests totaled eighty-two so far, and Candace was determined to keep the number below one hundred. With reluctance and out of politeness to Helen, she had included her and Monty, knowing they wouldn't attend. Fine. That worked for Candace. She had no plans to invite any of her extended family members. Her only aunt was her mother's sister, Stella, who had passed away single and childless. Jack had been an only child. However, relatives from both sides of Rob's family were on his mother's list.

Candace's mother had been raised in the Episcopal Church, but her father had grown up as a Pentecostal. However, neither he nor Susannah had had a strong faith connection. As a result, the family never spent much time in a house of worship. Candace's view was that a belief in God (or any higher power) was strictly personal and not subject to the rules of any particular church. But, hedging her bets, she considered herself a Christian and wasn't opposed to a wedding in Deirdre Chandler's New York City parish.

Thank God she had Jess to do the bulk of the planning and handle all the details. Jess would do the research, and Candace could just make the decisions, the same way she did with regard to business. She had much more pressing items on her agenda, like the launch of the new line—things were moving along well, so far. Among the designers and product development staff she sensed an excitement almost equal to her own about the product venture. Her people were the most creative and talented in the industry and they took her direction well. They were good listeners.

The sales team, with its in-house reputation for inflexibility and intransigence, was another matter. All nine members—led by Melinda—reported directly to Amanda, who had been at the company for over five years and was valued as a Team A player. Amanda was also in charge of the marketing team, led by Darlene, which handled PR, advertising, and social media. But an inherent adversarial relationship existed between Amanda's group and Paula's design staff. Sales personnel were often critical of new ideas and resistant to change; they preferred the easy route of established customer relationships. Designers, on the other hand, were emotionally invested in their creations, naturally defensive of them, and unable to relate to sales issues.

However, Candace was confident in her managers and in the new swimsuit line. As long as her vision was captured in it and its secrecy was maintained, orders from the department stores would fly after the line's unveiling at Fashion Week in September. SlimZ products enjoyed prominent display space in retail stores that were proud to carry them. SwimZ would be the hot new suit, the must-have for next year's spring and summer seasons, the line that would change the market. Candace knew that it would succeed, not just because of the appealing designs, but also because of the innovative way they would be displayed in the stores: by size, not pattern or color.

It made perfect sense, and she marveled that no one else had done something so sensible and smart. Every SlimZ product was sold that way in the stores and online, and Candace believed that all women's apparel should be as well. Men's clothing was always grouped by size in the stores, allowing the customer to look only at what would fit him. Why shouldn't women's clothing be sold the same way? Instead, for decades the stores had displayed products sorted by pattern and color, forcing women to dig through each rack to find her size. At best, it was frustrating and annoying; at worst, it was insulting.

Retailers had insisted on merchandising women's clothing that way, and they reserved size groupings for deeply discounted items they were trying to unload—but they took little care in maintaining those groupings. Candace felt that the whole system was flawed and led to lower aggregate sales. Her new swimwear line would be displayed in size collections only—this was a nonnegotiable in discussions with Myron, her chairman of the board. If a department store buyer of SwimZ refused to sign a contract promising to group the suits by size, he or she would not be allowed to carry the line.

Candace scrolled through her email inbox, skimming her messages and deleting some without reading the contents. Where was the information she had requested from David? Surely he had had time to send it to her by now. Then she spotted an email from him with the subject line "Fund Outlays." As promised, he had listed the amounts she had given, loaned, and was liable for. The total approached one and a half million dollars. He had also written a very troubling addendum:

I have forwarded an email from Whitney Jamison. I just spoke with her. I also received an updated construction budget of dubious validity from Monty. Let me know if you'd like me to send it to you.

Evidently they have drawn almost $65,000 more on the HELOC within the last few weeks. If you sign the new note, it would increase your total exposure on the property to $1,595,000. I strongly advise you not to do so.

In our conversation, Whitney gave me the following information:

Past due mortgage amount: $6,216
Past due interest on HELOC: $7,540
3 months interest on new note: $10,508
1 year property insurance: $7,126
1 year property taxes (Fulton County): $32,008

As you requested, I am working on a draft email to Monty listing items outstanding and specifying your requirements going forward. Look for it shortly.

In shock, Candace went back to her inbox, found the forwarded email, and read it in disgust. Damn her brother! What nerve to have negotiated a new home equity loan, expecting her to cosign, after defaulting on it and on his mortgage—while drawing sixty-five thousand more. This new loan would erase his mortgage payment and accrue interest only—interest that Candace would have to keep current until the house sold at some future date. It was a game of chicken, and she was losing.

She—David—needed to find out once and for all what exactly remained to be done to finish the renovation and get the house into marketable condition. She didn't want to take over the project, nor did she relish asking David to micromanage it—an additional task for which she would have to pay him.

She started to call David, but stopped. She wasn't ready to discuss it with him yet. The person she wanted to talk to right now was Rob. They had spoken briefly earlier today, but in the middle of a busy workday, he was probably unavailable. She sat back in her chair and took a deep breath.

Her laptop dinged, signaling a new message. Hoping it was David's draft to Monty, she leaned back toward the computer and opened her inbox again.

From: Helen Carawan <helen.carawan@vreden.com>
Sent: Thursday, April 15, 2010 2:15 PM EST
To: Candace Morgan <candace.morgan@slimz.org>
Subject: news

Candace:
I don't know if you have spoken to Monty, but I wanted you to know that we are expecting another baby this fall. I thought it might be a good idea for us to meet with you to discuss our current financial situation regarding the house. Please let me know when and where would be convenient.

Helen

Candace dialed David's number.

"David, I am appalled. The audacity of my brother to go to the bank and arrange this ridiculous new loan—don't worry, I'm not even considering paying their past due payments, interest, or anything else. This is complete bullshit. What I've gifted them alone is more than enough money to take care of it."

"I don't disagree. However, I'm sure that money is long gone. I take it you won't sign this new note?"

"Why should I? Can't these people pay their mortgage? My God. On top of all this, I just got an email from Helen saying she wants me to meet with the both of them about their 'current financial situation.' I'm not doing it, David."

"Hm. Actually, I think the fact that she's proposed it is a good sign. I dare say she's having a reality check now that she's pregnant, which I assume wasn't planned," said David. "Helen is the stable one in the marriage, though. She may not know everything Monty's up to. Perhaps she wants to have a come-to-Jesus meeting with him. I think it could be a positive step forward. If you agree but don't want to be there, I could attend as your representative."

"Have you finished the draft email you told me you're working on?"

"Just about. I'd like to add some questions for the two of them, though."

"Good. Ask questions like these: What is their combined net income? What are their monthly living expenses, and what is the breakdown? If I'm going to continue as a creditor in this fiasco, I think I have a right to know these things."

"Agreed."

"I realize I should have asked them a long time ago. I just hate being put in this position, though, and being manipulated."

"Candace, I strongly urge you not to sign this new loan."

"I shouldn't. And I won't—at least, not until I get some answers from them and you verify them. At best, they're dysfunctional. I don't want to keep financing their lifestyle."

"Then don't."

"But now that she's pregnant, how can I be so hard-line? Do I just throw them out of the house, take it over, finish it, and sell it myself?"

"That's exactly what I've been telling you, that you may have to do. We really need to tour the inside of the house—see what kind of condition it's in."

"Okay, but here's what we're going to do right now. You finish that draft and send it to me. I'm not sure if we'll send it to Monty or if you and I will just discuss it. Actually, yes, that's what we'll do, and then you'll use it as a guide for what needs to happen at this meeting."

"Fine."

"Also, I'm not going to answer Helen's email. I'm going to forward it to you, and I want you to respond to her, copying both me and Monty, with a date and time for a face-to-face at your office, say, early next week. She can take the time off work, and he'll be available—we know that for sure."

"Got it."

"I won't attend it. But in this email, say that you need to see the house, and propose a couple of days and times you're available to go. I may go with you or I may not, it depends on what else I've got going on. But when you go, take pictures of everything."

"Will do. You know, Candace, if you do take it over, bring in your own contractor and so forth, they can continue to live in the guesthouse while the work's being done. You won't have to throw them out—at least, not until the place sells. At that point, they can find a rental property. A house or an apartment. Once you know their income, you'll know what they can afford, and they won't be able to say they can't."

"Here's what I want, David. Ultimately. I want to sever all financial ties with them. I want this house finished, the C.O. obtained, the house listed and then sold as soon as possible for whatever it will fetch, even if that means I end up losing money and writing a little bit off. But I don't want to sink any *more* money into it—no catching up past due payments and no making future payments. I want to get out of this once and for all, baby or no baby. I want to cut them off, permanently."

"Then don't sign the new note."

• • •

Helen returned from the ladies' room to find an email from David Shepherd, Candace's personal financial advisor. Rather than replying to Helen's email, Candace had forwarded it to David, who had responded to Helen and copied Monty and Candace.

Imagining Monty's reaction, Helen's stomach dropped. Not only had David failed to congratulate her on the pregnancy, he had instructed both of them to be at his office at eleven o'clock Monday morning for the meeting that Helen had suggested; Candace wouldn't be there, but David would act as her representative. He also stated that he would come to see the house sometime on Tuesday afternoon "to evaluate its condition."

Distraught, Helen's hand went to her shoulder, her fingers massaging the scar that extended from above her collarbone to beneath her arm and under her bra strap. The ridged surface of her skin felt dry as the blood pulsated beneath. Two and a half inches wide and resembling a smeared road map, it had been a part of her body for so long now. The only person in front of whom she wasn't embarrassed about it was Adele.

When Monty had first seen it, back when the world was different and his only desire was to possess her, he'd briefly recoiled but then recovered, his lust taking over. The look on his face was painfully familiar to Helen, although she had never quite gotten used to it. All these years, she had tried to toughen herself emotionally to the reaction her disfigurement evoked, but the scar she carried within was more tender than the one she wore on the outside. It was her personal iron brand, and she would carry it to her grave.

Monty would have a tantrum when he saw what she had written to his sister. He would be furious that Helen had requested to meet, and even more irate that David, whom he hated, had called the meeting and was planning to speak on Candace's behalf. Helen shuddered, then felt hot anger rising. Why should she have to worry so much about Monty's childishness? Deep down, was she truly afraid of him, as Dawn had asked, or not?

She was. Now that she was carrying another child of his, the truth was that she felt vulnerable and alone. Tears began to form in her eyes as feelings of self-pity began to take hold. She had to be strong—she couldn't panic, no matter what her state of apprehension and alarm. She needed to take her sister's advice and open her own private bank account, then arrange with payroll to switch her direct deposit from the joint account she and Monty had to the new one in her own name.

She felt no shame in recognizing who her husband was and what he might do. The truth was that she had to anticipate it. She couldn't prevent it, but she didn't have to run from it or let fear take over. The smartest and most important thing she could do was to take control of the situation she was facing. The way Candace always did.

Her inbox dinged and she opened another message from David, this one written to Monty and copying Candace and herself.

Monty,
I just listened to your voicemail, but I will not be calling you back due to your unprofessional tone. Please call me when you are ready to have a civil and productive conversation.

I did receive the updated budget you sent, but I have several questions about it which I will bring up to you and your wife in person at the meeting. I will see you and Helen on Monday at eleven o'clock at my office on Capstone Road.

Regards,
David

Helen closed her inbox and tried to refocus on work, opening the graphic she had been working on this afternoon. What an absolute fool Monty was, on top of everything else. Was he just a narcissist? Is that what caused him to behave the way he did? He was more self-absorbed than anyone she had ever met; if only she'd really known who he was three years ago. But she and Dawn had agreed that a woman didn't really know a man until he was her husband.

Another ding. Shit! She had to get some work done today, sometime.

Monty had shot back a response, copying everyone.

David:
"Unprofessional tone?" Coming from you, David, that's incredible. I've kept all of your past, snarky emails in a folder. You won't tolerate from me that which you spurt off. Let's cut all this bullshit, since we don't have a "professional" relationship anyway, nor mutual respect. I am beyond pissed off at both you and your ridiculous client. If she hadn't persisted in ignoring me, we wouldn't be where we are today. I can't wait to be free of her and of you.

From now on I will speak in whatever way I choose and you had better keep your opinions about it to yourself. My sister pays you to handle her millions, not to be her bad boy. Let her talk to me directly or not at all. As for the meeting you are demanding, Helen can go if she wishes—it was her idea—but I will not be gracing you with my presence. Nor will you be allowed access to our home on Tuesday to "evaluate it."

Go fuck yourself.
Monty

7

Blood

Monty paced back and forth in the small living area of the guesthouse, running his fingers through his wet hair. Returning to Arcadia Lane from the ball field at least thirty minutes after Helen and Adele were due home, he'd been dismayed to see that her car wasn't in the drive. He had gone through the day's mail, drunk a bottle of water, showered, and poured himself a large cocktail. What the fuck was Helen doing, emailing his sister, trying to arrange a meeting? And where was his wife right now? She hadn't answered his call or his text. She rarely worked late, and she always let him know if she had to stay at the office to finish some stupid brochure.

Between the gym and the practice field with Chip and a bunch of seven-year-olds, Monty had retrieved and read Shepherd's email on his iPad. Helen didn't know that he had managed to get one of the first iPads available, nor how he had done it. As soon as he had it in his hands, he had immediately disabled the signature setting "Sent from my iPad"—no one needed to know he was in possession of Apple's newest toy before its official release next month. He had paid a premium to get it early. There was no way he was going to spend his time in a long line between two nerds at a mall, or at home waiting for an online shipment that could take weeks. He brought his iPad with him everywhere, surfing the web and managing his email whenever he was out and about. Handier than his laptop, it had become indispensable to keep up with the many projects he had previously filed solely in his brain, a brain that was so much *faster* than those of other people.

Which might have been a source of deep annoyance if it weren't for the very real advantages to be gained. Like with that moron Shepherd. That asshole hadn't taken Monty's call this afternoon, so he had been forced to leave a message; then Shepherd had attacked him in a patronizing email sent to all the parties. *That fucker is not going to micromanage me, no matter what his "boss" tells him to do.* It was clear that Candace's lackey was a fool, in over his head in his career. Monty took great satisfaction in the presumption that Shepherd had lost tons of his clients' money during the financial crisis of 2008. How many of them had taken their shrunken portfolios elsewhere? Monty surmised that it was a large number, and that Candace herself had lost a boatload.

Downing the last of the vodka in his glass, Monty refilled it with ice and poured another, then heard the approach of Helen's car.

"Come on, Boo," she said to their daughter as the two of them entered from the driveway. Monty couldn't stand this nickname she used—the only Boo he'd ever heard of was Boo Radley, the village idiot-recluse.

"What the fuck, Helen!"

"What the fuck, Mommy!" Adele parroted her father, her bright smile shining.

"Monty! Please!" Helen bent down to eye level with the little girl. "Don't say that, sweetie. It's not nice."

"But Daddy—"

"I know, but Daddy didn't mean to. Go on into Mommy's room now and turn on the TV."

Adele did as she was bid, skipping the fifteen feet through the bathroom and into the bedroom. Helen shut the door gently.

"Since we're having another baby, Monty, I just thought it's time to—"

"You *thought*? What *were* you thinking, Hel?" Monty knew she hated it when he called her that. "I can't imagine what was going through your mind. Did you think that Queen Candace would email you back? Or call you? She won't even talk to me! And why did you think it was up to *you* to tell her about the baby?"

"What do you mean? Did *you* call to tell her?"

"I just said, she won't talk to me! I had to leave a voicemail—"

"Monty, listen. I—"

"No, *you* listen. You are not to email her. Or that motherfucker who works for her. I'm the one busting my butt trying to get the house finished, the one who has to deal with the two of them. You don't. So, fucking don't."

Helen kept her voice low and even. "I can email her if I want to, Monty, and I can call her if I want to."

"I forbid you to. How's that? She's my bitchy sister, not yours. She's not Dawn. Dawn the bitch, just a different kind—"

Helen's eyes narrowed and her jaw set. "Leave Dawn out of it!"

"Ah, but you've called Dawn, haven't you? What did the Smart One say? Huh? Did she tell you to write to Candace, to request a meeting?"

"No!"

"Right," said Monty. "I really believe that. You know, I don't much care anyway. She and Frank can go screw each other in married bliss, and never get a kid—"

"I said leave her out of this!"

"How did she take the news? Was she jealous? Why don't we just let her have this one? We don't need another kid anyway, that's for sure."

Helen backed away. "I can't be around you. I'm going to go take care of our daughter."

He grabbed her above the elbow, holding onto her, his large hand closing around her bony left arm. "Let me go," she said quietly, her eyes filling with hate and fury. Then she pulled away slowly, but he tightened his grip and drew her back toward him in a snap. Her side was to him now, and her tender breast of early pregnancy hit against him slightly, just enough to evince pain. She let out a small gasp.

"Where *were* you this evening?" he asked in a low tone. "Why didn't you answer my text?"

"My phone died."

"Bullshit. Tell me where you were." Now he had both of her upper arms in his grip as they stood facing each other. "Tell me."

Helen took a deep breath. "The bank."

Monty's voice was harsh and menacing. "That's not true. The bank closes at five."

"I wasn't at our bank."

"Memorial, then? Where that cunt Whitney Jamison works? The loan officer?"

"No," Helen said. "American Trust Bank. I opened an account."

"Why? Why did you open an account?" Monty let go of her, pushing her back. "Did you switch ours?"

"No. I just—Monty, *I* make the money, and I'm going to manage it, from now on."

"What are you talking about?" He was staring at her now, his eyes wide.

"I'm taking over our finances. I'm having my paychecks deposited in my own account, and I'm paying our bills out of it myself, online. You don't have to do it anymore." She sucked in a breath, waiting.

"Well, this had to be Dawn's bright idea. Dawn, who couldn't stand me from the get-go."

"It doesn't matter. When *you* start bringing home an income, when you come clean with me on the house and the finances, we can talk about being a team again. Meanwhile, I've gotta manage the money I make, and this household's budget. I'm gonna start paying the bills. At the very least."

Monty gritted his teeth. "Whatever, Helen. We're still a team. We're in this *together*, like it or not. You paying the bills isn't going to change anything. However, the money we make belongs to *both* of us, not just to you—"

"You don't *make* any money!"

"Not currently, but when I sell the house, I will, and that money will belong to both of us. If we're still married, that is. What we need right now is the funds from my sister to get the damn place finished, so we can sell it! You're such a goddamn idiot. But then I always knew you were a stupid cow."

"Go ahead and insult me, if it makes you feel good—"

"And you go ahead and have your little meeting with what's-his-fucking-name. David. See if you can get them to be reasonable—being pregnant should help. I've already dealt with Whitney, and she's been in touch with them. All she needs is for Candace to sign off on it. So you go on Monday, alone. I have all of them where I want them. Candace will agree to pay the bank and sign the loan. I'm not going to lose any sleep over it."

Helen gave him a cold stare, then turned toward the bedroom.

"Just remember this, though," Monty said. "If you fuck every-thing up, *I* won't be the only one who suffers. That's for goddamn certain." He picked up his glass and swallowed the last bit of the liquid, then headed over toward the kitchen for a refill as Helen made her way to the bedroom and to Adele.

She caught me off guard, that's all. It's just a different checking account. There's got to be a way I can access it. He added a slice of lime to his drink, took a sip, and leaned back against the cheap counter-top, his eyes closed. *He* was the one who needed a separate account, not Helen. Well, he would just have to talk her into changing her new account into a joint one, to replace the one they already had. He couldn't let her have total control of the monthly income—or worse, permit her to give him an allowance.

But first he would have to undo the damage he had just done. Once Adele was finished with her bath and was in bed, he'd start the process. Maybe he'd even get her to blow him.

• • •

"Darling, I hate to stand by and watch you deal with this," Rob said before he took another sip of Scotch. "I know you can do it, and you will, but it's got to be awfully distracting. At a minimum."

Candace's ice-blue eyes glistened. She reached for her glass of sauvignon blanc and glanced around the restaurant. Chez Vincent was an Atlanta favorite of hers and her fiancé's. "David helps a lot. Truth told, I don't think I could manage it without him."

"Well, I'll have to thank him personally when this is all over. Which it will be soon. He's a good man, a very good man, to represent your interests."

"Mm-hmm," Candace said, nodding. "He understands me. The way I obsess, I guess, and the way I tend to micromanage things sometimes. He knows my background, and how I think about money."

"That's the kind of advisor to have."

"Something's bothering me, though, Rob. Something Monty could be right about."

Rob raised his eyebrows and set down his drink.

"That he and I may not be related," she said. "I mean, perhaps we aren't. Perhaps, at least, we only share one parent."

He cocked his head.

"I don't want to believe it," Candace continued, "but then I also don't want to believe that I'm related to Monty. He's so unlike me—"

"That's for certain."

"We've always been so different. Always."

"Love, that's obvious. To everyone. You've absolutely nothing in common with one another."

"Well, whether we share a father or not, Mother gave birth to us both. What if, in some weird way, some recessive or random way, a future child of ours might be like him? I couldn't have that."

"But our child won't be. Don't fret about it. And we've talked about this. You know I don't care whether we have any children— it's totally up to you. It's you that I want. Having a family is something we'll be open to only if it's your wish."

She looked straight into the deep blue of her intended's eyes, gauging his honesty. Satisfied, she exhaled. Why couldn't she have found this man a long time ago?

"I don't know if I do, though. Not yet," she said.

"We've got time."

"Not that much. In any case, I can't have a child like Monty. He's not just lazy and selfish. He's a pathological liar. He's evil. He inherited none of my father's qualities, nor my mother's good ones."

"Perhaps he was switched at birth."

Candace laughed. "Except, Adele clearly favors Mother, and so does he."

"A child of ours," said Rob, "if there is one, will inherit our qualities, not Monty's. You have my word."

"That's just it. We don't know what a child of ours would really be like, Rob. Dad probably never thought he'd have a son like my brother—"

"But he had a daughter like you."

"Still, our child would be who he or she *is*. What if there are issues that we can't anticipate right now, that we couldn't handle?"

"Candace. Having a baby would be wonderful, if and when we're both ready. Our child would likely inherit our qualities. However, we both know there are no guarantees. We'd have to be open. We can only do so much as parents—"

"I agree with you, but I wonder about nature versus nurture, and the degree to which one trumps the other. If it's nature, then whatever we did to raise our child—the best nanny, the best schools, the most attention—would it make that much of a difference? My college roommate Elizabeth doesn't have kids, and she's very judgmental of her sister, and critical of her sister's teenagers. Elizabeth says she made mistakes raising them and that's why the kids have drug and alcohol issues. But from what I know about it, their parents did everything right."

"Darling, we're getting way ahead of ourselves. Some people like to judge others when they haven't walked in their shoes. Of course we don't want such problems, and I'm sorry that they have them. Let's go back to the nature thing, though. I think we are all born as who we are. Our *brains* are what they are, from birth. Our personalities are basically set. Parents can only do so much—raise their children with love and acceptance, and do their best."

"I agree. And I know we would."

"Don't fret, love. We'll handle whatever comes our way, together." Rob reached for the goat-cheese-and-date appetizer the waiter had just set between them. "Now, have a bite of this."

Candace gave a gentle smile. "Will you always be like this?"

"Always. Now, I know you aren't fond of surprises—"

Her smile disappeared. "But?"

"But I have one for you, anyway." He reached into a pocket. "I took the liberty of purchasing something for you. Let's call it an engagement gift."

Candace looked down at the turquoise box Rob had placed next to her wineglass. "You shouldn't have."

"Ah, but I did. And *I* felt that I should have. Open it."

A moment later, she held two gorgeous diamond hoop earrings. Not too big, but definitely not too small and exactly what she would have picked out for herself. She removed the pearl earrings she was wearing and put the new ones on. "They're lovely. Thank you, Rob. I love them, you, and the surprise."

He sipped his Scotch, a twinkle in his eye. "Not in that order, I trust."

Candace smiled and sipped her wine. She fingered one of her new diamond hoops, then touched her lobe, as she often did when anticipating being alone, naked, and in bed with this man. She did love him. He was the only person with whom she could share her deepest fears and innermost feelings. Soon, when the time was right, she would share with him the one thing that so far she had kept to herself.

Three hours later, feeling very satisfied, the two of them lay together, legs intertwined, her head resting on Rob's broad shoulder as she fell asleep in his arms.

• • •

Adele was fast asleep in the dark bedroom. In her loose pajamas, Helen tiptoed into the bathroom and peed, then crept into the kitchen for a glass of water. The living room was dark except for the computer and television, which was turned on and playing at a low volume. Monty lay sprawled on the sofa. Helen turned on the faucet, her back to him.

In two seconds, he was behind her, one arm wrapping itself around her waist. She turned with a start, gasping. "Jesus, Monty! You scared me! I thought you were asleep!"

"Baby, I've been waiting for you," he whispered, taking her hands.

Hairs on the back of Helen's neck stood up. "You've been drinking. Let me go to bed. Please."

He looked into her eyes. "I'm so sorry. Will you forgive me?"

His eyes were red; the streak of a tear stained his cheek. Had he been crying? "It's not that easy. Let's just go to sleep. We can talk about it tomorrow."

"No, baby. We've gotta talk now. I need you. I'm nothing without you. I don't know what got into me. I was hurt, and I lashed out. I didn't mean anything I said. If you won't forgive me, I won't be able to forgive myself."

Don't answer him. Address the issues. "Monty, we've got to face our situation. We've got to figure out what to do. We don't have a choice. We *are* in this thing together, but if you don't face it with me, I'll have to do it alone."

"You don't have to. I *am* with you—I will be, from now on. I promise."

She braced herself, stiffening. "How am I supposed to trust you?"

He moved one hand up her left arm, caressing it. "I'll do whatever you want me to. I'm glad you emailed Candace about meeting. It was the right thing to do. I was wrong about it."

Stay strong. "Then why were you so angry at me?"

"I was frustrated, Helen. It's not you who made me angry—it was her. She made me furious today. She's selfish and she's evil. Somehow she brings out the worst in me, but I can't keep on letting her. For your sake, for Adele's sake"—he glanced down, then drew his eyes back up to Helen's face—"for the baby's sake."

"We've got to get on the same page."

"We do," said Monty, his voice tender. He rested both of his forearms on her shoulders. "That's why I was upset about you opening the new bank account."

Helen closed her eyes. *Don't back down.* "I have to manage the money I make."

"Yes! You do. But can't we do it together? Do a budget, pay the bills—map out a realistic strategy for finishing the house, together?"

Helen looked straight into her husband's eyes, wanting to believe him. "In the past—"

"The past is over. Let's just start fresh, tomorrow. Let's get on the same page. Let's go to American Trust and change the account a joint one. Let's go over our budget, like, twice a week. Can we do that?"

Like a brittle twig bent back to its breaking point, Helen's resolve cracked, then snapped. "Only if we manage *all* the money together—not just our living expenses. And only if you find a job. Bring home a paycheck."

He dropped his arms around her, pressing into her hips, his hands on the small of her back. "I will, I promise. I'll start looking tomorrow."

No, he won't! He never fulfills his promises! "Any job, Monty. I don't care what it is." Her lungs felt depleted, as if they were collapsing. How was she caving in so easily and so quickly?

"Right," he said, one hand moving up to her left shoulder, baring it. "Any job."

"Stop—"

"Don't stay mad at me," he pleaded. "I love you."

Her eyes glistened. Maybe there was a good man inside of him. The man she wanted him to be. "Then why do you hurt me?"

"I have no excuse. Let me make everything up to you." He leaned in to kiss her, then looked down at her breasts. "Do they feel tender?"

She pushed back, leaning away from him. "Monty, something feels different about this pregnancy—"

"Maybe because it's a boy. I'm sure it is, baby." Gently, he pulled her closer, then slowly removed her top, letting it fall to the floor. He looked at her breasts, then at her left shoulder. She flinched for a second, then he leaned down and kissed it. "Don't worry, baby. I'll be careful." He wrapped his arms around her, picked her up, and carried her over toward the sofa.

When it was over, she went to the bathroom again, but in the dim light, she didn't see the blood.

8

Two

David copied and pasted Candace's questions for her brother into the email draft he had written at her request yesterday afternoon. In light of Monty's staunch refusal to attend Monday's meeting, she had changed her mind again and decided that David should go ahead and send the finalized draft, rather than just use it as an agenda at the meeting.

But Candace had called early this morning with updated instructions: David was to write only an intro and a closing, edit her questions for continuity, and send the draft back to her. She would then proof it and send the final version back to him, which he was to send to Monty today, copying Helen and herself. David was bewildered about why she didn't just write the entire message herself. Was he no more than a glorified secretary in this instance? He shook his head. Whatever the wealthy wanted, they got.

He finished his coffee and set the mug beside his computer. He was sure that Monty would never offer up the income and monthly expense figures Candace was requesting, but there was a chance that Helen might do so at the meeting. Hopefully, she would also provide information about the missing vendor invoices, the status of the application for a certificate of occupancy, and the Carawans' plan to list the property for sale.

David had a favorable albeit ambiguous impression of Candace's sister-in-law. Secure in the creative, if unstable, profession of graphic arts, she must possess the talent required in her field. From what David could tell, she had a good work ethic. But on a personal level, she was an enigma. Why had she chosen a scoundrel such as Monty for a husband? She was slim and not unattractive, but her looks were only just above average. David had seen a photo of her with her sister, who was the prettier one by far. Perhaps Helen had been thrilled that a good-looking man like Monty had chosen her, and she'd happily fallen victim to his charms.

Yet Helen could not be happy in her marriage if she had half a brain. Monty's recent behavior alone demonstrated meanness and cynicism. One didn't write such emails and leave such voicemail messages and then go home to romance one's wife. Helen must be living a nightmare with that miscreant.

Did a woman's chance of finding a good mate—someone who was honest, faithful, and a good provider—depend solely on her looks? David possessed those qualities, and his wife Ellen was beautiful. Their daughter, Olivia, was almost ten years old and very pretty, resembling her mother. Olivia's future husband would have to be worthy of her—David would make sure of that. He and Ellen had wanted another child, but it was not to be. Her fertility had been affected after she had survived non-Hodgkin's lymphoma. But her spirit never faltered, and David admired her strength. She was his better half, by far.

Helen Carawan, by contrast, seemed weak enough to be blown over by Monty's shouting. Perhaps she had been rather beaten down by life. Candace had said that Helen was estranged from both her parents, who split up when she was young, though her mother remarried. Helen had worked as a waitress and put herself through art school. Then one day in her twenties, she'd walked away from a stable job and moved to Atlanta, where she knew no one, to accept a new position.

Maybe life had been going well for her at that point, but once she became entangled with Monty—well, David could only guess what she might have gone through. He glanced at the recent photo of Ellen and Olivia that he kept on his desk. He would protect the women in his life—he couldn't imagine losing either one.

• • •

Candace walked up to her assistant's desk. "Jess, get Paula and Amanda. Immediately."

Jess nodded as Candace entered her private office. It was eight-thirty. Jess deduced that her boss had risen early to work out before coming in. The heads of design and sales and marketing should be at their desks, though Jess had seen neither of them this morning. The entire company was humming with Candace present—a collective sigh of relief would escape once she was on the plane to New York and safely out of town.

Paula rushed past Jess's desk and knocked on Candace's office door before entering. Jess's eyes shifted the other direction. Amanda was approaching, ten steps behind her department head counterpart.

Jess looked back at her computer screen and focused on her agenda. Candace hadn't exhibited a worse temper than normal, but things would probably be tense in there. Design and Sales were often at odds, no matter what the project, and now that the new swimwear line was being developed, everyone at the company was a little more stressed. Of course, all employees were under very strict orders not to divulge anything about the line—not even to hint about it—before the unveiling to buyers in New York this September. Secrecy was imperative.

Jess glanced at Candace's door just as Amanda was about to turn the knob. Amanda was wearing a fitted, short orange top and tight, dark brown pants. Jess's eye caught on something white poking out of the back of Amanda's pants at the waist. A tag? No, it was the top of her underwear. Her thong underwear! It was a whale tail. Jess raised her eyebrows and turned back to her computer. Didn't Amanda know about the unspoken company-wide ban on thongs? Or didn't she care? Worse than panty lines, Candace hated thongs—they were a product competitor and unladylike (translation: skanky). More than once, Jess had heard her boss say with disdain that wearing a thong was like saying, "Here's my butt—deal with it!" whereas wearing a SlimZ garment was like saying, "I think enough of my ass to shape and contour it."

Whatever. Jess was young enough not to have to worry about it. She was slender but not without curves. No issues with underwear choices, thank you. Not all the women who worked at SlimZ were trim, but each one of them had either a pear or an hourglass figure—no one was an apple, with stick legs and a nonexistent ass. Could that be due to a subconscious discrimination policy? Surely some woman with that body shape had applied for a job here. But that type of woman probably didn't buy SlimZ.

Jess's phone vibrated. It was Beau Warren. Her "beau."

"How's your day so far?" he asked.

She glanced at Candace's closed door. "Fine, and getting better. She's off to New York this afternoon. But no one's leaving early or anything. How about you?"

"So-so." Beau was employed by Coca-Cola, working in the international distribution area. They had met during senior year at the University of Georgia. "Counting the hours until I see you tonight."

Jess smiled. Beau was taking her out to dinner at a new hot spot in Buckhead to celebrate their two-year anniversary. Then, most likely they'd hit a bar. "Me, too."

"How does eight o'clock sound? Is that cool?"

"Perfect."

"So, are you wearing underwear?"

Jess giggled. "See you at eight," she said. "I've gotta go!"

Just as she clicked off her phone, she heard Amanda's voice rising, coming from inside the nearby room. *Oh, shit.* Working in a virtually all-female office had its tensions, but all things considered, it was probably better than one with mostly men. Not that she knew what that was like—this was her first real job.

Now she heard Candace raising her voice, which was unusual. "This project is too big for the kind of quarreling I've witnessed here," came the boss's voice through the door. Jess bit her lip and shook her head. Using the word *quarreling* was just like Candace, who continued: "Amanda, you've heard Paula's issues. I'd like an email response to both her and myself by . . ." Her voice trailed off, the decibel level falling back to normal.

Ten seconds later, Paula left the room with a smile on her face, closing Candace's door behind her. Amanda stayed in the room.

• • •

"Helen Carawan?" the nurse announced to the waiting room. Helen rose from her seat, Monty at her side. They had driven together to Helen's obstetrician Dr. Joanna Russell's office, depositing Adele at school on the way over.

Helen felt faint and weak. Over an hour ago, she had awakened to find bloodstains. She woke Monty and told him—he surprised her with his attentiveness and evident concern, but he said few words. She called the doctor and was told to come right in. At eight weeks pregnant, Helen had only been to one appointment so far—the next one was scheduled for over a month from now. But the bleeding meant she was in danger of losing the baby. Monty had fed and dressed Adele while Helen showered and got ready. Now he was next to her, his countenance somber.

After weighing Helen in, a nurse ushered her and Monty into an examination room. Then a brief visit from another nurse who explained that, while the loss of blood was a very troubling sign, it didn't necessarily mean the end.

"Have you had intercourse in the last twenty-four hours?" she demanded of Helen.

Helen nodded and glanced at Monty. His face was stone cold.

The nurse scribbled down notes on a pad. "Well, before you see Dr. Russell, we'll do an ultrasound. The technician won't discuss it with you, but Dr. Russell will. Okay?"

Helen swallowed. "Thank you." She and Monty followed the nurse out of the small room and down the corridor to another room equipped with machinery.

Moments later, Helen was lying on a hard table between the technician and her husband. A swirly, fluidlike picture appeared on the monitor, but even though she had had a sonogram with Adele, Helen couldn't figure out what it meant right now or whether her baby was okay.

"Good morning, Mrs. Carawan. Mr. Carawan," the doctor said upon entering. "Let's see what's going on." She walked over to the screen, focusing on the image. "I'm happy to tell you, first of all, that we don't have a problem."

"You mean . . ." Helen began, then stopped, relief taking hold.

"I mean, you're not suffering a miscarriage. It's good that you called and came in, because the bleeding you experienced may well have indicated one. However, that's not the case."

Monty forced a smile. "That's great," he said, his voice wooden.

"But that's not all," Dr. Russell said. She smiled and looked from husband to wife and back again. "Helen, you're carrying twins."

Helen gasped. For a second, she couldn't breathe. *Three* children? "Are you sure?"

"Most definitely. Here are the heartbeats." She motioned to one, then the other. "Here's one baby, let's call him 'Baby A,' Danielle." She looked at the technician. "This one, we'll call 'Baby B.'"

"Did you say 'him?'" asked Monty. "I mean, can we find out if they're boys or girls?"

"Not yet. At least, not from this ultrasound. In another eight weeks or so, however, we should be able to—if you like. We'll probably do a second set of pictures at that point."

"Another sonogram?" Helen asked.

Dr. Russell nodded, taking Helen's hand. "Are you okay?" she asked the patient. "I know it's a surprise. I'm sure you're happy to know that the babies are doing fine, though."

"Yes," said Helen. "But what caused the blood?"

"It's more common than you think. Danielle's going to get some measurements, then she'll send you back over to see me. We have a few things to talk about: what to do about the bleeding, for one. Also, the fact that a multiple birth is a high-risk pregnancy. I'll see you back in the exam room in a few minutes." She left the room.

In twenty minutes, the couple was on their way home. Helen was to take the day off from work to rest, and the bleeding, which had subsided, should disappear. She could go back to work on Monday, providing that she experienced no more problems, and they were to take a week or two off from having sex.

They drove in silence for the first five minutes. Then Monty glanced over at his wife. "You look like you're still in shock."

"I don't know how we're going to manage."

"Well, it would have been a lot better if you'd had a miscarriage. Who knows? You still could."

She turned away and stared out the window. The future looked as bleak as the raw spring morning. Clouds had moved in and were threatening rain. She looked back at Monty, her eyes moist. "What a horrible thing to say."

He shrugged.

Helen took a deep breath and turned straight ahead. "Do you remember what you said last night? The promises you made?"

Monty glanced at her again. "What promises?"

Did he really not remember, maybe because he'd been drinking? Helen shut her eyes for a second, then spoke in an even tone. "You promised we'd go over our budget twice a week, do the bills together—"

"*What* budget? What are you talking about?"

"I'm serious, Monty. If you want a joint checking account, with access to my money—"

Monty pounded the steering wheel with his fist. "*Your* money? Damn it, Helen! Stop trying to control me! You know I need to access that money! Why are you doing this to me?"

"I'm not doing *anything* to you. You said last night, we're a team. We're about to have two more children. We have to start communicating about money—not just about our living expenses, which are gonna go up, but about the house! We need to manage everything together, Monty."

"You're at work all day, so *I* have to do that. Remember?"

Bullshit. "We can sit down together and go over everything on the weekends, once a week," said Helen, undeterred. "You also promised you'd start looking for a job today."

"Today's Friday," Monty said in calmer voice, his eyes cold. They approached the neighborhood entrance. "I'll start looking on Monday. Let's go to that bank this afternoon so you can change it to a joint account."

"You heard the doctor. I'm supposed to stay home and rest. You'll have to pick up Adele today."

Monty set his jaw. "Then, Monday. Speaking of which, when you go in to meet with Shepherd that morning, tell him we're having twins. He'll relay that to Candace. I'm not going to contact her." After a moment, he added, "You could email her again, of course."

"I'll tell him. But we're only going to change the bank account if we sit down this weekend and go over all the financial stuff together."

Monty puffed as he pulled the car into the driveway and parked. "Don't you realize that the money we're getting from Candace and the money we're gonna make when we sell the house is a helluva lot more than what you make at Vreden? And that I'm her connection to us? Me and Adele, but not *you*?" He looked over and down at her abdomen. "Now we're gonna have two more connections."

Helen turned away and looked out her window.

Monty stared out the windshield. "I was upset earlier when I said that about having a miscarriage. We'll go over the financials this weekend if you want. But you need to respect me, and you need to stop pressuring me. You need to trust me. I can't deal with all of this if you don't." He got out of the car and headed to the cottage without a backward glance.

Helen let out a deep sigh. She had to steel herself emotionally to get through what lay ahead. She had spoken to Dawn on the way to the doctor, but decided not to call again. She texted: *False alarm, not a miscarriage. Twins.*

Then she set her phone on silent and went into the bedroom to lie down.

• • •

Alone in her office, Candace opened the financial report she'd received this morning from Courtney, the company's CFO. Despite the economy's continuing poor performance, revenues at SlimZ were up from a year ago. Courtney attributed the higher earnings to the company's ability to cut production expenses across the board. Larger orders of the mainstay garment at the Brooklyn factories meant lower wholesale costs, and a slightly cheaper fabric blend in some of the newer product lines yielded a higher profit margin without affecting sales. Though less expensive, the new blend had a sleeker feel and was a genuine improvement. It was a win-win.

However, sales of the newer lines had plateaued rather than continued to rise. Candace believed that the marketing team, responsible for promotion and advertising, was only partially to blame. SlimZ enjoyed high brand recognition, but were consumers familiar with all of its products? The high-waisted shaper, the foot-less leggings, the contouring tights, the slimming camisoles—these were just a few of its many shapewear garments. And each product line came in multiple varieties.

But perhaps there were too many lines and too many choices for the customer. Candace had eavesdropped on shoppers in department stores thumbing through SlimZ packages, and more than once she had heard expressions of confusion and frustration. Tired of trying to make sense of all the choices, some women had just given up and kept their money. Discontinuing a product line wouldn't be easy. However, fewer rather than greater options might be the solution.

Simplicity had been key in the beginning. Psychology was a major ingredient in successful marketing; Candace knew that emotion was very important. A recent study she saw had proved what her instincts told her: when faced with fewer than five choices, a customer decides more quickly and feels more satisfied than when presented with more than ten. It was just too much information to gather in one's head, and most often baffling. The study was one of the reasons Candace had been adamant about limiting the design choices in the new swimwear line. Paula and her team were in agreement, but Amanda had resisted the philosophy, saying that department store buyers were always asking her salespeople for more options and more color selections rather than less.

But Candace was convinced she should offer only a small selection of swimwear. Each design must be appealing, flattering, and attractive. After years of planning, launching the line in a few short months was exciting but risky. However, Candace had never been risk averse when it came to business. Her decisions were fueled by her gut, refined by the feedback of others, and perfected by her willingness to adapt. Low barriers to entry existed in the industry, and competition surfaced often—all one needed was a sewing machine and a spare bedroom. The challenge was to create and sell a standout product that was worth the risk, that would sell, and that would last.

She opened another document from the marketing team. The report identified the target retail customer for the swimwear line: she was between 28 and 53, married, with 2.5 children. Her education level was a bachelor's degree or higher and her family income was in the top 7 percent. Each year, she shopped for new clothing 4.7 times and vacationed at a resort or beach 1.9 times.

Candace's inbox signaled a new email from David. She opened it and read his short message asking if she'd had time to proof the final draft email to Monty. Did she want David to send it by the end of the day, before the start of the weekend? Yes, she did, since the meeting in David's office was scheduled for Monday morning. In the draft, per her instructions, David had not requested but had instructed Monty to attend with Helen.

The fact that Helen was pregnant had nothing to do with anything—Candace had gotten over that small detail. Millions of couples all over the world were expecting babies, living up to their commitments and within their income, and there was no reason why her brother and his wife could not do the same thing. She was not going to enable him—them—by signing the new loan he had arranged with Whitney Jamison. The couple would have to catch up on their mortgage themselves and keep it current. She'd have to think about what she might be willing to do on the HELOC—once she decided, they could take that or leave it. She had many other, more important things on her mind right now.

• • •

Six hours later, Candace sat next to Rob in a first-class seat on a jet about to take off for LaGuardia. The extra legroom was a necessity for her six-foot-three fiancé, and she herself couldn't abide having to fold herself into a coach seat, though she had done it innumerable times, years ago. She glanced out the window, thankful that the skies were now clear of the day's early clouds.

"Would you like a drink?" asked Rob. "The stewardess is coming round. Or rather, the attendant."

"Yes, thanks." Candace smiled at him, but her eyes betrayed a distracted mind.

"You're tense, love." He took her hand and squeezed it. "And your hand is very cold."

"Yours is warm." She exhaled. Despite her earlier resolve, doubts about her decisions regarding her brother began to form. Rather than chase them away, she let them rise to the surface. "It's this thing with Monty. I just feel that, you know, I do have so much money. Maybe I should just be generous, give him the funds he wants, and be done with it."

Rob caught the flight attendant's eye and ordered their cocktails. Turning back to Candace, he said, "Well. That's an option. But not a very good one, not in the long run."

"Why, Rob? Tell me why."

"Candace, you have a lot of money, and so do I. Generosity is something that we both have an obligation to practice. It's a responsibility that comes with money. But you've already been very generous toward your brother and his wife."

Their drinks arrived, and Candace took a sip of hers before responding. "Is it enough, though?"

"I know you'll make your own decision, but my opinion is that, while one should be generous, one must also set and enforce boundaries. Especially with relatives." He sipped his Scotch. "If not, what will be the end, love? If you cosign the larger note, you'll be liable for it, and when it comes due, you'll pay it off, if the house hasn't been sold. They won't. Trust me."

"Wouldn't the bank just renew the loan for me until the house sells?"

Rob lifted her hand and kissed it. "They very well may, but you have no assurance of that. Even if they do, you'll continue to pay the interest and fees, prolonging the agony of the whole project, for God knows how long. Kicking the can down the road, as they say."

"True—and I don't want to do that."

"I don't believe you do. Listen, I've seen you deal with this for far too long. It would be different if Monty had a profession, or a trade—if he worked for a living. If he were an honest man. Then perhaps you'd see an end in sight, to everything. If he had been open with you and had lived up to his commitments on the project—"

"You're right," said Candace, shaking her head slowly. "I thought that when he married and became a father, he would finally grow up. That he'd get it. When I first got into this deal, I expected that he and his wife would behave like normal, responsible people. Not that he would lie and take advantage of me."

"Well, clearly your expectations weren't met, and I don't know how realistic they were, anyway. I hate to stand by and see him using you this way. I know that it's very hard to separate yourself emotionally. But you're here, now—*we're* here, and we must trudge on. The fact is, Monty isn't producing an income that we know of. Only his wife is. That's fine and it's their decision—we must look at it that way. Perhaps they plan to live solely on her salary while he takes care of the children. If so, then do that they must. It isn't up to you to finance a lifestyle beyond their income. No matter how large your fortune is."

"But don't I have a responsibility to help them, especially now, with the baby? I've always focused on making money as a measure of success. What's successful about watching them struggle in this situation?"

Rob gave her an exasperated look. "Again, their situation is not your doing. Can they not face the consequences of their decisions, as we all must do? Even if it means the house won't sell for a profit? If it sells at all?"

Candace's eyes widened. "It *must* sell, Rob. I wanted to help them in the beginning, but now I just want to be rid of this house—I don't want this situation to go on forever."

"Darling, if you really want to help them, then *don't* help them with more funds. Let them deal with the disastrous situation they face—let them succeed, or not, *without* you. It may sound harsh, but in doing so, you *would* be helping them, in the long run. You must let them go into the crucible, and come out of it, either as dust or as gold. They'll respect you, and themselves, in the end."

Candace closed her eyes, opened them, then took another sip of her cocktail as the plane taxied to the runway. She couldn't help but tighten her grip on Rob's hand as the plane took off; she clutched the armrest with her other hand. Never fond of flying, she felt most vulnerable during takeoff and landing. Nor did she enjoy the complete lack of control, hurtling through the sky in a metal tube encasing other people's germs, breathing the same air. She didn't have time to get sick right now. As usual before traveling, she had hydrated all day and taken antivirus pills along with her vitamins.

Without provocation, her thoughts shifted to two memories she had never been able to shake: the last words she had spoken to her mother, and the promise she had made to her father, never realizing what it would take to fulfill. Were other people haunted by such random flashbacks and recollections? Did moments from the past pop up without warning, invading their lives and wreaking havoc? Or was she different?

As the plane began to level off, she forced her thoughts back to the present. Rob had addressed the situation she was facing with Monty and Helen so well. If only he could just as easily remove the guilt she felt—the guilt she had lived with for over twenty years.

• • •

With Helen and Adele asleep in the bedroom, Monty unlocked his desk drawer and reached for his iPhone to check for missed calls. The private, second number was essential, but he had only given it out to a select few individuals. She was the only woman who knew it at the moment. His short contact list on this device identified her as RB. Good—she hadn't tried to contact him after his visit to her this afternoon. He put the phone back in the drawer and locked it.

He hadn't told her today about this morning's news at the doctor's office. She didn't even know his wife was pregnant—that by the end of November, unless something happened, he'd be the father of three. It was incredible. Candace had gifted each member of his family twelve grand a year for the past three years, the maximum amount she could give an individual with no tax penalty, and he had come to count on those funds. Now the total would increase from thirty-six to sixty thousand dollars. Sixty grand! It was a lot of money, but he wasn't sure it was worth the extreme hassle of what lay ahead for him during the next seven months, or thereafter.

He pulled up the email he had received today from Shepherd, ordering him to show up at that bastard's office on Monday morning with Helen. Maybe he should relent and accompany her after all. If she went alone, she might turn into a loose cannon, spewing information and possibly even bashing him. If he was there, he could control the narrative. He'd have to keep a cool head and not let Shepherd push him over the edge, and he'd insist that Candace sign the note.

Whether he went or not, he'd have to clue his wife in ahead of time about the new loan he had worked out with the banker. Since she was determined to talk about their finances this weekend, he would do it then. He'd tell her that he had proposed the new loan only to take pressure off their cash flow, since it would eliminate their mortgage payment. That the reason they'd fallen behind on that was because Candace hadn't come forth with the funds he needed to finish the renovation. That he'd had to use their mortgage money to pay vendors and suppliers. That Candace had left him no choice.

Of course, he'd have to promise Helen that he would use the money that would be freed up by the lack of a mortgage payment to finish the renovation. And that together with the rest of the funds they had available to draw on the HELOC, it would be enough to get everything done, despite his sister's stinginess. He would tell Helen that Candace had roped him into doing it this way—that she had lied to him. That he—they—couldn't let her keep manipulating them.

No matter what, he couldn't let his wife cut him off from access to the bank account and to her income. He had to get her to trust him again. He would say that he would show her their project budget anytime she asked. He'd also emphasize that it was imperative that Candace sign the new note, that since she was co-borrower on the HELOC, she'd have to—because if she didn't and then they defaulted, the bank would come after her for payment. With Candace's millions, it was the very least she could do for them. They were the only family she had.

He scrolled through Shepherd's email, grimacing at the list of questions, and saved it to a file he kept of all of his and Candace's messages. It was just the latest piece of bullshit, not worthy of any more of his attention. But he might need it, for the record.

9

Nonnegotiable

elen stretched her legs before getting out of bed early Monday morning and yawned. The bleeding had stopped late Friday night and hadn't come back. She felt relieved but very tired. Her eyes were bloodshot from crying, and every nerve in her body tingled. Veins in her scarred left shoulder pulsated, her neck muscles ached, and her temples throbbed. She hadn't slept well.

A hot shower would help. Adele was still asleep, thank goodness. Monty lay on his side, facing the opposite wall.

Just before eleven o'clock, Helen walked into the lobby of Elite Financial Planning on Capstone Road and glanced around. There was no sign of her husband yet.

David Shepherd appeared from around a corner. "Good morning, Helen. How are you feeling?"

"Hello, David. I've been better, I guess." She gave a weak smile.

He returned her expression, then dropped his eyes. "Is Monty on his way?"

Helen nodded. "He's never on time to anything, though." She swallowed and looked away, regretting the statement.

"Congratulations about the baby."

Her eyes traveled back to David, meeting his. "Babies."

"Yes, Adele's still very young—"

"No," she corrected him, "I mean, we're expecting two babies. Twins."

David's eyes widened. "Really? My goodness! When did you find out?"

"Friday morning. I had a small emergency and had to see the doctor. Nothing was wrong, except—well, I had a sonogram, and there they were."

"No fertility drugs or anything?" David bit his lip.

"No! It just—happened."

David nodded. "Well, that's wonderful. Let's go into my office and sit down, shall we? Perhaps Monty will join us in a few."

Helen followed him down a corridor and into a spacious private office, one wall of which was a glass window affording a view of downtown. Green tops of trees intermingled with city streets and sidewalks, some of them lined with the pinks and yellows of springtime in Atlanta. She sat down in one of two comfortable chairs facing a massive mahogany desk, and David took his seat behind it. Shelves and cabinets made of the same material lined the wall to his right and her left, and his thin, silver laptop sat on the desk within easy reach of his right hand.

David shut the machine and placed both his hands in front of him on the wood. "Both Candace and I are glad that you requested to meet. She's in New York right now, so I will be speaking for her, acting on her behalf, as I so often do." He smiled.

"Okay."

"Now, I assume you know about Monty having dealt directly with Whitney Jamison over at Memorial Bank and having discussed a new arrangement with her?"

Helen nodded and raised her eyebrows. Was there something Monty hadn't told her when he explained it on Saturday?

"Have you seen the email Candace had me send to him late Friday, with her questions?"

"No, I don't think I have. Was I copied on that?"

David shook his head. "You should have been. That would have been an oversight." He opened his laptop, clicked the pad a few times, then pivoted it toward her. "Here it is. I'm sending it to you now." She leaned forward. "You see the list of questions—"

At that moment, Monty barged through the open office door and plopped down next to his wife, who leaned back in her chair. He stared at David. "So, I'm here. Happy now?"

David regarded him, stole a glance at Helen, and looked straight back at her husband. "Hello, Monty. Glad you could join us."

"Could? I guess I do what I'm told at times, just like you do, Dave."

David cleared his throat. "I was about to go over this list with Helen, but now that you've arrived, perhaps we can tackle it together."

Monty sneered. "Perhaps. Or, perhaps we could stop wasting time, and Candace could just sign the fucking note."

Helen dropped her eyes, then gazed at David, who offered Monty a faint smile. "If you had answered the questions via return email, we wouldn't have to 'waste time' on them now."

Monty leaned back, crossed his arms in front of him, and stared at David. "What the hell. Fire away."

"First, here are the items we've received, including your most recent project budget." David pointed to the message, visible to husband and wife on the laptop. "The invoices you sent are only for the windows and the plumbing fixtures, though. When can we expect them for the rest of the work that's been completed so far?"

Helen looked at the floor. Monty shook his head. "Are we really going to go there?"

David narrowed his eyes. "Yes. We are."

A few moments of silence followed as Monty stared at him without blinking. "Tomorrow. Okay?"

"Number Two: We need to discuss the fact that you are four months behind on your mortgage, and interest is past due on the HELOC."

Neither of the Carawans spoke. David cleared his throat and looked from husband to wife. "What's the story on that?"

"Here's the story, Dave," said Monty. "The HELOC had about eighty-five left to draw, but we needed to keep availability on it. However, we had to pay for some work that had to be redone. Your client wouldn't take my calls or answer my messages, so we were forced to make these payments from our income. So we wouldn't get sued."

"Exactly what work had to be redone?" asked David. He crossed his arms and stared at Monty.

"Does it matter?"

"Monty, for inexplicable reasons, Candace trusted you in the past. But at this late date, we need to establish accountability."

"Look," said Monty, "I'm trying to answer your question. We couldn't pay the interest or the mortgage because workers and suppliers had to be paid. They were threatening us."

David looked straight into Monty's eyes. "Send me the supporting documentation. Including an explanation of what had to be redone, and why."

Monty's face didn't move. "Next?"

"Number Three: You did, in fact, draw additional funds from the HELOC, totaling sixty-five thousand. We need the invoices tied to those draws."

Monty exhaled. "I'll get that to you later this week."

"What was the money used for?"

"Various items. Next?"

David looked at Helen. "What is your combined income?"

"Don't answer that," Monty said to her. "That's private, and none of Candace's business."

"To the contrary. It *is* her business, since she is guaranteeing your existing loan. If you want any further consideration from her, I'd advise you to be open about this. You can send me your 2009 tax return," David said to Helen.

"*Don't*," repeated Monty.

David turned to Monty. "Are you generating any income?"

"You can tell Candace that I'm being hugely undervalued right now."

David's eyes shifted to Helen. "We also need a listing of your monthly living expenses."

Monty stood up. "This is ridiculous. Get my sister on the phone."

"Sit down, please. Candace is unavailable."

Monty leaned toward the desk, placing his hands on it and drawing close to David's face. "I *demand* that she participate in this meeting. Get her on a conference call, or Skype. *Now.*"

"Monty, calm down. You're not in a position to demand anything. You need to comply with Candace's requests if she is to do anything more for you. That's just the way it is, and the sooner you accept that, the better it will be for all concerned." He looked at Helen.

"I can send you the tax return, David," said Helen.

Monty whirled around and faced her, a snarl on his face. "What?"

"They need to know—"

"No, they don't! That's off the table," Monty said. He turned back toward David. "So is what we do with our money—"

"But—" Helen began.

"Shut up," Monty said, staring at David. "Look, we aren't going to be micromanaged by that bitch. I simply refuse to let it happen. Nonnegotiable." He sat down again, his eyes menacing.

Unruffled, David spoke in a low tone. "Helen, why don't you send me a PDF of your last six months' bank statements? I can have my assistant go through them and plug the numbers into a spreadsheet. That should suffice."

Monty rose and lunged toward David over the desk, but stopped short of physical contact. *"Do you fucking understand English, you prick?"*

David sat immobile. "The last time you were here, Monty, I had to call security. I hope I don't have to again." He reached for his cell phone.

Monty stood up straight. "Go ahead," he snarled.

Helen scooted back in her chair, her eyes wide with fear. David threw her a reassuring glance, then spoke into his phone, pronouncing his assistant's first name as he always did: *en français.* "Geneviève, please have Joe come to my office."

Monty sat down and leaned over, clasping his hands together between his knees. "Hey, I almost forgot. Did my wife mention that we're having twins?"

Helen looked away and David nodded slowly, studying Monty. "I congratulated her. How wonderful for you."

"Don't worry about telling my sister—I will, today. Call Joe off. I'm ready to cooperate."

David stared at Monty and paused. "Last item: I need to come to see the house tomorrow." He brought up a calendar on his computer, surveying his agenda for Tuesday. "I'm available between two and four thirty. Let's say, three?"

"Fine," said Monty. "What's the purpose?"

"To assess the status of the renovation. Take photos and come up with a list of what remains to be done to get the certificate of occupancy and to list the property with a realtor as soon as possible."

"Now it's my turn to ask questions," said Monty. "Is Candace going to sign the note? Is she going to see us through on financing the project?"

"We'll be in communication with you."

"What does *that* mean?"

"Of course, our shared desire is that the house sell quickly. A lot depends on what we find out tomorrow as to what remains to be done. Once it's sold, all the creditors, including Candace, will be paid." David turned his attention to his office door, where a uniformed guard had just appeared. "Hi, Joe. I think we're okay here, after all."

Joe nodded. "Yes, sir. Let me know if you need me. I'll be in the hall."

Monty gave David a hard look. "As I've said in the past, Helen and I need to come out of this deal on the plus side. We're buying our next home with the cash we take away from this one. What amount is Candace willing to write off so that can happen?"

"And as I've said, there's no point in discussing any such situation until the project is complete, and we get a contract on the home."

Monty gave his wife a sideways glance. "Are you satisfied? This was what you wanted, wasn't it?"

Her lips tightened into a thin line as she looked from her husband to David. "Should I be there tomorrow afternoon?"

"It's not necessary," said David, "but it might be a good idea."

"Are we done?" Monty asked while rising. "I have places to be."

Helen rolled her eyes at David, then caught herself, looked down, and picked up her purse. "I'll try, David. It may be closer to four before I can get there."

"Then I'll plan to arrive around three thirty or so. See you tomorrow."

• • •

Back at the office, Helen spent her lunch hour at her desk trying to catch up on work. At a quarter to one, her cell phone buzzed. It was Dawn.

"So, how did it go with David?"

"Okay, I guess. He went over a list of requested items with us, and Monty cooperated."

"That's hard to believe. I'm sorry, Helen—I didn't mean that."

"Yes, you did. But that's fine. He did have a mini-meltdown when David asked about our income—"

"Your income."

"Right. That, and our monthly budget. But then he calmed down. He said he'd send David the info they want. Receipts and stuff."

"Do you think he will?"

"Dawn, I hope so. He's got to. David said Candace won't do anything for us if he doesn't."

"What's she gonna do? I mean, do you need her to front more money to get the renovation done?"

"It's complicated. But yes. At least, it looks that way. David's coming out to see it tomorrow afternoon, and we're going from there."

"Helen, I'm glad you emailed Candace, and that you had this meeting. You need full disclosure, too."

"I know. Anyway, I've got to eat my sandwich while we talk. I'm famished."

"Eat, eat. You're carrying two babies! How do you feel?"

"Better than I did. But hungry all the time. It's irritating, to say the least."

"Does Candace know that it's twins yet?"

"Probably. Monty said he was gonna call her. I told David this morning. But let's talk about you and Frank."

"Nothing to tell. Except I'm pissed off at him right now."

"What happened? Dawn, he's perfect."

"No, no, he has flaws."

"Like what?"

"Like, reneging on promises."

"I don't believe you."

"It's not a big deal," said Dawn. "It's just—you know how I hate that! He'll say he can do something, and then say he can't. I'm like, don't tell me you can, unless you really can. Plus, as long as I'm bashing, he hates to travel. Says he can never get away from the office for long. But I shouldn't bitch."

"Are you talking about going on a trip?"

"We were, but now he claims it's not a good time. Too much going on at work. Even though *I* can get away."

Helen took the last bite of her sandwich and pictured Frank arriving home in his suit at the end of the day. Dawn had said that he wasn't a workaholic, but she had complained before about the short-to-no vacations problem. On the reneging issue—well, Frank didn't break the big promises, as far as Helen could tell. The guy traveled a lot for business, and if he didn't want to travel much otherwise, it was understandable. He was a good man—he worked hard and earned a good living. Dawn was lucky.

"I'm sorry, Helen, I'm just in a bad mood. Forget what I just said."

"Don't worry. I'm fine." Some of her coworkers were returning from lunch. "I should probably hang up, anyway."

"Look. I meant that about being able to get away. I can come down to Atlanta. Anytime."

"Maybe you could, later on. Like, when I get closer to the due date."

"Of course! But should I come before that? This spring or summer?"

"Not now. We'll see. Okay?"

"Okay," said Dawn. "I guess I'll go to lunch. Love you."

"Love you, too." Helen placed the phone back on her desk and tossed her paper plate in the trash can underneath it. She shut her eyes. Dawn was always going to be there for her. She always had been, as long as Helen could remember.

Although she loved her older sister, Helen had been jealous of her back in their younger days. Dawn was without a doubt the more attractive. She had flawless skin, lovely features, perfect dark brown hair that never misbehaved, and an ideal figure that was effortlessly maintained. Unlike her, Helen had struggled over the years with a slight pudginess and had worked hard to maintain a slim figure. Her mousy brown hair was fine and thin, and her eyes were slightly too close together.

But a long time ago, Helen had come to terms with her appearance. There was a level of prettiness that she could achieve, and no more. At least her complexion was clear and smooth, a sharp contrast to the big patch of skin on her left shoulder, starting below her neck and reaching to the top of her breast. Her right hand moved to the area, her fingers feeling the warped flesh underneath her blouse. The scar had branded her, made her fundamentally different from other women. Past boyfriends had politely pretended it was a nonissue, and so had Monty, back in the beginning.

But it had aged her skin so prematurely, dispelling her youth like an ugly loss of virginity. It was just an irregular blotch of flesh—the slap of a grisly palm with long wiry fingers. It wasn't a disease, like leprosy (though she'd been asked if it was). Helen had grieved over it for a long time before she accepted it. Her teen years had been the most difficult; what used to be embarrassment had developed into shame and anger. She had directed those emotions toward the person whose careless mistake had cost her any chance of beauty. Now that she was a grown woman and a mother, Helen was sure that no man who saw her disfigurement could ever desire her.

She was stuck with the man she had.

Luckily, he hadn't brought up the subject of going to the bank this afternoon to add his name to her new account. But she knew he would bring it up later. She knew she would acquiesce, too, if only to keep communication going between them. On Saturday, he had shown her the paperwork on the project and they had gone over all the bills online. She'd been very upset when she found out about the past due payments, but now it made sense why he'd been secretive and stubborn about wanting autonomy. But he had explained everything and outlined his objectives in working out the new loan. Once that was in place, he said, they could catch up and get the house done and ready to sell.

She would have to keep on him about it, no matter what, and she would have to make sure he at least went out looking for a job. As for her new account, it would be simpler just to close it rather than to add him—she hadn't gotten payroll to switch her direct deposit over from their joint account, anyway. She pushed her thoughts aside and refocused her attention on her seemingly endless task list. She had to stay busy and produce what she had been assigned. She couldn't afford to be identified as a superfluous employee.

• • •

David returned to his office after a quick lunch at the food court downstairs. For the next several weeks, because of his allergies, he planned to avoid exposure to the high pollen levels outside and stay within air-conditioned buildings as much as possible. As usual, he wouldn't get to enjoy the beautiful spring days. Before too long, the city would be enveloped in summer's oppressive humidity, which lasted through the end of September. Autumn was David's favorite season, the only one he didn't like to see end.

He had left Candace a voicemail after this morning's meeting, saying he would email a concise summary. She would call him after that, he was sure, to discuss it and his visit to the property tomorrow.

Her brother was a truly amazing individual, if one were amazed by depravity. She claimed he was a pathological liar, and David was beginning to believe it. He certainly doubted whether the guy would send him the information Candace had requested. Even if he did, David would be wise to check on its validity. He'd assign Geneviève to track down the vendors and confirm receipt of any funds Monty claimed he had paid. He made a mental note to ascertain whether she had done that for the invoices already received, as he had directed.

He looked over his email to Candace before sending it. He had included the fact that the couple was expecting twins because, if he omitted it and Candace found out he had learned of it today but didn't tell her in this email, she would probably be very annoyed. As for letting Monty tell her himself—well, that wasn't a priority. Hopefully the news wouldn't cause Candace to back down in her demands for accountability. However, David suspected she might acquiesce about signing the new bank note or, at the minimum, forking over some more money. Her stocks were up lately, and her judgment could possibly be off by an inverse amount. It had happened before.

An hour after he sent the email, his fears were realized. Candace called and said that depending on what he found out tomorrow afternoon when he visited the property—and in the interest of expediting the sale of the place—she would be willing to talk with Whitney Jamison at Memorial Bank.

10

Poor Relations

Rob Chandler hailed a taxi on Tuesday evening and instructed the driver to take him to the St. George Hotel in Manhattan, where Candace was meeting him for cocktails. Afterward, they planned to look at the hotel's banquet room that her assistant had reserved for the wedding reception. Dinner would be at eight o'clock at Manaque, a hip new restaurant that a partner at the firm had recommended.

Checking email on his phone, Rob saw a new message from Candace. Evidently her money man had met with her brother today at the house she had financed to evaluate his progress on the renovation. Shepherd had taken several pictures of the rooms and had forwarded them. According to Candace, the place was a literal mess: half-done floors, tile and other materials stacked in corners, and piles of rubbish everywhere. Rob put the phone down and glanced out the window at the pedestrians bustling about the city streets. Undoubtedly, Candace would want to discuss the situation this evening, but he felt confident that she had already made her decisions—especially now that couple was expecting twins, as Shepherd had reported. Candace was so tough and strong when it came to business, yet so much the opposite when it came to that blasted brother of hers and his family.

After generously tipping the driver, Rob stepped into the hotel and made his way over to the bar. He selected a corner table, sent Candace a text, then ordered a single malt on ice. When it arrived, so did she. He stood up and leaned down to kiss her.

She smiled. "Did you see my email?"

"I did." The waiter appeared and Candace ordered her usual martini: Grey Goose up with a twist.

"Well, the situation is worse than I'd imagined," she said. "David said there was debris everywhere. Also that Monty was very uptight and defensive."

"I'm not surprised. Did Helen show up?"

"She got there after David, and left when he did. He said she's being very cooperative."

"Poor girl. Hope she can manage the pregnancy," said Rob. "However, it's better that you know the facts about the place. Did you give David any instructions?"

"Not yet. He's waiting on more information from them, later this week." The waiter placed an ice-cold martini on the table, then disappeared. Candace lifted the glass and sipped her drink, her sapphire-and-diamond ring shining under the bar's diffused lighting. "This whole thing is so awful, Rob. And so *embarrassing*. I mean, really, who has a brother like this?"

"I think you'd be astonished at how many people do." Rob sipped his Scotch. "Especially wealthy people. As Dickens said, 'It is a melancholy truth that even great men have their poor relations.' I'm not saying that all of us 'great men' have a Monty, but many have a moocher, even a manipulator, in the family."

Candace shook her head. "So, I'm not alone."

"No. But . . ." Rob looked straight into her eyes.

"What?"

He took her hand. "It's just that I can't believe that guilt is what has driven you to get so deeply involved with him in this project. While the accident was a tragedy, Candace, you were not at fault for your mother's death. It just happened. You were very young at the time, an inexperienced driver, and you made a mistake. The weather that day was a huge factor in it. You have to accept it and put it in the past where it belongs."

"I *have* put it in the past, Rob. But still—that event changed my brother's life—"

"It changed your life, too. And your father's. Every year, millions of people throughout the world lose a parent—or a spouse—through an accident or illness. It's unfortunate, but true."

Candace sipped her drink. "I know. It's just, my feelings of guilt are deeper than you know. There's something else about the accident. Something I've never told you."

"Why, darling? What is it?"

She breathed deeply, then clasped his hand more firmly. "The day before the accident, Mother had asked me to go and have the tires replaced. All four of them were bald, or almost. But I didn't do it."

Rob squeezed her hand and gave her a tender look. He was grateful for this woman's trust in him, and for her resolve and commitment to the truth even when it hurt.

"Dad didn't know she had asked me, and neither did Monty. I never told Monty that she had—"

"Candace—"

"But after the accident, I told my father. I felt terrible—if I'd done what she asked, the accident might never have happened. I felt that I was to blame. But Dad blamed himself for it. He said that he knew the condition of the tires, and *he* should have gotten them replaced."

"Did Monty ever find out that Susannah had told you to get it done? Did Jack say anything?"

"No. I'm sure he didn't."

"Then—"

"Wait. There's more. Right before the accident, as we drove through the pouring rain, Mother and I were arguing. But not about the tires. It was about my future, and what I thought was her indifference to it. I didn't think she cared about me. I attacked her, Rob. I called her horrible names." Candace paused and blinked away tears. "I don't know exactly what, though. I've tried to block out the memory for so long."

Still holding her hand, Rob gazed at her. "Don't try to remember. You were a teenager—a child."

"But I wasn't a good teenager. I was very self-focused and self-absorbed, and not very forgiving—"

"Like all teenagers. You were normal."

"Anyway, after her death, Dad was in deep grief. While I was out in Texas, he went through hell with Monty. When Monty started screwing around, Dad suffered even more. He didn't bankroll him, though, or enable him. Mother was the one who did that. Monty was her project. I didn't relate to her—I've told you about how she and I never got along."

"Like many mothers and daughters."

"Yes, well. I had so little in common with her. I blamed her for so much, too. She was a spender, and Dad was a saver. The fact that they never had any money—that was clearly because of her. We all knew it, and Dad had to deal with it." She sipped her martini.

"And I'd say, you inherited—or adopted—his attitude about money."

"I agree. I mean, I do spend a lot of money now, but I didn't back when I didn't have much. And I've always kept track of it.

Anyway," she continued, looking into Rob's eyes, "the year before he died, Dad redid his will."

Rob took another sip of his Scotch, his eyes trained on his fiancée.

"SlimZ was in its second year, and sales had more than doubled, from a very strong start."

"I remember."

"Yes. So, I was already making a lot of money. Dad told me that he was dividing his estate equally between Monty and me. He didn't have many assets other than his home. It was paid off, and he wanted it to be sold upon his death. I told him to leave all of his money to Monty, that I didn't need anything, whereas Monty might, someday. Dad argued with me, but I did talk him into leaving almost everything to Monty. Rob, I didn't think he would die so soon after! I thought he would live for at least another twenty years." Candace brushed a tear away as another fell down her cheek.

"Candace, I—"

"I also made a promise to him," Candace said. "I told him I would take care of Monty financially. For the rest of his life."

Rob leaned back in his chair. "You mean, support him? Why make such a vow?"

"I shouldn't have. And no, I didn't mean I would support him. I meant I would help him if he ever needed money."

"And you feel bound by this promise."

"Yes. But then, Monty never seemed to need any money. He was always supported by some girlfriend. When he and Jeanine split up—"

"The one before Helen?"

"Right. Jeanine had a good job. When they split and he married Helen, with Adele already born—well, I guess Helen's salary wasn't enough for him. He had known—or thought he knew—how much money I had made for some time by then. When I agreed to loan them six hundred thousand so they could get into that house with a two-hundred-thousand-dollar mortgage, I thought I was done with him. I didn't want the money paid back until sometime in the future, whenever they sold the place, eventually. I expected them to just live their lives and leave me alone. I didn't expect that they would come to me for even more money, to redo it."

"Looking back, I'm wondering why they wanted to do a renovation, anyway," said Rob. "What with a new baby and everything."

"Exactly. They didn't need to do it at all. But as you know, he talked me into it. He said he knew the market, that it was on the rise, and that once the renovation was finished, he'd be able to sell it for so much that we'd all make money. I felt that when that happened, he'd be okay—and in the meantime, he'd be fine, too. I'd be fulfilling my promise to Dad."

Rob let out a deep breath.

"But then he roped me into cosigning the home equity loan—"

"Which David advised against."

"Yes. But which I did anyway." Candace finished her drink and set down the glass.

"Yes. Well. Back to your promise. To fulfill it, you didn't need to lend your brother over eight hundred thousand—nor guarantee another loan for five hundred—to allow him to speculate on real estate. That is not 'taking care of him financially.' Candace, Monty's had his hand out to you ever since you achieved your wealth, and you've been very generous. I don't know exactly what your father meant by his request, but I don't believe he wanted you to fund your brother's risky endeavors, or buy an expensive home for him. Ever."

"So, given Monty's personality, background, and abilities, and given my fortune—what do you suppose my father *did* want?"

"You've said Jack wasn't Monty's enabler. My guess is that, because he knew his son, he feared that Monty might end up alone and penniless—I don't mean to be harsh, but there it is. I assume

Jack felt you were the only one who would provide his son a safety net." Rob shook the ice in his drink, took a sip, and put the glass down. He looked directly into Candace's eyes. "Did Monty know about the promise you made?"

"I don't think so, but I don't know. *I* never told him."

"But Jack may have."

Candace shut her eyes for a second, then stared straight ahead. "It's possible. I try not to think about that."

Rob squeezed Candace's hand again. "Siblings—even those that despise each other—usually have each other much longer than they have their parents. As an only child, I'm fortunate enough—or unfortunate enough—to escape the situation. Whether Monty knows about your promise to Jack or not, I just don't see your responsibility in this. We've talked about this. Are you to keep funneling money to him? What if his pattern with the house continues—the deceit and manipulation? What if, God forbid, he uses your money for illegal activities?"

"I can't believe he would do that. But, Rob. Am I to stand by and let my brother spiral down? Perhaps end up penniless?"

"If he chooses to spiral down, you must let him. A safety net does not equal the assurance of a certain lifestyle that he's unwilling to earn for himself. He's far from penniless, and I don't expect he'll ever get close. I don't understand why you're afraid he may—I'm not. He's not of low intelligence. He's a capable man in his thirties with some amount of charisma, and is the brother of a very successful woman. Despite his spotty work background, he can get a job and support himself. You *know* he can."

Candace shut her eyes for a moment, then smiled. "Yes, I do know. Let's go see the banquet room, shall we?"

• • •

On Thursday afternoon, Monty drove to the Little League field to meet his buddy Chip Duncan and the Pirates for baseball practice. Chip's kid Sonny was the biggest and probably the most talented seven-year-old on the team, but Chip went to great lengths not to show favoritism. The rules decreed that all the players get equal time on the field, which wasn't hard to do. But the Pirates wanted to win every game and to become the league champions. Chip said he'd tried to recruit the best kids he could find, but Sonny had persuaded him to choose his friends for the roster, regardless of athletic ability.

Monty emerged from his five-year-old gray BMW, ball cap on his head. "Hey, Coach! How's it going?"

"Not bad," said Chip, grinning. None of the players had arrived yet. He handed Monty a sports bag full of bats and balls. "What's up in your world?"

Monty cleared his throat. "My man, you're looking at the father of twins."

Chip stopped short. "You're shitting me."

Monty smiled broadly. "Absolutely not."

"Well, goddamn. Congratulations, man!"

"Thank you." Monty glanced at the parking lot and waved to one of the team's stronger players, who had just stepped out of a minivan.

"Three little Carawans. I can't believe it," Chip said with a laugh. "You've outdone me again."

Monty laughed and puffed out his chest. "When you got it, you got it."

More players began to appear and trickle onto the field, carrying their gloves. "Well," said Chip, "I found out something a lot less interesting last night from Kristin."

"Oh yeah?"

"She's got a nephew named Beau Warren. One of her older sister's kids. 'Bout twenty-five or so. Works at Coke. We never see him. With all of her sisters and brothers, I can't keep up. Anyway, the dude's girlfriend works at your sister's company."

"Really," said Monty, as a statement. "What's her name?"

"Jess Copeland. Kristin said she's Candace's personal assistant. Beau's been dating her for a couple years."

"She young and hot?"

"What does that mean, man?" asked Chip, laughing. "You got a wife and kid, and now two more babies on the way."

Monty laughed. "You need to get out more."

Chip directed five of the boys over to a batting cage and picked up his own glove. "Man, you'll never change. Let's get some balls in the air!"

Monty smiled again and jogged out on the field to join Sonny and four Pirates. Maybe he'd look this chick up on Facebook—chances were that she *was* hot.

• • •

Candace exited her New York apartment building a few minutes after seven and entered a waiting taxi the doorman had procured for her. She and Rob were meeting some friends for drinks and then dinner in the hip Meatpacking District. She reached inside her bag for the hand sanitizer she always carried. The interior of a Manhattan taxi had to be as full of germs as an airplane lavatory. She glanced out the window as the cabdriver darted in between other vehicles, daring pedestrians to block his path.

She leaned back in her seat. This trip to the city had been productive, but she was looking forward to getting back down south on Sunday evening. Much as she hated to, she had made the decision to give up her Manhattan apartment this fall and move into Rob's much roomier one. Candace was a minimalist, so combining their belongings shouldn't be an issue.

She crossed her ankles and smoothed her skirt, her thoughts shifting to a memory of her mother getting dressed to go out to dinner one night back in the eighties. She had skipped a slip that night and donned only a pair of nude panty hose under a slinky red dress, laughing about her own mother's instruction to wear panties underneath panty hose. *"Grandmother didn't care if anybody could see the lines of your panties through your clothes—she cared if they couldn't. Because then, they'd know you weren't wearing any!"*

She shook her head slightly and closed her eyes. Her mother must have felt very risqué when she went commando under a pair of L'eggs. Candace couldn't remember if she ever did wear panties under panty hose. She had always thought that underwear was a very important part of a woman's wardrobe. A great outfit looked horrible with the wrong thing underneath, bottom or top. All SlimZ shapers and bras were designed to be invisible under clothing and to avoid the appearance of any lines. Candace hated the recent trend of letting bra straps show.

Her phone vibrated, signaling a message from David. Apparently the banker, Whitney, would be available for a conference call tomorrow between nine and one o'clock. Candace checked her schedule and sent a one-line response. Eleven thirty would work, otherwise it would have to be Monday. She put her phone on silent and placed it in her bag as the taxi slowed to a halt in front of her destination. The conversation with David and the banker wouldn't be a pleasant one, but it was necessary, unfortunately.

She paid the driver, exited the vehicle, and walked into the bar, oblivious to another message just received from David, this one marked as urgent.

• • •

Helen arrived at 710 Arcadia Lane as the sky was darkening, early for this time of year, and noticed that Monty's car wasn't in the driveway. Then she remembered it was Thursday, the day he helped out his friend at the Little League field after school. Either practice had run late or he had gone out with Chip for a drink afterward, or both. Fine—she would have more time to herself this way and wouldn't have to deal with him yet.

She got out of the car, unbuckled her daughter from her car seat, and looked up at a gathering sea of clouds in the sky, threatening the approach of a storm. Once inside the tiny guesthouse, the toddler scurried in front of her mother and into the living area. Helen turned on the big-screen television and then went to the bedroom to change clothes. Just before she lowered the window shade, a flash of lightning startled her. Within seconds, a loud thunderbolt cracked and Adele came running to find her.

"Mommy!"

Helen reached down and picked up the little girl, hugging her. "It's all right, Boo. That just means it's about to rain, and we're safe here inside. Don't worry." She kissed her, then put her down. "Let Mommy get into her comfy-cozies, and then we'll snuggle up on the couch."

Adele traipsed back into the other room just as the deluge began outside. Furious raindrops pelted the roof and slashed at the windows as the tall pines surrounding the house swayed in the wind. Thunderstorms were a fairly common occurrence in this city, and Helen was thankful to have made it home before this one hit. Whenever it rained, drivers went berserk, most going way too slowly and taking forever to get anywhere. Others drove way too fast. But Atlanta almost never experienced tornadoes, something Helen always feared growing up, and the aftermath of which she had seen firsthand.

She checked her phone for messages, set it down, pulled on her hoodie, and joined Adele on the sofa. The house was chilly. Another flash of lightning and bolt of thunder, this one sounding sooner than the last, frightened Adele into her arms again. Helen calmed her down again and stroked her hair. The wind howled outside as branches snapped and fell to the ground and leaves swirled.

Crack! That bolt struck and the sky lit up. Lightning was hitting way too close now. Helen's arms closed reflexively around Adele as she told herself not to alarm the child, who was glued to her television show.

Pop! Adele whimpered and Helen pulled her close. "The roof is protecting us, baby. Everything is okay. Are you getting hungry?"

Adele nodded.

"Let me see what we should have for dinner." Helen moved from the couch to the small kitchen and opened the freezer, where a vegetable lasagna sat waiting. She took it out, turned on the oven, and went back over to sit down with Adele.

Maybe the lightning was moving away from them. Helen started counting the seconds each time a flash appeared. The wind was almost as worrisome, however. She looked out the window and saw the tall pines bending and more branches falling to the ground. Why hadn't they had the bigger trees taken out? Because of the money it cost, she told herself.

The oven beeped, signaling it was preheated. Helen got up and opened the frozen dinner package. Just as she was about to put it in, another crackle-flash popped loudly and the power went out. Adele ran to the kitchen and Helen grabbed her up.

"Honey—" began Helen. Another flash of lightning hit just as the unthinkable happened. A horrible crash brought down the living room ceiling as wooden beams and debris fell through. A huge tree landed with a boom, destroying the sofa and the coffee table, and an avalanche of thick rain rushed into the room.

Adele screamed and shook in Helen's arms. They had to get out of here! Lightning flashed as Helen ran into the bedroom, holding her daughter. She grabbed her purse, and in two seconds, they were out the cottage's side door. Helen ran to the car with the sobbing child clutching her neck. Pulling her keys from her purse, she held Adele tightly as they slid behind the wheel and Helen shut the car door.

Don't panic! Calm her down, and calm down yourself. She took a deep breath as she saw more tree branches falling around the vehicle, missing it. She put the keys in the ignition with a trembling hand and spoke reassuringly to Adele, coaxing her to climb into her car seat. Then she put the car in reverse and reached in her purse for her phone.

It wasn't there. She had left it in the bedroom.

• • •

Late that night, Monty left his sister a voicemail.

"Hi, Candace. Not sure where you are right now, or if you're aware of the huge thunderstorms that pounded Atlanta tonight. Just thought you'd like to know that an *enormous* pine tree fell on the cottage my family is being forced to live in because *you've* withheld funding for the renovation. The roof totally caved in and almost *killed* Adele, the place is completely flooded, and virtually none of our possessions are salvageable. Not that you give a damn. But hey, call me when you get this, in the unlikely case that you *do* give a shit."

He dropped the phone and then checked his other, private one for messages—there were none. Thank God he hadn't left it locked in his desk drawer. When Helen had called his public phone a few hours ago from a neighbor's home number, he hadn't picked up. She should have realized that he never answered an unknown caller.

It was after midnight and the storm had long passed before he got around to listening to her hysterical message.

After he did, he jumped out of bed and raced from the Midtown condo to Arcadia Lane. Tree limbs and debris littered the roads, and the neighborhood was dark and devoid of emergency responders or police. Monty turned into the cracked driveway and parked behind the two-story home. At least *its* roof was intact. He popped open the glove compartment and reached inside for the flashlight. Careful to avoid the downed power lines, he walked around to survey the damage. The cottage was in ruins. Two exterior walls near the kitchen and bath were intact, but the place was mostly a huge pile of rubble.

He made his way over to where the living room had been. All the furniture was wrecked and the TV demolished. His desk was in pieces on the ground. His laptop was destroyed, and so was his iPad, which had been locked inside his desk. The framed picture of his mother was broken and ruined.

He reached down and moved the slats of wood, searching for the birthday card he had saved for so many years. The one she had given him when he turned seventeen. There it was—the front was wet and dirty, but thankfully, the card was basically intact, the inside damp but readable. His eyes fell on the last words she had penned to him.

Happy Birthday to my brilliant son! Life holds many wonderful opportunities for you, and such a bright future!

I can't wait to watch as you design and create buildings and skyscrapers. I know you will become a very famous architect. Never forget that I love you and will always be here to help you, in every possible way.

—Mother

Monty stood still for a few more moments, a tear forming at the corner of his eye. He wiped it away, feeling dark and lost.

He put the card in his jacket's breast pocket and went into the bedroom, just beyond the bath, to look for his clothes. He was able to save only some of them, which he gathered up and threw into the backseat of the BMW. Then he slumped behind the wheel, put the key in the ignition, and threw his head back against the headrest.

He had done all that he could here. Before starting the car, he put the card in the glove box and sent Helen a text saying that he'd gone to Chip's house over in Morningside for the night. On his way back to the condo, his thoughts wandered and his mood lifted a little. He had to be practical. Disastrous as it was, the situation afforded a perfect way to get a lot more money from Candace, and he wasn't going to waste the opportunity.

11

Sex

Against his better judgment, David Shepherd began writing a response to Monty Carawan's latest email. Then he stopped and decided instead to forward the written tirade to Candace, telling her that he would like to give it the twenty-four-hour rule before replying.

Her brother was incredible. Two months ago, when David's assistant Geneviève discovered that the vendor invoices the office had received were phony, David had momentarily become unhinged. Then he'd chided himself for not having authenticated the documents himself or following through. That evening, he emailed Candace about the issue, flagging the message as urgent, but she hadn't contacted him until the next morning.

In the intervening hours, David had researched all the invoices Monty claimed to have paid since the beginning of the project back in early 2008, including the most recent one, supposedly funded from an equity line draw. A few of the early vendor invoices were legitimate, but no record existed for most of the rest, and one supplier had disappeared—or had never existed. The next morning, David had been prepared to be the recipient of Candace's wrath, expecting her to threaten pulling all of her accounts because of his mistakes.

But that hadn't occurred. Before their conversation, she had learned that the guesthouse where the Carawans resided had been destroyed by the ferocious storm the night before. The sorry plight of her niece and sister-in-law, if not her brother, had evoked her sympathy. She had instructed David to hold off on confronting Monty about the invoices, deciding that it wasn't the right time.

She returned to Atlanta the next day, saw the devastation for herself, and announced that she would cover all costs not paid by homeowner's insurance to level the cottage and take out the remaining tall trees. She also provided funds to make the home's basement livable again, and for household items and replacement furniture. Within a week, the Carawans moved back into the basement.

David shook his head and switched his focus to the day's agenda. Like most Mondays, he had a million things to do and a busy week ahead. Candace would soon let him know how she wanted him to handle her brother's latest tantrum, he was sure.

• • •

Helen had to get some bleach.

She pulled out her shopping list and added Clorox to it. She planned to swing by Walmart on her way to pick up Adele after work. She checked the time: it was almost four—just over an hour left before she could close up shop and call it a day. Then her phone vibrated.

"You busy?" asked Dawn.

"Not too. Tired, though. Make that exhausted." Helen stretched in her seat. Her desk was situated in a corner, which kept her invisible to most of her coworkers here at Vreden.

"I'm sorry. When's your next doctor appointment?"

"Friday. I'm having another ultrasound."

"Everything okay?"

"Fine. They just want to see how the babies are doing, measure them and everything." Helen smoothed her top against her stomach, which was growing exponentially. She felt a tiny flutter, then another. "Wow. I just felt some kicks."

"Oh my God! That's so wonderful!" said Dawn.

"Yeah, it's about the right time for that to start, as I recall."

"Helen. How are *you* doing?"

"Okay. Hanging in there."

"Have you guys bought all the stuff you need yet?"

"Yeah, we have, just about. We're fine. Except—"

"Except what?"

"Except, it's harder to keep the basement clean than it was the guesthouse. It smells like mildew down there."

"Are you sure it was adequately waterproofed before you moved in?"

"Dawn, I'm not sure of anything to do with the place. Plus, all basements down here are mildewy. It's humid, like, year-round."

"Go get a dehumidifier. Can you?"

"I should. Maybe I'll look for one at Walmart."

"Wait," said Dawn. "If this house is supposed to be so high-end, why wouldn't you have one installed? A good one, I mean?"

"I don't know why. Dawn, here's the situation. Monty is working with David now on all the details. I'm in the loop, but I'm not getting involved. I just—I can't." A single tear ran down Helen's cheek, and she quickly wiped it away.

Dawn's voice softened. "You're dealing with so much, Helen. Maybe you could talk to David, not to get involved, but just to touch base. Would that work?"

"I dunno. I guess I could. He's been so nice."

"Good. And forget the dehumidifier, for now."

"Well, maybe I do need to get on that. I noticed some mold on one wall of the bedroom."

"Oh my God. You can't have that, Helen."

"I'm getting some Clorox on the way home today, and treating it over the weekend."

"Is that safe? I mean, shouldn't you have someone else do it?"

"You're right."

"And get the cause of the mold identified and fixed. See—this is the type of thing you can go to David about. Couldn't you? Like, just tell him what the issues are, and see what can be done?"

"I'll try it." She glanced around. "Look, I gotta go. I have to finish a design before I can get out of here today."

"Just let me know what happens, okay? I love you."

"Love you, too."

Helen put the phone down and stared at her computer screen. She couldn't go to David about the mold. He hadn't been to the property since that day back in April to take pictures for Candace, and Monty would be livid if he came over again. Anyway, David was a financial advisor, not a construction expert. In the big scheme of things, was a little mold in the basement bedroom that big of a deal?

Surely they wouldn't be living down there for very much longer anyway. She would take care of the problem, or get Monty to, and she wouldn't mention it to Dawn again. Since they'd moved back in to the basement, Monty had been more focused on getting the renovation completed. He was dealing directly with David now and cooperating with him to manage the funds. As long as David didn't get in his face, it seemed to be working. David copied her on everything, but when she asked Monty any questions, he was evasive. She had no idea what was really happening while she was at work. What she saw around the house looked half-done and seemed to remain that way. When she remarked about it, Monty said she didn't understand how construction worked.

Her victory in getting him to go over the bills and the renovation budget together had been short-lived—they'd only done it twice. After the tree fell on the cottage, things had gotten crazy. Monty had talked her into letting him handle the money again, saying she could log into their account anytime she wanted, to see what was going on. He claimed it just didn't make sense for them to take the time to recalculate what the bank account already reflected. His job search was temporarily on hold—it had to be, he said. He was just too busy.

Once the house was finished, Helen was afraid he would dig in his heels and refuse to put the place up for sale until the market recovered to the point where they could sell it for as much money as he originally planned. If he did dig in, he'd have to find a job and start helping her to support the family.

• • •

Candace dialed David's number at five o'clock.

"Hello, Candace."

"David, I know you wanted to wait until tomorrow to respond, but I'd like you to write an email to Monty now and send me a draft to review."

"Okay. But—"

"I've thought about it, and here's what I want you to say. First, I want you to ask these questions: 'Why are you blaming Candace for your financial problems, when she has come to your rescue time and again? Why are you blaming her for the numerous bad decisions you have made, decisions which she had no part in? What monies do you and Helen have in savings or retirement funds that you are unwilling to use to finish the project? When are you going to find a regular, full-time job?'"

David began to rub his temple. "The reason I wanted to wait to respond—"

"I know, David, and I don't care anymore. I also want you to list for him all the monies I've loaned, paid, and given to them as of right now—dates and specific amounts, including the most recent ones to the bank. Then, I want you to state that they have put my initial investment at risk. I want you to say that Monty's pattern of lying, withholding information, and sending angry emails and messages has got to stop. I want you to say that no more funds will be made available to finish the project until he furnishes valid receipts for work already done, a verifiable completion budget, and their tax returns from 2009. All things which we have previously demanded yet still haven't received."

"What makes you think—"

"I know. I want you to say all of this, nonetheless. In addition, I want you to demand that Monty come clean with whatever is still required to be done to get the certificate of occupancy. That day I went over there after the storm, he assured me that the C.O. was on its way, that everything had been taken care of. Yet we still don't have it. You told me that it's illegal for them to be in the place without it, and here we are two months later, with no sign of it. When I walked through the first floor that day, I was appalled at what I saw, and I'm afraid that nothing has changed."

"We ought to take this thing over, Candace."

"Well, before I make that decision, I want you to send this email so I can go on record. The last thing I want you to demand is a current income-outflow budget. They simply *must* start to live within their means. Monty needs to face reality, and apparently Helen can't get him to do it. I am not the bad guy here, and I refuse to allow him to paint me as a greedy villain."

"I will send you a draft email this evening."

"Good. I'll review it in time for you to send it tomorrow. Copy Helen and myself on it."

"Got it."

"That's it for now. I've got to run."

David put his phone down and looked over the notes he had made while Candace was speaking. Within ten minutes, he crafted the email and sent it to her. When she was in a semi-manic mood, it was best to get her what she wanted right away. She'd read it later, revise it, and get back to him about when to send it. He doubted that the final version of the email would resemble the rant she had just unleashed, and worried that it wouldn't make much difference in her pattern of enabling Monty.

• • •

At six thirty Tuesday morning, Helen woke up in a pool of warm blood.

Panicked, she called Dr. Russell's emergency line. The doctor told Helen to come in as soon after seven o'clock as possible—Friday's scheduled ultrasound would happen this morning. Helen cleaned up and got dressed, dropped Adele off at school, and drove as fast as she could to the obstetrician's office. Monty met her in the waiting room, and in a few moments a nurse ushered both of them back to the ultrasound technician, who greeted them in a soothing tone.

Helen settled herself on the table, fighting back tears. There was more blood this morning than there was the first time. Monty stood by her side, his eyes glued to the monitor, not touching her. The technician started the process and the room filled with the quiet dread of impending tragedy.

Searching for clues, Helen kept her eyes trained on the technician's face, which was stone cold and still as she studied the screen. A few seconds passed, then Dr. Russell entered the room, her eyes focused on the images of the babies. "Good morning," she said. "Danielle?"

The technician looked up. "Good morning, doctor. We have two heartbeats, and they're both strong."

Dr. Russell grabbed Helen's hand and gave it a quick squeeze. "All's well. No worries. What do you think happened to cause the bleeding?"

"I don't know," said Helen, her eyes glassy.

Dr. Russell smiled. "You need to take things easier. Do you have help with your toddler?" She glanced over at Monty.

"She goes to day care while I'm at work."

"What about when you're not at work?"

Helen shut her eyes. "She's not that much trouble. Really."

"Well, you need to let others help you with her. Like your husband." She turned to face Monty. "You can do that, can't you?"

"Of course."

"Good. You both know that this is a high-risk pregnancy—all multiples are. We all need to work together to make sure everything goes well, and Helen gets as close as possible to her due date. That means a lot of rest, and less stress. Okay?"

Monty nodded, narrowing his eyes.

Dr. Russell turned back to her patient. "Helen, you're not going to work today. I want you to rest for the day and don't go back to your regular schedule until you've seen no blood for twenty-four hours. Now, would you two like to know what they are? Or not?"

"Yes," said Monty.

Helen nodded.

"Paint the room blue!"

"Both boys?" asked Monty.

Dr. Russell smiled and nodded at Helen.

Thirty minutes later, as they rode the elevator down together, Monty made an announcement. "I've picked out their names. You named Adele, first and middle."

They weren't married when Adele was born. Helen was still Helen Piper, and she had named her baby Adele Marie Piper. When Monty became her husband, they had changed the surname to Carawan.

Monty watched the floor numbers change and spoke again, almost talking to himself. "Broden Henry, and Parker Owen. We'll call them Brody and Park."

Helen gave him a quizzical look. "How did you come up with those?"

"They'll play football, too. Those are good names for football players. And they don't sound like each other. I don't want twin-sounding names for them."

The door to the elevator opened on the ground floor, and Monty stepped out first. "I have some things to take care of," he said without looking at her. "See you at home later."

• • •

Monty slipped behind the wheel of the BMW, locked the car doors, and placed both his private phone and public one between the two front seats. After picking up a fully caffeinated latte at Starbucks, he drove over to the high-rise Midtown condo building and entered the underground garage. The woman who currently occupied his newest real estate investment would just now be getting up, or, if he was lucky, she'd still be in bed.

He had met Rachel Benton last summer at a bar in Buckhead. Eight weeks later, he'd purchased the condo for a song, paying cash, and by December, he had filled it with expensive, modern furniture. Rachel worked as a decorator for the most affluent Atlanta residents and was able to find unique pieces and art—the best of the best.

Twenty-five years old, she had moved here from Philadelphia three years ago and had gotten started in the design business with the help of a rich, society-conscious aunt.

Rachel had an amazing body and her youth was intoxicating. She was almost as tall as Monty and had gorgeous legs and the best ass he had ever seen—and he had seen several. She had long, silky blonde hair and perfectly formed, perfectly sized tits. He felt a stiffening as he imagined her naked, lying in the queen-sized bed, waiting for him.

He ran through a light that had just turned red on Peachtree. He was in the mood to celebrate: he was going to be the father of twin boys. How awesome was that! He'd send his sister an email later today announcing the news, while Rachel was away at a client's home.

He parked the car and took the elevator up to the fourteenth floor, then bounded down the hall, unlocked the door, and almost raced into the bedroom. She wasn't there. Then he heard the shower running and entered the luxurious Italian-tiled bathroom that was quickly filling with steam. Through the glass doors he could see the profile of her flawless, nude body. He watched for just a second or two, then stripped quickly and stepped inside, startling her. Grabbing her around the waist, he moved his arms up just under her breasts, pressing himself against her back, her wet hair in his face. She turned around, pulling him toward her.

An hour later, she sat in front of her vanity applying makeup, wearing only her pink bikini underwear. From the bed, he studied her reflection. Her only imperfection was a faint rose birthmark on the side of her face, just in front of her ear. She camouflaged it with makeup and covered it with her hair, normally pushing her tresses forward—she never pulled her hair back. She didn't wear earrings, but she loved necklaces and bracelets, and over the last year he had indulged her with many.

"Monty," she said. "Stop staring at me. You know I have an appointment with a client."

"When will you be finished?"

"I'm going to the gym after."

"And then?"

Satisfied with her mascara, Rachel put the wand down and turned to face him.

"You're killing me, baby," he said. "Let's go again—"

"I don't have time, and you know it." She stood and walked over to the dresser. "If I don't hurry, I'll be late. I'll see you tonight. And don't forget the cash you said you'd give me."

"Yeah, I'll call you." Annoyed, he gathered some clothes to put on. "I have a meeting, and I have to catch up on email." After getting dressed, he regarded his image in the mirror. He'd get in a workout today, too. He certainly didn't want to hang out at Arcadia Lane with Helen lounging around. He had promised to pick up Adele after school, but once he delivered her to her mother, perhaps he would just come back to the condo and hang out. He could take Rachel out to dinner, and after another round in bed, he'd go home after Helen and Adele were asleep.

His public phone vibrated with the receipt of an email. David Shepherd. Fuck. He wouldn't read it right now. He didn't want anything to spoil his good mood.

12

Exit

fter a working lunch with Amanda and Darlene, Candace returned to her office, closed the door, and checked her inbox for messages. A new email from Monty with the subject line "Twins" caught her attention. Candace shook her head slightly as she opened the email, skimming it. Her brother had chosen not to reply to David's message marked with a red flag, the one she had edited and finalized this morning. Without even acknowledging receipt of that email, Monty had sent her a two-paragraph personal update.

In the first paragraph, he outlined in dramatic detail another emergency rush to the doctor this morning. Evidently, Helen was prone to bleeding during her pregnancy, but this second episode was another false alarm; a sonogram revealed that the babies were fine. *Perhaps all women carrying twins were more likely to experience spotting.* Having never been pregnant, Candace had no idea.

In the second, shorter paragraph, Monty announced that both of the babies were boys. Of course, he and Helen were thrilled and "couldn't wait to share the news." Apparently, they could wait to share the specific financial information Candace had just had David request again in writing.

She dismissed her frustrations for the moment and refocused her attention to more urgent company issues. She needed to make a decision about whether to ratify Darlene's position that no advertising was necessary to promote the new swimsuit line. The company had never engaged in advertising, print or otherwise, but in recent years a presence on social media had been key. Darlene was in charge of the marketing team under Amanda's sales and marketing division and had proven her worth as a valuable employee. She was in charge of the website, Facebook page, Twitter account, and all public relations. In Darlene's opinion, any money spent to promote the new swimwear line in magazines or other print media would be a waste of money and utterly unnecessary.

Amanda held a different view. With years of retail sales experience and a traditional professional background, she was probably the most old-school employee in the company. She had worked in Texas and California before moving to Atlanta to join SlimZ. Candace felt she understood Amanda professionally, but on a personal level she had little in common with the woman.

Amanda was in her late forties and was divorced with a teenage daughter. She dyed her longish hair a peroxide-ish shade of blonde, tanned excessively, and often displayed a muffin top above too-tight pants. More than once, Candace had seen her with camel toe. Amanda was a former smoker and was on the slim side but not fit. An array of cigarette wrinkles fanned out from her hard, thin lips that she coated in red lipstick. But she was a hard worker, focused on results, and very confident. She was also blunt, which was both a good and bad quality.

Today, it hadn't been good. Whenever friction surfaced between Amanda and Darlene, Candace felt annoyed. The underlying tension between the two women had been a problem for some time, and today's meeting seemed to showcase their differences. Candace wished they and all her employees could work together more like men did: once men resolved a conflict, a clear winner emerged and all parties continued to show professional respect for each other.

With women, it was different, and being a woman, Candace understood that. But that didn't make dealing with personnel and management issues any easier. Candace hadn't created her company to be a referee or to tap-dance around people's feelings. She glanced out the window, then began composing an email to both women. She would back Darlene's opinion.

At thirty-six, Darlene was closer to Candace's age than Amanda was. Darlene was from Atlanta, had married young, and had a middle-school-age son; her husband was an engineer. She was tall with a proportional figure, dark hair, and a pale complexion, as if she regularly wore sunscreen. Her professional wardrobe was more conservative than sexy, with a not-trying-too-hard French touch. She wore attractive high heels and scarves of all lengths in an unconscious, effortless manner. Her thoughtfulness and poise perfectly reflected the company image Candace had worked hard to construct. Darlene's group had jumped on a social media marketing plan after Shelly's very astute product development team had come up with the SwimZ tech pac (technical package, or actual samples of the new line, complete with patterns, fabrics, and size specifications).

Shelly's people had worked closely with the designers, viewing their swimwear designs via the company's internal computer-aided design (CAD) system—these were the swimsuits that design wished to "sample," or show to buyers, in September. Shelly reported to Paula, the head of design, and their close working relationship was ideal. Candace was grateful for it and wished that Darlene and Amanda could develop the same type of bond. The CEO had been very satisfied with the marketing work done by Darlene's group in the past; Darlene's leadership and vision had been one of the key components in their success and in the company's bottom line.

Candace buzzed Jess with a request for water and a cup of green tea. The green monster, jealousy, factored into today's testy session with Darlene and Amanda, Candace believed. Despite Amanda's talents, she was flawed with a deep insecurity that manifested itself in her pushy attitude. But she was valuable, and Candace couldn't afford to lose her. She'd have to massage her ego. Yes, Candace was sure that in male-dominated businesses, the typical hierarchy experienced jealousy, backstabbing, and grudges, too. However, that didn't compare to the cattiness and even nastiness of a group of ambitious, high-achieving women. Her team was smart, though, and very good in a crisis. Perhaps that was because of the way they were wired as women: adaptable, resourceful, and clever.

Candace opened David's email to her brother, which David had copied her on, then forwarded it to Rob. Monty was going to respond to her questions. If he didn't, she was done with him. No matter how many babies he and Helen produced.

• • •

On Thursday afternoon, with Candace safely on a commercial jet bound for LaGuardia, Jess skimmed her task list for the week and checked off the last assignment. She would tackle the next few items today and then have all day Friday to work on the rest. With her boss away, Jess might even be able to take some personal break time and relax. Normally, Candace bombarded her daily with urgent messages to get this or that done. In between, Jess stayed busy anticipating her orders and frantically putting out small fires before they became explosions. It was exhausting at times.

Tomorrow morning, Candace would be on her way out of the country and wasn't due back in Atlanta until almost the end of the month. Candace planned to spend a long weekend in France with

Rob, then would be in New York for a week. Rob's assistant Julia had emailed Jess the itinerary. Through NetJets, Julia had booked a private jet departing New York at nine o'clock in the morning and arriving in Nice seven hours later, at ten p.m. local time. Jess knew that for Candace, it was the only way to travel across the Atlantic: much shorter and more comfortable than first class on a commercial carrier overnight. An added bonus was the avoidance of crowds and their germs. When the jet touched down in France, it would be only four o'clock Eastern time, so the couple would be fresh and ready for cocktails.

The itinerary showed they planned to stay at Château Eza, a five-star boutique hotel in Èze, a village just east of Nice. Jess pulled up the website Julia had linked to in her message and clicked through the photo gallery. Located at the height of the Moyenne Corniche and perched on top of steep rock cliffs, the Château boasted panoramic views of the French Riviera from private terraces floating high above the Mediterranean. For Rob, the trip was combination business and pleasure: he had a client meeting in Monaco on Monday. Candace would be checking in with the office then, but tomorrow she'd be out of touch for most of the day.

Jess pulled up her Facebook page and settled back in her chair. She hadn't checked it in days—she was just too busy to post much on it. Since her twenty-fifth birthday was in two days, she expected to get lots of Facebook birthday wishes. Beau was taking her out to dinner to celebrate that night, and on Sunday they planned to go to Lake Lanier.

She had a new friend request. It was from Beau's uncle, Chip Duncan. Jess checked him out. Jeez. He looked to be in his late thirties or forties. His profile picture was of him and his family: he was married with two kids, one of them a baby girl. Jess recognized his wife: she was Beau's mom's younger sister, Kristin. The kids were named Sonny (how original) and Sawyer.

Jess shook her head slightly. Who named their baby daughter Sawyer? It must be Kristin's maiden name. Jess had met her at a family thing last winter at Beau's parents' house, and then they had friended each other. Chip had only ninety-one Facebook friends. Jess had over nine hundred.

Most of her Facebook friends were her age and younger—very few were her adult family members. Why did so many married adults insist on getting on Facebook, and worse, on friending young, single people like her? Didn't they realize that Facebook was developed for people in college and in their twenties, primarily single people?

Jess believed that older, married (and divorced) people who had a Facebook page (and who friended people who weren't relatives) had one of two motivations: to reconnect with their high school friends or to establish themselves on the dating market. Well, maybe Chip Duncan felt that since he was Beau's uncle, he was almost like family to Jess. She didn't feel that way, and wouldn't until she and Beau were married, or at least engaged.

Although she was sure that Chip's reason for friending her on Facebook was benign, she was now in the position of having to accept or deny his request. She much preferred Twitter. There, when someone followed you, you could choose to follow or not to follow them—no questions asked, and no hard feelings. As for Facebook, no matter what group of people it was intended for as a social media, it was used by zillions of people now. Jess was kind of over Facebook, anyway—she was drowning in stupid updates and photos.

She looked over Chip's page again, hovered the mouse over the "accept" icon for a few seconds, clicked on it, and forgot about it.

• • •

Helen arrived at Vreden Management on Friday morning a few minutes early. She had taken off Tuesday and Wednesday, returning to work yesterday. The spotting had disappeared twenty-four hours before, and since then she'd had no more issues. She must have really needed the rest, especially with two babies in her womb.

She had bought Clorox on Monday evening, but after Dawn's admonition, was wary of using it to scrub the mold off the walls. What if just smelling the bleach triggered another episode of bleeding, or caused something worse? Then again, living in a dank, moldy basement couldn't be good for her, either. She would get Monty to take care of it while she took Adele to a park or something. She'd have to pick the right time to ask him.

She picked up her coffee mug and clicked on her email inbox. She was over the worst of the nausea she had experienced earlier in the pregnancy, and coffee tasted good again, thank God. She wasn't a big coffee drinker, but she needed a little caffeine in the morning to get going. No one at work had suspected her pregnancy yet, which was fortunate. She smoothed her loose, dark blue dress over her expanding abdomen. Pretty soon she would have a serious babies-bump, but she didn't plan to wear tight, stretchable clothes that would show it off, as was the fashion. People could just think she was getting fat. It wouldn't bother her in the least.

A new email popped up from her supervisor, Peter McPherson. She was to come and see him in his office as soon as possible. What could this be about? The brochure she had been working on this week was almost ready, despite her time off. She had planned to finish it this morning and have it ready by noon, even though it wasn't due until five o'clock. Had something more urgent come up? Had she forgotten about another assignment that was overdue?

With a nervous step, she made her way to Peter's office and knocked on the door.

"Come in," he called.

She entered and approached the nearest chair. "Good morning, Peter."

"Good morning. Close the door, please."

Helen turned, shut the door, and turned back to her boss, hesitating.

"Thanks, Helen. Sit down. How are you feeling?"

She dropped to a seat. "Much better, thanks."

"What was the matter? Flu?"

"No. Well, not really sure. Exhaustion, I guess. I just needed some rest. But I'm back to normal now."

"Terrific. You have a toddler, right? All those germs. I'm sure he keeps you busy."

"She. Yes, she does. But she's fine, too."

Peter smiled and glanced over at his computer screen, pausing. "Well, the reason I needed to see you this morning was to discuss some changes happening here at Vreden."

Helen nodded, her lips in a tight line, her eyes fixed on Peter.

Peter cleared his throat and looked right at Helen. "As you probably know, some reorganization has been going on over the last few months."

"Well, I've heard some rumors—"

"Which were just that—rumors. I don't know how they get started, but they seem to have a life of their own." He offered a weak smile. "In any case, let's talk about reality. Which is that the company is downsizing."

Helen sucked in a breath, bracing herself.

"Which means," continued Peter, "that certain positions are being eliminated." He picked up a pen on his desk and clicked it on and off, looking at it. Then he exhaled and turned his eyes back to Helen's.

"I'm sorry, Helen. You've done great work here—"

"Wait. Are you saying I'm being laid off? Fired?" Helen said, her voice trembling.

"I'll give you a great recommendation. You're on LinkedIn, right? You'll get something right away, I'm sure. You can leave anytime today, but you'll be paid through the thirtieth."

In shock, Helen stood as her eyes welled up with tears. She was having trouble breathing. Could this be happening? What if Peter knew she was pregnant with twins? She fought the urge to blurt it out, then spoke calmly.

"Peter, my situation—"

"I know you're under a lot of stress. So is everybody. But Vreden is under stress, too. The real estate crash has affected our business, I'm sure you're aware. We just don't have the luxury right now of keeping nonessential employees. Not until things turn around." Peter put the pen back on his desk and started to rise, signaling that the meeting was over.

This is it. You have to tell him. "You don't understand. I'm not able—"

"Sure you are. Look, the decision's been made—my paperwork is in. Don't worry, though. You're very talented. You'll have a job by July first, I just know you will. Go ahead and stay at your desk today if you want. You'll be locked out of the network, but get on the job sites later and get the word out. Then shoot me an email and tell me what you need from me." He walked to the door and opened it, smiling.

Helen's legs began shaking as she somehow made her way to the door. She stopped and looked at Peter right in the eyes. Would it change anything if he knew? Should she beg?

"Chin up, Helen. I'm confident that you'll be fine." He stood aside, looking down and waiting for her to leave. She stepped out and walked back to her desk, sat down, covered her face in her hands, and cried.

• • •

On Sunday morning, Monty dropped Helen and Adele off at the Lindbergh MARTA station, where they could catch a train to the airport.

Even though there was no traffic, he wasn't about to drive them all the way down there, several miles south of the city. The train would take them straight to the terminal, and in about an hour, they'd be on a plane bound for Chicago. Helen's sister, Dawn, had insisted on flying her and Adele up for a visit, now that Helen had been canned from her job and had nothing else to do.

Monty pulled over to the curb in the "Kiss and Ride" lane and watched distractedly as Helen struggled with her suitcase and took their daughter's hand.

"Bye, Daddy!" called Adele.

"Bye-bye, sweetie!" Monty said, then blew his daughter a kiss. Helen shut the car door and began rolling her bag toward the ticket machine, Adele at her side.

He let out a deep breath as he guided the car out of the lot, happy to be free of them, for a while, anyway. Helen hadn't told him about being fired on Friday morning until that evening, when she and Adele got home at the usual time. Evidently she'd stayed at the office, on the phone with her sister, devising a plan to go stay with Dawn and her dimwitted husband Frank for the next two weeks.

Monty was looking forward to the time alone, and to spending more time with Rachel. He'd stay over at the condo the whole time Helen was away. Staying at the house was just too depressing, and the condo was more comfortable, to say the least. He would head over there later today—Rachel would be waiting for him—but this morning, he needed to go to the house and finish some research.

He'd started it on Friday, just after he looked at Chip's Facebook page. He spent an hour guessing Chip's password and finally cracked it, kicking himself for ignoring the obvious: Chip's real name, Chester, plus the number 1—Sonny was a junior. Then he logged on and saw that Chip had recently friended Candace's assistant, Jess Copeland. He checked out her page. The chick had just turned twenty-five and had gotten tons of Facebook birthday wishes. She had long dark hair, was gorgeous, and was in a relationship with Chip's nephew—a fact that Monty assumed Candace didn't know. Why would she? Candace didn't care about *anyone* other than herself, or *anything* other than her company. It was her whole world.

A world he was getting ready to shake up.

On Friday afternoon, while Helen was still at work, not working, he found out everything he could about Jess. It wasn't that difficult. She was on Twitter and her tweets were public. She had gone to the University of Georgia and was probably ecstatic to have a job at SlimZ, even if it was as Candace's bitch. It had to be an incredibly stressful job, no matter what kind of bullshit she had to do. Who could put up with Candace all day, every day? She'd probably gone through a dozen other assistants before this girl came along.

Jess had been with Candace for a few years, though. Long enough to have learned a lot about the workings of the company, but also long enough to be relaxed about what she knew. To be a little sloppy, like a lot of people her age were—at least, while the boss was away. She probably knew a ton about what was going on over there and had access to a myriad of confidential information. Information that the CEO trusted her not to share.

She looked just dumb enough to provide a way in for Monty, but smart enough to do it without leaving a paper trail.

He was sick of Candace nickel-and-diming him; it was about time he got some real money. He made a decision. He wanted more than the house and more than a few hundred thousand dollars. Candace could spare a few million—maybe even ten—and still go on with her decadent, obscene lifestyle. She wouldn't even miss the money. Then, he would have the funds he needed to live the way he ought to. He could study architecture at an elite school, apply his knowledge, and get the recognition he deserved, at last.

To make all of that happen, he needed to connect with Jess on a personal level—on the phone, or better yet, in person.

13

Decisions

On the last Monday morning in June, Candace stepped toward a black Escalade parked in front of Rob's Manhattan apartment. Dominic, the driver, stood outside of the vehicle, waiting to take her to LaGuardia. Her phone buzzed.

"Hey, David," she said. "What's up?"

"Hello, Candace. I wanted to let you know I'm forwarding two quotes from the contractors we discussed last week—"

"Are both available immediately?"

"I'll find out."

Dominic opened her car door and she flashed him a smile. "Still no word from Monty?" she asked David.

"No, and it's been almost two weeks since I sent that email to him. Would you like me to follow up with a phone call?"

"No," Candace said while settling herself in the Escalade's backseat and putting on her seat belt. She turned to the tall driver, who had placed her Louis Vuitton valises in the back of the vehicle. "Thank you, Dominic." She spoke into the phone again. "David, here's what I want to do. I'll look at the quotes you sent and I'll call you back this afternoon. We can discuss them then. I'm scheduled to arrive in Atlanta before noon."

"Fine."

"Also, we can talk about a timetable. So, it's important that you find out how soon work can begin on the house, and how long it will take to get completed. I want us to know the plan before Monty finds out this is going to happen."

"Got it."

Candace removed her new iPad from her bag and entered her passcode. "I'm pulling up your email right now; I can look the quotes over on the way to the airport. The other thing I need you to do is find a realtor. A good one. Someone familiar with that area of Atlanta and that market."

"You want me to start looking now?"

"Why not? I want this thing done, David. I want it finished and sold and out of my life."

"I don't blame you."

"Oh, wait. I almost forgot. Find a rental—house or apartment, I don't care. Something that fits their income. I mean, Helen's income. She sent you that tax return, right?"

"Yes."

"It doesn't have to be in that area, but keep it in inside the perimeter. Or at least close to Helen's office. Can you have Geneviève work on that?"

"Definitely. She should be able to find something. The rental market here is huge right now."

"I want to be able to tell Monty where they can live while the work on the house is being done, and how much the rent is. Since I assume the workers will need them to be moved out. Monty and Helen can live in the place Geneviève finds for them, or they can find a place themselves." Candace took a breath. "Finally, just in case it comes up later, which it better not: I am not gifting the family any more money, ever. That's over."

"Anything else?"

Candace looked out the window and down at the dirty water as the Escalade traveled east, over the Triborough Bridge. "Yes. As you know, I don't want to put one more dime into that house than is absolutely necessary. I'll look over the quotes you got, but I'm counting on you to negotiate with whichever one of them we choose, to bring the price down."

"Candace, you're going to get sticker shock when you look at them."

"That's fine. I know that contractors need to make a profit, too. What I'm saying is, with the housing market being what it is—the lack of new construction, renovations, whatever—and with the state of the economy in general, these guys are lucky to get *any* work. So, whatever their quotes are, I expect you to get them to take ten to fifteen percent off the top. Just to get my business."

"Understood."

"That's all for now. I'll call you later today." Candace placed her iPhone in her bag and began scrolling through her email on her iPad. A signal sounded as a new message came in. It was from Helen.

Candace read the five lines twice. Helen had been laid off from her job a week and a half ago. Two days later, she and Adele had flown to Chicago to stay with Helen's sister for a few weeks. Helen had updated her resume and begun searching for a new position, but she felt doubtful about having much success before the babies were born.

Candace sat back in her seat and shut her eyes, then let out a deep breath. Odd that Monty had kept this news to himself, but she wasn't surprised that Helen had. It fit her personality. Given the chaos, she was probably still in shock about having been let go, and Candace couldn't blame her for wanting to get away from Monty.

However, with Helen and Adele up in Chicago, it would probably be easier for David to get the family moved out of the house and into a rental. He would have to expedite the process. Maybe the loss of Helen's job would be the catalyst Monty needed to go and get a job of his own. In a few short months, he'd be a father of three. It was time for him to starting acting like one, to start providing for his family. Until he did, however—or until Helen found a job—somebody would have to pay their rent.

Candace had paid the bank fourteen thousand dollars to catch up their mortgage and HELOC a couple months ago, and she trusted they hadn't fallen behind again. However, she hadn't signed the new note to roll the mortgage into a larger home equity loan, despite Monty's pleas.

"Ms. Morgan?" said Dominic, interrupting Candace's thoughts. "You said Delta, correct?"

"That's correct, Dominic. Thank you." Candace propped her Fendi sunglasses up on top of her head and inspected her nails, which were due for a manicure. She'd have to have Jess schedule one today or tomorrow.

She had a busy week ahead of her in Atlanta. Late last week she had visited the Manhattan sample room that Shelly's product development team had been working with on the swimwear line. This week she would meet with Shelly, Paula, and Amanda to discuss the timeline and any remaining issues, but everything was on track for the unveiling of the new line in September. Candace also needed to meet with her direct reports to talk about long-term business development and how the new line fit in. With the end of the quarter two days away, she would meet with Courtney, the CFO, to go over financials as well.

Money. Candace's thoughts shifted back to the plight of her brother and sister-in-law. Surely they had some savings or a 401(k) they could draw on to get through the next few months, until after Helen gave birth to twins and could get a new job. Whether they did or not, it was imperative that David find a rental immediately that was available and affordable for them to move into so the house on Arcadia could be completed. Candace sighed. If they couldn't pay the rent, she would pay it and keep the HELOC and mortgage current until the house sold in late summer or early fall. David would just have to add those payments to the total of their debt to her.

She knew that they owed a lot more money—to the bank and to her—than what the market would bring upon the sale of the house. The place was underwater, as millions of other homes in the country were. It was a fact that most homes in Atlanta had lost significant value. Monty and Helen would not be coming out of this deal with any money. If they were to emerge from it unscathed, with no damage to their credit, Candace would have to write off a very large sum. Something they should be grateful to her for doing, when it was all said and done.

Then, she would cut all financial ties to the family, and they would have to support themselves without her help.

The question was, how much was she willing to write off? How much would she *have* to write off, so that the couple could emerge from it unhurt and wouldn't be left with a major debt to the bank after the house sold? She shook her head slightly and answered her own question. That wasn't going to happen, because the bank wouldn't make an unsecured loan to them. Once the house sold, the collateral would be gone. Candace wouldn't be able to get out of this deal without writing off the entire loss on it. As for them paying her back and sharing in the loss, that wasn't going to happen, either.

Her only other option was to walk away and force a foreclosure, but she'd already committed to sink more money into the place. So that was off the table. She'd have to price the house to sell, and pray that it would.

It bothered her to no end to lose that much money on something she never wanted to be a part of, something she felt she'd been roped into. But what bothered her even more was that, in so doing, she would be enabling her brother's manipulation and his avoidance of working an honest job. Her father hadn't enabled him, yet here she was doing that exact thing, or about to. Her mother had done it by regularly handing over small amounts of cash to Monty, ensuring that he never felt the punch of empty pockets. She'd also blamed his teachers for any bad grades—and his coaches for failures on the football field.

Dominic took a left and pulled up in front of the Delta curbside check-in counter at the airport. He parked, hopped out, and took care removing Candace's elegant luggage from the back of the Escalade. Candace reapplied her lipstick, placed her personal items in her bag, and stepped out of the vehicle as Dominic held her door open. The air was heavy and warm, the sun climbing higher in the hazy sky. The humidity was high for New York, but Candace knew it wouldn't reach the oppressive level that would blanket the city of Atlanta today. But like most people from the South, she was accustomed to it.

She walked to the counter, presented her driver's license, and then turned to her chauffeur, putting a hundred-dollar bill in his palm. "Thank you, Dominic."

"My pleasure, Ms. Morgan," Dominic said with a nod and a smile. "See you next time, now."

Candace smiled and turned back to the Delta worker as he handed back her license. An hour later, she took her seat in the first-class section of a jet bound for Atlanta. She had already perused the two job quotes David had emailed. One of the contractors identified several more items to be done (and a higher bottom line) than the other. While Candace didn't want to pay for more any more work than was necessary, she also didn't want a backfire situation if corners were cut.

She accepted a glass of ice water offered by the airline attendant and tried to shift her thoughts from the half-built, decaying disaster on Arcadia Lane. Worries about her other investments, real estate in particular, seeped into her mind. She had purchased her Atlanta condominium several years ago, and with the declining market it had lost almost half its value. Condos were overbuilt in the city and weren't selling. She wasn't interested in selling hers at the moment, but if she were, she couldn't unless she was willing to lose a lot of money. David handled the fees and utilities for her, and those amounts added up. She didn't spend enough time there to justify them. If she didn't own the place, she could stay in one of Atlanta's finest hotels during her visits and be out much less money annually.

Her Manhattan apartment was a different situation. It would fetch some money, hopefully a little more than she had paid. Her country home in France was a money pit, though. She had parted with a large sum of euros for it at the wrong time. Every few months, it required this or that repair, or a fee or tax paid to the bureaucracy, and she trusted neither French construction companies nor government officials. She didn't spend enough time there either, but she planned to start doing so next year.

She always enjoyed going to France, and so did Rob, who loved practicing his French. She was looking forward to future trips there together and vacations exploring the countryside. The Luberon Valley was particularly beautiful, and the nearby region of Languedoc had its charms; less touristy than Provence, it was quaint and picturesque. The relaxed pace of a *séjour* there would be a welcome change to her high-powered life, and a reward for her hard work on the new line. In France, she didn't feel as pushed to stay busy as she did at home.

She gazed out the window and took another sip of water. Her thoughts shifted to her other investments, most of them liquid. Many were down and had been since the crisis of 2008. Her worth as the president and CEO of SlimZ was high—and highly publicized—but it didn't indicate her true financial picture. Her personal portfolio had run into some rather large bumps, and it wasn't stable enough to suit her. David would continue to manage it after October—she and Rob had agreed to keep their funds separate—and she would require that her financial manager earn the high fees she paid him.

If she didn't care about losing money, she could get rid of the whole fiasco on Arcadia Lane with the stroke of her pen. She could write a check to Memorial Bank to pay off the home equity loan, and she could pay off the first mortgage, too. She could authorize David to hire the more expensive contractor to complete the renovation in record time, and she could take the first offer she got. She could sell it for a huge loss. She could be done with it more quickly and more easily than the way she was proceeding now.

If she wanted to, she could be even *more* generous and give Monty and Helen half a million, say, to buy another home for cash. Some house in an upper-middle-class neighborhood with decent public schools. She could pay the 35 percent gift taxes on it and then forget about it. She could pay zero attention to whether her brother ever got a job. She could believe that she'd fulfilled her promise to her father, and that Monty had no power make her feel guilty anymore. She could tell herself that she *wasn't* enabling him, and hope that he'd never ask her for money again.

She could hope.

• • •

"Hi, this is Dawn Mitchell with Meridien Wealth Management. Today is Monday, June twenty-eighth. I will be out of the office today, but please leave your name and number and I will return your call as soon as possible. Thanks." The recorded message complete, Dawn put the phone down and turned to see her sister entering the kitchen. "How did you sleep?"

"Okay," Helen said while stretching. Adele was still upstairs. "How long have you been up?"

Dawn smiled. "I can't sleep much past my usual time." She had worked every day last week, meeting Helen and Adele for lunch twice. She had decided to take a long weekend and stay home today and Tuesday. "I haven't even checked email yet, though. Guess I should."

Helen poured a glass of skim milk and sat down at the round kitchen table. Dawn placed her coffee mug on the table, sat down, and opened her laptop. She clicked on her email and began scrolling down the inbox.

"Well, here's a surprise," she said. "Something from Mom."

Helen bit her lip. "What did she say?"

"Oh my God," said Dawn.

"What?"

Dawn sighed. "She and Rich are splitting up. Getting a divorce. After thirty years."

Helen's eyes widened. "She's telling you that in an email? Did she send it to me, too?"

"No," said Dawn, her eyes on the screen. "'Tell Helen the news when you talk to her. I'll call you both next weekend.'"

"It's typical of her to ignore me," said Helen. "Let me see that." She scooted closer to her sister and read the cryptic message. "I wonder what happened?"

"It's so like her not to explain. My God." Dawn shook her head, then took a sip of her coffee. "Actually, it's amazing they've stayed together this long, when you think about it."

Neither of the sisters was close to their mother, Diane. She had married their father, Tim Piper, when she was only twenty and he was twenty-four. After six years and two children, they divorced and Tim moved to Maine, leaving Diane to raise the girls. He had never been part of their lives, and when Diane married Rich Corrigan in 1980, the sisters had welcomed his presence as a step closer to stability, accepting him as a substitute father. Once Helen grew up and finished art school, Diane and Rich had moved to Southern California.

"Has it really been thirty years?" asked Helen.

"They were celebrating their twentieth when Frank and I got married. Remember? They went on that cruise?"

"Oh, yeah. She got sick?"

"Right," said Dawn, focusing on the laptop screen. "You know, I wonder what would have happened if she and Rich had been able to have kids of their own. I remember when they were trying."

Helen swallowed and studied her sister's face. Dawn had had five miscarriages. To Helen's knowledge, Diane had had two, in her thirties.

"I don't care," she said. "You and I never hear from her unless it's bad news, or they need money. Or both. I'm sure she's still pissed at us for telling her to stop asking, and mad that we told Rich how often she had." Helen leaned back and sighed, pushing away the possible parallels between her marriage and her mother's. "She hasn't seen Adele since she was a baby, and she never calls."

"Well, I'm guessing this is about money. Or she's having a late-life crisis. As ridiculous as that sounds."

"I know. I wonder how Rich is doing," Helen said while reflexively placing her right hand under her top and resting it on her scarred skin. Rich was a private person and said that he didn't believe in talking about his problems because, when it came right down to it, no one was really interested—everyone had their own. Helen felt the same way, except with Dawn. "Anyway, what a mess."

Dawn turned to look into her sister's eyes. "Helen, have you forgiven her? I mean"—she glanced down at Helen's hand on her shoulder and then back up at her face—"she was twenty-six then, and taking care of two toddlers all day. Tim was away so much—"

"Let's not talk about it, okay?" Helen cast her eyes down. "I try not to think about it, or her. Ever."

"I don't blame you. She's been out of both of our lives for so long anyway—"

"Which is fine with me."

"Me, too. It's just, well, I know you suffered. Really, I *know* you did. But if you could just let it go, completely—"

Helen looked back up at her sister, gazing at her with misty eyes. "I have."

Dawn cocked her head, pausing. "We both know she was a terrible mother. But she never meant to hurt you, Helen. It was an accident."

Helen looked away, blinking back tears. "I know it was. But Dawn, she didn't—she didn't *damage* you. You don't carry a scar."

"You're right. I don't carry a physical scar, like yours. I *was* damaged by her, though, in a different way."

Helen exhaled, then looked back at her sister.

"You've said you don't really remember that day. I do. You were standing next to her at the stove, holding on to her legs like every two-year-old does. I ran in the kitchen toward both of you. She had a glass of wine in her hand—I'm sure it wasn't her first. She was angry at me. She whipped around toward me and, by accident, she knocked over a pot of hot oil—"

"Stop," said Helen.

Dawn grabbed her sister's arm. "We've never been able to talk about it. Don't you know how guilty I've felt, all these years?"

Helen gazed into Dawn's eyes. "Why do *you* feel guilty? She was the one who did it. She was the adult."

Dawn's eyes welled up. "I startled her. I ran in—"

"Like any little kid in any family does."

"But it wasn't any family. It was *our* family. You, me, and Mom—Diane, a single mother in the '70s. Helen, she just couldn't handle raising two kids alone. She burned you by accident. She didn't take you to the doctor because she was broke. She was probably also afraid she'd be accused of child abuse. She had a fucked-up life, and we paid the price. *You* paid the price."

"The thing is, Dawn, I don't care about her. I've lived with this for so long"—Helen glanced down to her left, then back up—"that it doesn't matter. *She* doesn't matter. I don't care what happens to her. If she and Rich split up, that's their problem—or maybe, their solution. Whatever. I don't want to know."

"But can you forgive her, for what she did to you back then?"

Helen shut her eyes for a second, then opened them. "She's never asked me to forgive her. She's never said she was sorry. She's *not* sorry—"

"I'm sure she is."

"How do you know? She doesn't care, Dawn. Not about me, not about you, not about Adele."

Dawn reached for Helen's hand and held it. "Look, I'm not defending her. But you can forgive her, anyway. You *need* to forgive her, not for her sake, but for yours."

"Why?"

"Because, when you do, you'll be getting rid of a huge burden, a burden you've been carrying around since you were two years old. And as long as you don't forgive her, you're letting her have power over you. I know you don't want that."

Helen bit her lip and stared at Dawn. "Is this something you heard on *Oprah*? It's not that simple. Mom doesn't have any power over me."

"Come on. I don't pay attention to Oprah."

"Dawn. You're the one of us without flaws—"

"That's not true—"

"Hear me out, okay? You're beautiful. You're smart. You have a perfect figure, and yes, perfect skin. And you're successful. You've got a great career and a fantastic marriage."

"I'm human, Helen. I'm not perfect."

"In my opinion, you are. You always have been. Everything you've touched has turned to gold."

"No. I don't have a beautiful baby girl like you do."

"You will, though."

"How do you know that? You don't know, and neither do I. But I do know something about forgiveness, and it's not something I heard on television. I've been married for ten years now. I know things aren't great between you and Monty, and I'm not going there. But because I've been with Frank so long—because of what we've been through together—I know how important forgiveness is, in any relationship. Blame isn't the answer. I'm telling you."

"Mom and I don't have a relationship."

"Our relationships with her aren't ideal, but she is our mother. She's your kids' grandmother. Even if she doesn't act like one."

Helen clasped her hands behind her head and leaned back in her chair. "It doesn't matter."

"Let's be honest. We both care about her, at least a little bit. Maybe we even pity her. *I* care much more about *you*. You suffered because of the way she is, the way she's always been. She's irresponsible and self-absorbed. She doesn't care about anyone but herself. She's a narcissist. We don't have to love her. We don't even have to like her. But you can let go of the hurt she caused you." Dawn leaned toward her sister. "*You're* beautiful, Helen. No one sees the scar on your shoulder the way you do. *No one*."

"Dawn, I want to believe you. But you're not me—you haven't seen the looks I get, the looks I've gotten all my life. You can wear sleeveless tops. You can wear spaghetti straps and strapless dresses—strapless *bathing suits*. It's cold most of the time in Chicago, and that worked out for me when I lived here. It's not that way in Georgia. I can't even wear comfortable clothes. *Sexy* clothes. I always have to hide this."

"That's exactly what I'm saying. You *don't* have to hide it."

"Why? Because I'm married? Because everyone who knows me knows about it? Because I'm not supposed to care how someone reacts—*cringes*—when they see it? I dress the way I do because I want to. Let me be modest. Let me hold on to some semblance of vanity. Please."

Dawn looked into Helen's eyes and held her gaze for a moment. "I do. I will. You make your own decisions, and I'm not trying to criticize you. I'm only saying that it's really not so horrible. It's not so bad as you think. It's a scar, and it's not a small one. It's not a disfigurement. It's not a handicap. Maybe it would help you if you let it show. *Let* the world see it. Don't worry about how people react. That's their problem, not yours."

"You don't understand—"

"You're right. I don't know what it's like to be you. I wish I did. I do know you can change your attitude about it. You can just say, 'Fuck it.' Don't let it be a negative. Make it positive. It's part of you—of your body. Fine. Is that all we are? Physical? Beauty is fleeting, Helen. You think I'm physically attractive. But what's going on, on the inside of me? Why can't I have a baby?"

Helen let out a breath. "Dawn—"

"I want to adopt, and Frank doesn't. There. Now you know."

Helen looked into her sister's eyes, leaned toward her, and grabbed her hand.

"We're at an impasse," said Dawn, her eyes filling with tears. "I didn't want to burden you with my problems, so I didn't mention it. The thing is, we both want a baby so much, but we don't agree on what to do. And I'm afraid. You have Adele, and soon you'll have two more babies. But I may never have one. I may *never* have the deep happiness that you have—as a mother."

"Oh, Dawn." Helen reached her arms around her sister. "You *will* have it, I know you will. You and Frank will work this out. He loves you. He won't—"

"I know he loves me," said Dawn. "But love doesn't create perfect solutions. You've got children. You're beautiful—to Adele, to me, and to everyone. Please believe me."

Helen pulled Dawn close and the two hugged for a long moment, neither wanting to lose the other's touch.

14

Information

At a quarter to twelve on Wednesday, David Shepherd pushed his chair back from his desk, stood, and put his suit jacket on. To avoid today's ninety-five-degree heat, he planned to grab a sandwich at a deli in the building's lobby.

Geneviève looked up from her computer as her boss appeared outside his office door. "I just emailed you a list of fifteen rental properties for Ms. Morgan," she said. "Rent prices ranging from about a thousand to a little over thirteen hundred."

David stopped at her desk. "Thank you, Geneviève. Would you start making inquiries after lunch, and let me know what you find out?"

"Certainly. *Bon appétit.*"

David smiled, turned, and headed to the elevator. The door opened and, pleased to beat the midday crowd, he stepped inside to an empty space.

His assistant usually took a late lunch, around one o'clock. Like most Frenchwomen—old or young—she was either naturally thin or she paid close attention to her diet, or both. In her fifties now, she dressed in professional but attractive clothing, with an effortless

French flair: colorful scarves were her trademark. She was also a hard worker with an easygoing disposition, and had been with him for years.

He hadn't reprimanded her for failing to verify Monty Carawan's false supplier receipts a few months ago—though he had asked her to do it, David felt himself responsible for the mistake. However, it was a small oversight in the big picture of Candace's situation with Monty.

On Monday afternoon, Candace had called and instructed David to offer the less expensive contractor a fee 12 percent lower than his quote. He had advised that a cut in price would likely result in a cut in quality, but Candace was firm. Not wishing to argue, he had acquiesced. If he were wrong, she could deal with the ramifications of her decisions later on, when a buyer was found and a property inspection was done.

At the moment, getting the Carawan family into a rental was priority number one. On Monday, Candace said she had just learned that Helen had been laid off, so a location convenient to her office wasn't important anymore. David shook his head slightly as the elevator door opened to the lobby. That poor girl. Why in God's name had she married such a weasel as Candace's ne'er-do-well brother? It was a mystery.

Strangely, after Candace learned of her sister-in-law's ill luck, she hadn't changed her mind about taking over the renovation, kicking them out, and cutting off funds. For the last two days, David had been bracing himself for such a turnaround. He knew his client's idiosyncrasies, and second-guessing herself was one of them. Given the current circumstances, her newfound resolve was surprising, though welcome.

He hoped it was her last stand, so to speak. With a toddler underfoot and his wife unemployed and carrying twins, Monty

Carawan would simply have to find a job, support his family, and stop his constant pleas for cash.

Because it looked like Candace was finally done parting with it.

• • •

Monty had learned all he needed to know—for now—about the new product line his sister's company was developing.

While Candace was fucking her boyfriend over in France and up in Manhattan, he'd been busy. Staying at the condo with Rachel during the last ten days had helped. The constant sex was good for his mind. Rachel left in the morning—not early, though—and stayed away until five or six in the evening. Then they'd have a drink or two, screw, and get ready to go out. She'd dress up in something sexy, then strip for him again a few hours later. He loved her firm yet soft body, her scent, her femininity, her youth—and her perfect skin.

He owned the place and had paid for all the furniture in it. Rachel paid the utilities, the homeowner dues, and the twice-monthly maid service. The condo was in his name, and she was living here as his guest, an arrangement that suited him well—at least, until he got tired of her. Last week, she had been away for seventy-two hours. During her absence, he had accomplished his goal: he met Jessica Copeland and found out some valuable information.

It hadn't been easy to connect with her, out at night and unaccompanied by Beau Warren. But he had been patient. When he learned that she planned to go out to dinner with the girls on a Thursday night for a friend's birthday at Plunge, a Buckhead hot spot, he had acted. He surprised Rachel with a ticket to Philadelphia to visit her best friend from high school. Then he arrived at the restaurant bar early and hung out, watching a Braves game and eavesdropping while Jess and her friends drank cocktails. When the gaggle broke up at around eleven o'clock, he watched them hug and listened as they moaned about having to get up early in the morning, to go to work or take care of their infants. Then, when Jess made her way back from the restroom, he snagged her.

He had used the sincerity method—at first. Looking distracted, he stood quickly and blocked her path, almost causing her to tumble off of five-inch heels. He grabbed her arm with just the right amount of firmness, righted her, and apologized. Then he feigned recognition of her as his sister's employee. Introducing himself, he insisted on buying her a drink. She sat down next to him at the bar, and once he got a cosmo in her hand, things had gone swimmingly.

At first, he listened more than he talked, and he learned a lot. Jess knew that Candace had a brother, but she didn't know much about him. Evidently, Candace never spoke of her family. She didn't display photos in the office and Jess had never seen any on the computer. The little bit Jess knew of Candace's personal life was only because she was her assistant—Jess had met her fiancé only once or twice.

Monty cracked a few sarcastic jokes about his sister, making Jess laugh but not crossing the line. She bought his story: that he was Candace's behind-the-scenes adviser, but that because he was her brother, she rarely spoke of him to anyone but top management at SlimZ. That he was a fashion industry consultant and traveled to Paris, London, and Milan. That he and Candace had had a special relationship for years, ever since their mother had died. That Candace had told him how hardworking her assistant was, but *hadn't* mentioned that she was gorgeous.

He'd kept on flattering Jess, keeping her glass filled and working his magic until her initial nervousness vanished. Believing he knew about the new swimsuit line, she started yammering about how company secrecy had been driving her nuts. About how she couldn't wait for the damn swimsuits to be public after Fashion Week, so life around the office could get back to normal. About how excited she was to be working in the industry, though, and how she hoped to become a designer.

That segued the conversation back to Candace and how she depended on Jess to do everything for her, even log her into the company's computer system. Monty said he had advised his sister to pick weird, long passwords like he always did, and to change them regularly, of course. Then Jess told him that Candace had exempted herself from the company policy of frequent password changes, and that in reality, her boss wasn't all that tech savvy. Monty joked about Candace's naiveté and inexperience with technology, saying she was a rather late adopter. Jess laughed, then gave him the hint he needed: that Candace had never graduated from the spell-it-backwards trick when picking a password.

When Jess got up to leave the bar, Monty walked her outside and got her a cab, then hired a valet to take her car home. He gave her a lingering hug and a kiss on the cheek, and as she drunkenly waved good-bye, she called out that she would see him at Candace's wedding this fall, if not before.

The next day, if she remembered talking to him, Monty was sure she would tell her boyfriend, who might even tell his uncle Chip. But that was fine. Neither of them would put anything together about his ultimate goal: to show Candace what he was capable of doing. If Jess told Candace about their meeting—it was unlikely, because he had made her promise not to, since they both knew how much Candace liked her privacy (". . . *if she wanted you to know about me, she would have told you*"). If she did and Candace confronted him directly, he would just deny the whole thing.

Today was Friday, more than a week after his encounter with Jess last Thursday night, and Candace hadn't contacted him. Rachel had returned from Pennsylvania last Saturday. She'd gone to the gym this morning, then come back to the condo to shower and dress for a one o'clock lunch and afternoon appointment. He sat in the expensive brown leather chair in the corner of the condo's spacious bedroom and watched her touch up her makeup. Then she rose, stepped into a pair of peep-toe nude high heels, and regarded herself in the mirror. "See you at five?"

"Sure," he said, smiling. "I can't wait to get you naked again."

Rachel turned, cocked her head, and raised an eyebrow. "Is that all you ever think about? Me naked?"

"There's nothing else I *want* to think about. Or see."

She smiled and walked toward the bedroom door, swinging her hips. "*Ciao.*"

"Bye, doll."

He listened to her unlock the door to the condo and shut it behind her. Leaning back in his chair, he closed his eyes, visualizing her bare body. He needed money to live the life he was meant to live—lots of money. Years ago, he should have been given the chance to earn his own fortune as an architect. He would have been famous by now—more famous than Candace, wealthier than she was, and much more admired.

But he'd been robbed of his future, and Candace was responsible. Jack Carawan had unfairly allowed her to use up all the inheritance money from his aunt, whose death had been a convenient, life-changing event for his sister. Because of it, Candace had gotten to go to an elite college and had been able to lay the groundwork to start her business. Because she had come home the next summer, had gotten behind the wheel one day, and had cut off a pickup truck in the pouring rain, his mother had been killed. Candace had killed her, and in doing so, she had ruined his life.

Susannah had always been his advocate. In an instant, she was dead. Her blood and brains had splattered everywhere in the car, even on him, lying in the backseat and bleeding himself. Once his mother was in the ground, he was forced to deal only with his father. Jack had almost relished destroying his dreams—dreams that

Susannah had encouraged. He refused to send Monty to a private architectural school. His only option was to go to a state school, the University of Georgia. Was it so surprising that he hadn't been motivated there, so of course he couldn't succeed academically? After one semester, Jack had yanked him out of Athens and insisted that he learn the construction trade. But Monty's talents lay elsewhere: in drawing and visualizing buildings, not in painting drywall or hammering wood.

Thank God he had gotten away from that in his twenties. Then Jack had kicked the bucket early. Monty had come into a small sum of money, but only enough to pay off his credit cards and buy a better car. Weeks had turned into months, and months into years. Now Monty was almost thirty-eight years old, and he hadn't accomplished what he was meant to do. It was all because other people had stood in his way, undermined him, and sabotaged his plans.

If he didn't resent them for it, if he didn't want justice, if he didn't want to even the score, as best he could—well, then he wouldn't be human. He was sick and tired of being looked down on by the other person left alive, the one who had quashed his dreams and crushed his future.

• • •

Candace took a sip of water and turned her attention to her laptop on the desk in her Buckhead office. She skimmed David's latest email and dialed his number.

"Hello, Candace. You got my message?"

"Right. Tell Geneviève that yes, the lease will have to be in my name alone, now that Helen's unemployed. However—"

"It needs to be month-to-month," David finished her sentence.

"Correct. Now, how soon can the workers start on the house? What's the guy's name again? Ben?"

"Ken. He said they can begin as early as next week. All of their belongings need to be out of the house first."

"Then I suggest you have your assistant find a rental today. If not today, Monday."

"She's on it. What about the move itself?"

"What do you mean?"

"Shall I have her find a mover, get that process started?"

Candace huffed. "I suppose so. I'm sure Monty won't move their stuff himself."

"Geneviève will get some quotes, and we'll go with the lowest."

"Fine. But shoot me an email with the amount first."

"Definitely."

"Once Ken gets his people over there, how long will it take to get the place ready to list?"

"His estimate was six weeks. Unless they find something they don't anticipate."

"Surprises, you mean?"

"That, or just—well, if they find any issues."

Candace shut her eyes for a second. "I don't want any issues, David."

"Of course not. I'm not saying there will be any."

"So if all goes as it should, we're talking about, what, late August? How's the search for a realtor going?"

"Geneviève is researching agents. We'll start talking to them next week."

"The earlier, the better. I want everything in place."

"Oh, Lord," said David.

"What?"

"I just got an email from Monty. He didn't copy you."

"What does it say? Read it to me."

"I'll forward it—"

"No," said Candace. "Read it now, before you do. He doesn't have an inkling about me hiring a contractor, or having to move out, right?"

"I haven't been in contact with him. Here's what he says: 'David, as you and your client have known for some time, annual property taxes and insurance fees are due on the house. Candace has ignored my repeated requests to pay these. With Helen out of work and our current situation being what it is, we are powerless to handle them. We also have the added expense of paying high COBRA health insurance premiums for the remainder of Helen's pregnancy—'"

"Stop," said Candace. "I don't give a fuck about the COBRA. What are the tax and insurance amounts?"

"I have to look back at those, then I can tell you. They aren't low. I want to say, over thirty thousand for the taxes and at least six for insurance."

"This is never going to end!"

"Yes, it is, Candace. It's getting close."

Candace let out a deep breath. "Okay, here's what I want you to do. Write him back, copying me, and say that I will agree to pay the taxes and insurance on July thirty-first, under this condition: that he find a job by that date, and that he be *working*. I need proof, and I need to know how much money he's making."

"Anything else?"

"Yes. Obviously, tell Geneviève, the cheaper the rent, the better. Since they're going to have to pay it themselves, once Arcadia sells."

"Of course. But Candace—"

"I know what you're going to say, David. That Monty will agree to my condition, just to get me to pay the fees. I know he will. However, this time we're going to follow up. Do you know when Helen is due back from Chicago?"

"No."

"Okay. Then copy her on your email as well, and at the end of it, ask her when she plans to be back. I'm sick of not knowing what those people are doing, and I can't wait until the time when I won't have any reason to care."

• • •

Helen Carawan put her pen down next to her notebook on the seat-back tray, which was horizontal above her lap on the flight to Atlanta. Adele was in the window seat to her left, practicing writing her name on a piece of paper. Thankfully, the aisle seat to Helen's right was empty.

Adele looked out the window, then up at her mother's face. "Look at the clouds, Mommy!"

Helen smiled and leaned over toward the window. "Aren't they pretty?"

"I'm going to draw pictures of them."

"That's a good idea, Boo. Draw lots of them." She turned back to her own paper, at the letter she had written to her mother: a letter that she didn't plan to send—but one that she knew was important to write.

Although Helen worked—used to work—at a computer all day (or maybe because of it), she preferred to write letters by hand. She loved the feel of her favorite pen in her hand as she transcribed her thoughts onto paper—it was so much more satisfying than tapping out keystrokes in front of a blank screen. She was also a list-maker, keeping an ongoing grocery list on a notepad, and she loved to sketch. Since her art school days, she had preferred paper over a device. It was therapeutic.

It was also safer: she could destroy a handwritten letter if she wished—there was no electronic paper trail. Later today, she would tear up this letter expressing her deepest thoughts to her mother.

But first she needed to finish it and reread it. She needed to process her feelings.

As promised, Diane had called last Saturday, a week ago, at the end of Helen and Adele's second week in Chicago. Dawn hadn't replied to her email, leaving Diane unaware that the sisters were together until she called. When she did, Helen sat listening to Dawn's side of the conversation, then took the phone herself when Dawn handed it over.

Diane didn't ask any questions about Helen's life or family—not surprising—or why she and Adele were visiting the Mitchells. Saying she didn't want to go through the story of her split with Rich all over again, she gave Helen the abbreviated version: they had grown apart. They didn't like the same things or have the same friends, and neither wanted to live the rest of their lives with the other. After the divorce, Rich planned to remain in California and Diane was moving to Hawaii, where she would work part-time in the travel industry and hang out with her vegan and breatharian friends.

Helen had never heard of breatharians. Apparently they were people who avoided not only meat and animal products, but all food and water. Diane was a vegan and fasted at least once a week, but she hadn't made the full leap (yet) to breatharian. However, she wanted to learn more and expose herself to the breatharian community, who supposedly found an inner peace not possible to people who chose to nourish and hydrate themselves.

Helen had hung up the phone as quickly as she could. Her mother was really going off the deep end. Diane had always been overly concerned about gaining—and losing—weight. In Helen's view, she was anorexic. She had nagged and fussed at Helen and Dawn when they were in junior and senior high school about food choices and portion sizes—being only a few pounds overweight was unacceptable. Dawn had always had a slim figure, but Helen's teenage body had been on the pudgy side. Diane claimed Helen took after her father's side and not after hers, as Dawn did.

Helen glanced at Adele, smiled, and rested her hand on her pregnant belly. These babies were active, kicking her often, and sometimes it hurt. Her stomach was expanding more quickly than it had with her first pregnancy, and even though she knew that was to be expected, it was getting hard on her back—and her skin. If Diane could see her now, she would disapprove of her size and demand to know how much weight she had gained. In the past, Diane had almost bragged about how little she had gained during her pregnancies, gleefully admitting that smoking and drinking had helped. Helen wondered if any of Diane's breatharian friends were former smokers, alcoholics, or both.

In the letter she had penned, Helen described all her emotions toward her mother. She expressed what it was like to grow up feeling unworthy and unloved. Saying she received unconditional love only from her sister, she described how she had searched for it in her twenties, moving from one bad romantic relationship to another. She'd felt unacceptable physically and had willfully taken abuse of one kind or another from each of the men she had dated. She was baffled by the apparent self-confidence of other women who were clearly less attractive than she was. Her self-image was horrible, and she blamed Diane for planting the seed. No matter what problems her mother may have had, her treatment of Helen had been neglectful and inexcusable. Her carelessness had manifested itself on one fateful day, leaving a physical mark on Helen. It was a mark that grew over time and a wound that would never heal.

The last part of the letter had been the most difficult: forgiving Diane for what she had done and for how she had treated her. Helen had listened that day when Dawn brought up the power of forgiveness, and had thought about what she said. Over the next few days, Dawn had opened up about her infertility issues and miscarriages, and for the first time, she confided in Helen about what she'd gone through emotionally.

She told Helen that she'd been angry at God for not allowing her to have a baby. After years of asking, "Why me?" she had woken up one day and decided to let it go. She had forgiven God. She had accepted the reality that she wouldn't bear a child. Once she had done that, life had gotten so much easier. Though she and Frank didn't agree about whether to adopt, Dawn felt a sense of peace about it. In time, she knew they would come to the right decision.

Helen had realized then that she needed to stop asking why, too. She needed to stop hoping that Diane would apologize one day. She needed to let it go, to forgive Diane. She could do it first with pen and paper, and then in her heart. She finished rereading the letter just before the plane began its descent. Then she folded it up and put it in a zippered compartment of her purse.

She would tear it up tonight, after she unpacked. Monty had said he would pick her and Adele up today, but he had told her to text him when their plane was on the ground. He would drive up to the curb outside of baggage claim once he knew they were there waiting for him.

Almost an hour later, she and Adele climbed into the car. Wordlessly, Monty threw their suitcases in the trunk and got back behind the wheel, a grimace on his face.

"Daddy, why is it so hot here?"

"It's summertime, baby. It's always hot in the summer."

"Not at Aunt Dawn's."

"Well, that's Chicago, sweetie. They only have two seasons: winter, and the fourth of July."

Helen looked silently out the window, her arms folded on top of her pregnant belly.

"Daddy, I want to go to Disney World!"

"Not this year," said Monty. "You just got back from vacation."

"Boo, we don't have enough money to go to Disney World," said Helen.

"Well, that's easy!" said Adele. "Let's go to the bank!"

Helen turned to look at her daughter, who was sitting in her car seat behind Monty. "What did you say?"

Adele smiled and cocked her head. "You know, Mommy! Let's go to the bank! That's where the money is!" she said slowly, as if she had to explain. "Whenever we need some, you always say that's where we have to go. So let's go!"

"What are you telling her?" asked Monty.

"Nothing," said Helen. "I guess I tell her we have to stop and get money at the bank sometimes. That the bank is where we go to get cash."

"Aunt Dawn said *she* would take me to Disney World," said Adele.

Monty rolled his eyes, then exhaled. "She's not going to take you, so forget that. You just got home. But we're going to our new house, and you have your own room now."

"Okay, Daddy. Don't get mad at me!"

Monty's hands tensed on the steering wheel. He looked over at Helen, then spoke in a low tone. "*What* are you telling our child about me?"

"Nothing. I don't know why she's saying that."

The family traveled on in silence for the next twenty minutes. Then Monty pulled the car up to a 1950s ranch house with a one-car carport. "I've started unpacking, but there's still a lot left to do." He parked in the driveway, then got out and unbuckled Adele, who ran over to the door.

"Where's my room?"

"Hold on," said her father. "Let me unlock it."

An hour later, Adele lay on her twin bed, books and stuffed animals surrounding her, and fell asleep. In the kitchen, Helen stopped unloading boxes and filled a glass with tap water.

"So, I spoke to Candace today," Monty told her from his seat at the small kitchen table. "And I've got some news."

Helen turned and regarded him. "What is it?"

"She's changed her mind about Arcadia Lane."

Helen's eyes widened. "What do you mean, changed her mind?"

"Don't get upset. It's a good thing. She told me that after seeing this place—"

"She came here? When?"

"I don't know. Maybe she just saw pictures of it or something. Anyway, she said she's been thinking about us, and since we're about to go from one to three kids, and you don't have a job yet—and since we have to go on COBRA—she's decided to give us the house."

"Arcadia?"

"Right. She's got the contractor in there, and after the work's all done, we can have it. Move back in and live there, with no debt owed. She's decided to be generous, for once."

"I can't believe it. Are you sure? Why didn't you tell me?"

"I just talked to her. You were on the plane. And I didn't want to talk about it in front of Adele."

Helen sat down at the table, studying Monty's face. "What got into her? Why is she suddenly willing to write off all the money she put into the place, after all these months?"

"It's not writing off. It's a gift. Plus, I told her that when we do sell it, someday—could be a long, long time from now—we'll pay her back her investment. Because we wouldn't ever sell it unless we were able to get what it's really worth. Then paying her won't be a problem."

"But why didn't she decide to do this a long time ago?"

"I don't know, Helen. She's a bitch. She wanted us to suffer. She's selfish. But she's finally come around. Maybe she realized how hard we're trying. We're her only family."

Stunned, Helen sat in her chair. She felt another kick and placed her hand on her stomach. "What about the mortgage? And the bank notes?"

"She's paying them off. Writing a check. At the end of next month—or by September, at the latest—the house will be finished and we can move in. No house payment, no loan payment."

"We still need money coming in, Monty—"

"Damn it, Helen! Can't you just enjoy this good news? At least for one second?"

Helen stared at him, her face expressionless. Could it be true? After all this time, had Candace decided to drop all her efforts to get paid back? Helen's mind flashed to the tense meeting in David's office. Why had Candace changed her mind? "I can enjoy it. I guess we still have to pay the taxes and insurance ourselves—"

"No. She did that."

Helen exhaled, looking up at the ceiling. There was an old water stain over to the left, near the window that overlooked the backyard. "In that email, she said she would do that only if you got a job."

"I do have a job."

"You do? Since when?"

"I start on Monday."

15

Generosity

On Tuesday afternoon, while her daughter was taking a nap, Helen started writing an email to Candace.

She had spent Sunday and Monday cleaning, organizing, and unpacking, and she was almost done. Fortunately, Monty had labeled the boxes as the movers had packed them. Since they would only be living here for a month and a half, she didn't have to get everything out. The kitchen was operational and the three-bedroom, one-bath house was livable. Though it was small, the place would be easy to manage and keep clean.

Now that she had a few minutes to herself, she sat down at the table and opened her laptop. The news that Monty had told her on Saturday had sunken in. She was grateful to her wealthy sister-in-law, ever so grateful. The least Helen could do was to thank her, on the record, for her generosity.

She would send Candace a private, short message to thank her for her decisions and for having come to their rescue. Helen had existed on autopilot ever since that day over three weeks ago, when Peter McPherson had let her go and sent her home and into shock. While she was up in Chicago, she'd had time to process her situation, and she had returned to Atlanta ready to deal with her problems. She had planned to sit her husband down and demand that they come up with a repayment plan on Arcadia, and that he go out and get a job—immediately.

But she hadn't had to do that. Candace had done a one-eighty about the house and the money, and Monty was working. He hadn't told Helen much about his new job and had evaded her questions. But he left every day at seven thirty in the morning, and he didn't return until after six. Last night, he told her that he would have to spend some weekday evenings at work learning a program, and that he wasn't sure how long that would go on—it could be for a while. He wouldn't have to do it every night, though.

He did tell her that the company was brand-new and was developing a social media marketing application. It was backed by some investors that he had met last year. They had contacted him while Helen was in Chicago and had hired Monty and two other people that he had never met. The investors were still deciding what to name the company.

Helen didn't plan to mention any of that in her email to Candace. She knew Monty wouldn't want her to, and there was no reason to, anyway. Monty had stressed that Candace hadn't asked about their income; it was understood that he and Helen were on their own and were responsible for their own monthly expenses. Helen intended to work as soon as she could find a job, whether that occurred before or after the twins were born. She'd have to work—at least, she didn't want to depend on Monty to support the family. But that was another piece of information that she didn't need to include in her email to Candace.

She finished the message and saved it. Later, she would reread it, polish it, and send it. She picked up her glass of skim milk and took a sip, thinking about the changes in her husband. Well, fundamentally he hadn't changed, but—perhaps triggered by Helen's job loss—he seemed calmer, more stable. He hadn't had a tantrum when he learned that Candace had hired a contractor to finish the renovation, when she had effectively fired Monty from the project. He hadn't gotten mad when she found them a rental house, one that Monty probably wouldn't have chosen, and when she demanded that they move out of Arcadia. He was cooperating with Candace now, and Helen wondered if Candace's decision to give them the house and write off all her debt had a catch.

If so, what could it be? Surely not anything that would bother Helen. If it bothered her husband, well, then he would just have to deal with it.

• • •

That night, over drinks in her Midtown penthouse condo, Candace read Helen's email out loud to Rob.

"'I can't tell you how much your generosity means to us, Candace. When Monty told me that you had offered to pay off the loans and fees, pay the contractor, and give the house to us, a huge boulder was lifted from my shoulders. We deeply appreciate your financial assistance. It makes such a difference in our lives and in our future as a family. Thank you so much for your kindness and compassion in helping us through such a difficult time.' Rob, what am I supposed to do now?"

Rob shook his head, then took a sip of his Scotch. "Darling, your brother is a scoundrel."

"I know he is! Lying to his wife, and making me look like a greedy ogre when she finds out it's not true."

"Do you think he put her up to this?"

"What?"

"Writing you that email. Telling her to thank you for something you haven't agreed to, to manipulate you into doing exactly what he wants?"

Candace took a sip of her martini, then set down the glass. "Well, that's possible. But I just don't see Helen as participating in his schemes. Do you?"

"I don't know. I don't want to believe it. But—well, we do know what Monty is capable of. And desperate people do desperate things."

Candace huffed. "I need to sleep on this. I'm certainly not going to respond to her email. But I don't believe he put her up to it. I think I should give her a call sometime tomorrow, and start by telling her that all I've agreed to pay is the taxes and insurance—and only because Monty told me he's working."

"Be ready for her reaction on the phone," said Rob.

"I know. That boulder's going back on her shoulders, and it's going to crush her. I hope she doesn't start crying."

"Has David verified his employment?"

"Not yet. He's working on it."

"Well, I hope it's true that he's found a job. But we know how much he's lied in the past. Candace, he's a miscreant. He may be a psychopath."

Candace shook her head. "I think he may be, too."

"In light of this development, I think it's more important than ever for you to enforce boundaries. You've got the renovation under your control now. Let it be done, and put the house on the market. David will figure out what your loss will be—you know it won't be small. However, when it sells, you're done. You will have saved Monty and Helen from financial collapse, and they can start over. Meanwhile, he can earn an income to support his family. You must let them go on living their lives. It will show that you respect them as adults who are capable of supporting themselves."

"Rob, I'm ready to enforce boundaries, and to stop enabling him. Helen will understand that the house needs to be sold, and after she gets over it, she'll accept that I'm not giving it to them.

She's going to have to. I don't think she was ever as emotionally invested in the house as Monty was, anyway. She knew the neighborhood wasn't right for their income level, even if Monty got a job making what she did. She just believed what he told her—that they could sell it for a profit, and then buy a house that was more appropriate for them."

"I hope you're right about the emotional part," said Rob. "In any case, she's the one anchored in reality. She knows there's no requirement that you give them a much larger portion of your fortune than what you may wish to, just because of Monty's demands and manipulation. I'd even say she also knows that if you forgave all debt and gave them such an expensive home, you'd be doing them a disservice. I'm sure she wants their children to respect them and to accept the lifestyle they can afford without your help."

"Well, I agree with you. She does seem realistic, and grateful for what I've already done."

"You've been very generous and have made a difference in their lives. She knows it's not your fault they chose that house and began a costly renovation that wasn't even necessary in the first place. She also knows it's not your fault that the market declined. Millions of people all over the country are dealing with the depressed real estate market, yet somehow those people survive. Let Helen and Monty do the same. They will thank you for it eventually—at least, she will."

Candace humphed. "I'm not holding my breath." She leaned back on the sofa and stretched. "Rob, I'm just so ready to be *done* with this nightmare. I can't think about it anymore."

"Let's go to dinner, and let's have some champagne tonight. A little bubbly will take your mind off of it."

"I agree." Candace finished the last of her drink. "Let me get my purse."

• • •

The following afternoon, Candace shut her office door and dialed Helen's number.

"Hello, Candace."

"Is this a good time, Helen?"

"Yes, it's fine. Adele's taking her afternoon nap."

"How are you feeling?"

"Pretty good. So relieved, too—"

"Before we talk about that, let me ask you a question. What's the name of Monty's new employer?"

"It's a new social media company, but he said the principals don't have a name for it yet. They're working on a logo and thumbnail for the app."

"What are the principals' names?"

"I don't know."

"Helen. I don't mean to sound suspicious, but—"

"It's okay. I'm concerned about it, too. Monty's been kind of secretive about the whole thing. As you might imagine, I don't fully trust him."

"Okay. So, what *has* he told you about it?"

"Virtually nothing. He says he has to keep quiet about it, that it's going to be launched soon, and before then they can't have a leak. He won't even tell me where his office is."

"Well, David is following up, because I need to know. David won't leak anything about it, you can be sure of that."

"Good. Candace, no matter what's going on, we need money coming in, and I don't really know what to do about it. Monty hasn't told me how much he's going to be making. When I asked him, he just walked away. We're so grateful you're handling the rent on this place, but we have to pay COBRA premiums until the babies are born, until Monty gets enrolled in a health benefits plan." She paused. "I'm sorry. I don't mean to unload our personal problems on you."

"It's okay. However—that brings me to what I called you about. Yes, the rent is taken care of, and so are the taxes and property insurance on Arcadia. I'm also paying the contractor to complete the renovation. But you need to understand this, Helen. I never told Monty that I would pay off the bank loans and give you the house. Once it's finished, the house is going on the market. You're not moving back in."

"What? But Monty said—"

"I know what he said. And thank you for that email. I'm glad you sent it only to me, though. I'm sure he'd go ballistic if he saw it, because he knows good and well that I never agreed to give you the house."

"So, we're still in the same position we were in."

"Here's what's going on. The contractor should be finished by the middle of August at the latest. That's in six weeks. Then the house will be listed by a realtor that I choose, for a price that I decide. I know Monty's not going to like that."

Helen took a deep breath. "You're right."

"Anyway, that's what's happening. Then, once a buyer is found, if there's enough money, the bank will be paid off—the mortgage and the HELOC. The money you owe me is different. If we don't recover enough cash from the sale of the house to pay me back, I'm prepared to write it off. You and Monty can come away from the closing table with your credit intact. Needless to say, I won't be giving you any more money, or making you any more loans."

"That's fair."

"Yes. It is. It may not be as generous as what you would like, or what Monty told you. But it's what I'm willing to do. The house won't go into foreclosure. It's underwater—much more is owed on it, to the bank and to me, than what the market will bring. Fortunately for you, I'm willing to take the hit."

"Thank you, Candace," said Helen, her voice wooden.

"You're welcome. Now, a piece of unsolicited advice. I think it would be in your best interest to demand to see your husband's paycheck, and verify exactly where he's working and what he's doing every day."

"You're right."

"David will see what he can find out, and I will let you know. I assume you've decided not to look for a new job until later on, after you have the twins."

"I've been sending out resumes, but I don't have a lot of hope right now. I just want to get through the pregnancy and then find a new job by January, at the latest."

"When are you due, again?"

"The end of November. But twins are sometimes born prematurely."

"Well. I hope I haven't upset you. I just needed to let you know the truth."

"It's okay. We'll make it. We don't have a house payment, and now that we don't have to make payments to the bank, we should be able to get by, especially with Monty working. We're going to have to downsize and cut our expenses. When I get a job, we can start to get back on our feet."

"Monty simply has to bring in an income. Once the house sells, you'll be responsible for your rent payment over there. I'm not going to pay it anymore. That could happen before you start working again. You can't do everything, Helen. Not with three kids."

"We'll figure it out."

Candace paused. "I'm sorry."

"It's okay. I don't know how we would have maintained that house on Arcadia anyway, even if we did own it free and clear. The property taxes are exorbitant, and the utilities won't be cheap. Even if both of us are working, after day care costs, it would be a huge struggle to live there and keep it up."

"You can rent for a while and save your money. Then buy a house you can afford. Since housing prices are down everywhere, you'll probably be able to find something when you're ready."

"We should never have gotten into that house on Arcadia. I'm sorry we've put you through all of this, Candace."

"Let's just focus on the exit strategy. Now you know what's going on, and I'm glad you were able to digest it."

"If David finds out anything—"

"I'll call you. Oh, and Helen?"

"Yes?"

"I'm not going to tell Monty we've spoken, or that I've told you anything. Our priority is verifying that he's working, and I don't want anything to happen right now to set him off."

"Believe me, I don't either. I won't say a word."

• • •

At one o'clock on Friday night, Monty slid behind the wheel of the BMW parked in the garage at his Midtown condominium. He had just spent the evening with Rachel, who was asleep upstairs, naked. They'd gone out for dinner and drinks at a hot nightclub two blocks away, then returned for a two-hour session of mind-boggling sex.

He turned the key in the ignition and backed out of the parking space. Helen and Adele should be asleep now. He had told his wife that he'd had to go out with Mack and Jeremy, the two guys who ran the fictitious media company he said he was working for. She had been bugging him the last two days to tell her more about it, but so far he had gotten away with saying little. He had claimed that everything was very hush-hush, and that he had been ordered not to divulge anything about the business, not even to his wife.

When she gave him questioning looks, he'd ignored her. As long as he made deposits in their joint checking account, he said, she should be happy, and he would be getting paid once a week, on Fridays. He'd made a deposit in their checking account today, in cash of course. He knew she would freak, but he planned to tell her that Mack and Jeremy were Dutch and the company wasn't even registered yet in the U.S.

He had taken the money out of his other bank account, the one he used for the condo and for his purchases for himself and Rachel. He also had cash in a safe deposit box there. That way, he could keep it hidden with no one tracking it and there was no trace of it online. He'd decided to pay himself a weekly salary of $1,920. Annually, it worked out to about a buck and a quarter—$125,000—with a tax rate of 20 percent. A take-home monthly pay of almost eight grand should satisfy Helen, and would be more than enough to keep them afloat. It was also plausible compensation for the kind of job he'd created for himself.

It didn't matter, though. In a couple of months, he would tell her that his employers had decided to go back to Europe, but that before they did, they had paid him a large consulting fee. By then, he would have millions of dollars in the bank. His family would be living in comfort at 710 Arcadia Lane, with two new cars and no debt. He didn't care anymore that Candace had forced him out of the renovation project. Once he moved back in, he could change anything her cheap contractor had done; all it would take was enough money, and by then he would have plenty.

He approached a red light and slowed to a stop. The night air was sultry. The weather in Atlanta would stay hot and humid until at least mid-September. But when the weather changed, so would his life.

Finally.

16

Leak

David Shepherd sat down at his desk on a Thursday morning. Checking his email, he saw a message from Ken Samuels, the contractor on Arcadia. The work over there wasn't finished, even though Ken had promised it would be done by the fifteenth. Today was August nineteenth, and Candace wasn't happy.

David opened the message and braced himself for bad news.

He got it. Evidently Ken's team had found some issues that required more time to address: an active leak had been discovered, the result of a drain that had been improperly installed by Monty. There was also some damage behind the drywall and under the carpeting, and the wood floors in the den were cupped due to moisture. Mold had been found all through the home, although it had only been evident in the basement initially.

Ken had been working hard during the last two weeks to finish the cabinet installation, repair and re-stain the trim, and reinstall some windows that had been set incorrectly. Earlier, his team had had to spend their time removing debris and redoing the electrical wiring as well as the waterproofing. With the latest mold and leak discoveries, Ken believed the waterproofing had to be redone again, unfortunately. The bottom line equaled an additional $30,000 and at least three more weeks.

David sat back in his chair and reread the message with its list of bullet points. Candace was going to be furious. He would tell her what Ken had explained to him the last time they had spoken: that the moisture issues were due to shoddy work previously done by her brother, or by the people he had hired before Ken's team took over. She would still hit the roof, and David would be the recipient of her wrath. She would require him to argue with Ken about the additional charges, and to micromanage all the remaining work on the house—two things David didn't want to do.

He had to tell her about the situation, though, and he had to do it today. Earlier this week, she and Monty had argued over how much to list the house for, exchanging emails and copying David. Candace had instructed David not to forward them to Helen—she was six months pregnant now, but looked as if she were eight and a half months, according to her husband. Candace had said that she would personally handle any communication with Helen by phone and that she didn't want to upset her right now with any bad news.

When the house was ready to go on the market, Monty wanted to list it for $2.1 million, with the expectation of getting just under two. Candace believed the house wouldn't bring in half that amount. David felt she was right. The Carawans weren't going to make any money, and David's task was to minimize how much his client lost. Then she—and he—could remove it from her list of investments.

However, Ken needed to finish the work first, and then he had to be paid. A contract had to be signed with a realtor, who had to locate a buyer, a task that wouldn't be easy. David just hoped that potential buyers wouldn't meet the neighbors and find out how long the renovation had taken to complete.

• • •

Fashion Week was scheduled to begin in just over three weeks, and Candace was looking forward to unveiling SwimZ.

The samples were ready in every color and pattern that she had approved. She had tried on each style and was pleased with all of them. Of course, no one in the industry (or the general public) knew about the line—everyone at SlimZ was sworn to obey the commandment *thou shalt not leak.* Breaking that commandment meant losing one's job.

Previous new garments the company had shown to buyers during Fashion Week had wowed everyone, creating that sought-after buzz before the product became available in stores a few months later. The new SwimZ line would do the same. Candace was proud of her achievement in making it a reality; it had been in development for years, and now was the right time.

She looked over the photos on the SlimZ internal system. Everything looked great. Her competitors would be stunned with the new line and would scramble to imitate the designs. But they wouldn't succeed. In the spring, SwimZ would be the must-have swimsuit, and no other apparel company's product would come close to its customer appeal. The SlimZ brand name was a major positive in marketing and was worth quite a bit of money. With an average unit retail price of $200, Candace expected to sell about 1.25 million units, yielding sales of $250 million, which equaled a gross profit of $125 million.

She enjoyed making a profit, but money wasn't what she worked for—at least not anymore, and not for its own sake. The money was an added bonus, a way to measure success, like an SAT score or an index of accomplishment. Candace liked earning high scores. As long as she kept working and SlimZ kept thriving, her money kept coming in, and her success increased.

She had a passion for her products and for the company she had founded. She was proud of the fact that she had done all the research herself and had created products that had never existed before. The fact that she had been financially secure at the time and could afford to take a chance on a new idea had helped, but it wasn't the reason for her success. She had been a creative visionary then and she was still one today. She thoroughly enjoyed the process; *that* was the reason she kept on working. Besides, if she ever stepped aside, what would she do? She didn't want to retire. She had created her ideal job.

She also enjoyed her social connections to the super-wealthy in business and to many New York and Hollywood celebrities. She thrived on their admiration for what she had done professionally. She couldn't imagine herself without the financial status she had achieved. It was an integral part of who she was, like her IQ or the shape of her nose.

And in recent years, she'd grown very accustomed to the finer things: well-made designer clothing, bags, and shoes; luxury vehicles; private jets; fine hotels; expensive wine. She'd become quite used to getting exactly what she wanted, when she wanted it. The things that she wanted added up to thousands of dollars—tens of thousands—but that wasn't extravagant, given her net worth. They added up, but she didn't intend to live without them, or to feel guilty for the lifestyle she led.

She didn't see herself as pretentious in any way, though, or as a snob. She had never hidden—or been ashamed of—her middle-class family upbringing. She couldn't help it if she counted her pennies; she had inherited the trait of frugality from her father. Like him, she had an irrational, deep fear of losing everything that she had saved and everything that she had built for reasons beyond her control. It was a fear she had had to push away more than once. The French had an expression she often repeated to herself when her fear surfaced: *gardez votre sang-froid.* Keep your sangfroid, your composure. Your cool.

Her inbox signaled a new message. It was from Darlene, who handled public relations and social media, and it was marked urgent. She clicked on it, skimmed it, and reread it with alarm.

Candace,

I just saw this blurb on woohoo.com:

"SlimZ, the fabulous shapewear company founded by Candace Morgan, is about to unveil a new line to store buyers at New York's Fashion Week: Swimsuits! We can't wait to see them, and we know you can't, either. No word yet on colors, designs, or even the new logo, but check back often: we will post more info as we get it!"

Darlene

Candace rose from her desk, her heart racing, and walked from her office straight to Darlene's desk. Then she leaned down to her.

"How did this happen?" Candace whispered.

"I don't know."

"Someone must have talked."

"Everyone here knows not to say a word about the line. Not to their friends, not to their families, not even to their husbands."

"Evidently, someone did, and now it's on Woohoo, a site millions of people read every day."

Darlene bit her lip. "What do you want me to do?"

"Nothing, yet. I'm going to have Jess call the department heads in, and after I talk with them, I'll send for you to come over. So stay here, and stay mum."

"Oh my God, Candace."

Candace gave her a stern look. "Continue your work, as if nothing's going on."

"Okay."

Candace walked to Jess's desk and stopped in front of her. "Call Amanda, Paula, Ginger, and Courtney to my office, right now."

Fifteen minutes later, Darlene's phone buzzed. It was Jess.

"Candace would like you to come to her office right away."

Darlene rose from her desk and walked down the hall toward the CEO's office door. Passing by Jess, she glanced at her with a nervous smile, then paused before opening Candace's door.

The four SlimZ department heads stood opposite the CEO, who was standing behind her desk. "Darlene," she said in a low tone. "Come in, and shut the door."

Darlene did as she was bid, then turned and stopped, looking around.

"Have you seen anything else online?" asked Candace.

Darlene shook her head. "Not yet."

"Okay. As we all know, this is a very unexpected and unwelcome development. It's not the end of the world, though. Before we get to how it happened, we need to talk about what to do next."

Darlene nodded.

Candace continued to address the group. "A leak like this has never happened to us before. We've always been able to control the news of what we're doing and manage our narrative. We can still do that."

Amanda piped up. "We need to know who leaked it."

Candace held her hand up, palm out. "First, we need to know exactly what got leaked. The fact that we are about to unveil a new line of swimsuits is out there. What else?"

"The blurb on Woohoo said, 'We will post more info as we get it,'" said Amanda. "They've got a source. When they get more info, they'll disclose more, and that means our competitors will know more."

The other women in the room looked at each other with worried expressions. Candace leaned toward them and placed her hands on her desk. "It's important that we keep calm. The SwimZ line will be shown in three weeks. That's going to happen. Somehow, Woohoo knows about it. We don't know if they know anything more. If they had renderings of our designs, I suspect they would have already put them out there. They've made a connection with someone who wanted to make some money, and evidently that person hasn't given them anything else yet."

Darlene looked at Amanda. "We can take control of this. We can act like we meant to let it out, to garner attention pre–Fashion Week. A teaser."

"That's exactly what we need to do," said Candace. "But we do need to trace this."

Paula looked around. "No one on my team would leak it."

"Nonetheless," said Candace, looking from Paula to Amanda, then to Ginger, then Courtney, "I need for all of you to take a new look at each of your direct reports. You know them. You know their personalities. You know how long they've been here. You know who they live with, who they call on the phone." She paused for a few seconds. "I'm sure that no one in the company did something stupid like talk about SwimZ in an email or on their Facebook page. But someone told Woohoo—or they told someone else, who told Woohoo. It may not have even been someone here at the company. It could have been a seamstress, or even a fabric vendor who wanted to make some cash. So we need to widen the search beyond SlimZ employees. Paula, see what you can find out. Get Shelly on it, too, and get back to me as soon as you know anything."

• • •

The following Friday afternoon—eight days later—Monty dialed Candace's number.

He wasn't surprised when she didn't take his call. After the beep, he left a message, speaking in a cheerful tone. "Hey, Candace. Just wanted to ask how everything's going over at the company. I've seen some stuff about you online. Something about a new line of bathing suits coming out soon? Good luck with that. Call me back as soon as you can. I need to talk to you about a proposal. And about Helen."

He clicked the phone off and put it down. It was almost four o'clock, and Rachel would be getting back to the condo soon. She never worked much past four on Fridays; none of her decorator clients would schedule an appointment so close to rush hour at the beginning of a weekend.

Ten minutes later, his phone buzzed.

"Hi, Candace. Glad you had a minute. I'm sure things are busy at the office—"

"What about Helen, Monty? Is she okay?"

"Well, not exactly. The doc says she may have to go on bed rest in a few weeks. She's an emotional mess."

"Monty—"

"She's stressed. She can't believe she's going to have to give birth to twin boys, then come back to live in a crumbling three-bedroom ranch house with three kids. We need to move into a house that's big enough for our family. One that's safe, and one that's clean. One that's right for us."

"If you don't like the house I'm paying the rent for, go out and find yourself another one. You said you have a job, so—"

"The house we want to live in—the house we *deserve* to live in—is the one on Arcadia. Why are you so against us moving back in to it, once the work over there is done? You and I both know this isn't the right time to put that house on the market. My family needs to live there, until that time comes."

"Are you saying that you'd pay me rent to live there?"

"Do you need the money? I don't think so. You don't even need that house as an investment. Let's stop bickering about all this. You know what you ought to do: give us the house and forgive all the debt."

"We're not bickering. You've strung me along and manipulated me out of hundreds of thousands of dollars. I don't trust you anymore, and I never should have. I've made my decision: you're on your own now. I'm not going to enable you to live a lifestyle beyond your means. Giving you the house would be doing just that. You couldn't afford to maintain it, anyway."

"You're a presumptuous bitch, and you always were. Our ability to maintain the house is none of your concern, and neither is our lifestyle. You don't get to control us simply because you made an investment that you could well afford, and one that you don't even need."

"You're the one who's presuming here."

"Whatever. You've screwed me long enough. You need to give us that house, and we need to move back into it before the twins are born. You also need to give us a tiny portion of your obscene fortune—the fortune you've been paying what's-his-fuck to manage for you. Share the wealth with your blood relatives, Candace. Pay me ten million, and then we're done. For life."

"Are you out of your mind?"

"Which one of your employees leaked the news about your new swimsuit line?"

"What are you talking about?"

"I'm just wondering how that happened."

"What goes on at SlimZ is none of your business."

"So, you *don't* know how it happened. I bet there's a *lot* going on over there that you don't know about."

"I don't have time—"

"If you don't give me what I'm asking for, you're going to lose a whole lot more than just trust in your employees. You'll lose ten times the amount I'm asking for. I guarantee it."

"Are you threatening me?"

"All I'm saying is, I wonder what else could go wrong over at SlimZ. Think about it. Do you want to take that chance?"

"Monty—"

"You don't have to give me your answer right now. I know you're very busy getting ready for Fashion Week. By then it will probably be too late, though. Take the weekend and think about my proposal. I'm sure you'll decide to do the right thing." Monty hung up and put his phone down. Then he poured himself a few fingers of vodka and sat down at his laptop to wait for Rachel.

• • •

That evening, Candace sat on the sofa across from Rob in her living room in Midtown. He had arrived in Atlanta an hour earlier, and he planned to stay in the city for the next two weeks. She placed her martini on the glass cocktail table and regarded him.

"I can't prove it yet," she said, "but I'm convinced that Monty found out about the new line from someone at the office and leaked it to Woohoo."

"Does anyone at the company know him?"

"I don't know. I didn't think anyone did. People are aware that I have a brother, but I never talk about him."

"Well, if you're right, then someone at the company does know him—or someone knows someone else who does. Are you any closer to figuring out who leaked it?"

"No. I've been too busy to worry about it lately. Once the news was out, we had to manage it, and the publicity. Plus, I've been busy making sure everything's ready for New York. But if Monty found out about the line from someone at the company, what else does he know? What did he mean by saying I would lose a hundred million dollars if I don't give him the money he wants and the house?"

Rob shook his head. "There's no way he can cause you to lose money. Has David found out who his employer is?"

"Not yet. All Helen had for him was the principals' first names, and a cock-and-bull story Monty told her about what they do."

"You didn't ask Monty about it today?"

"No. I should have, though. It was just—I was flabbergasted when he made his demand. 'Pay me ten million, and then we're done.' Who does he think he is?"

Rob took a sip of his cocktail. "A genius. But he's a fool."

"When I spoke with Helen the other day, she said he'd been making cash deposits once a week in their checking account, saying it's his salary. He told her he's being paid in cash because the principals are European, and they're not set up yet with the IRS."

"Sounds far-fetched."

"Exactly."

"If it's true that he's working, good for them. If it isn't, which I suspect, then I wonder where he's getting the money." Rob set his glass down and leaned toward her. "But that's Helen's concern, not ours. I'm certain there's no way he can hurt you or the company."

"I hope you're right."

17

Plans

On Labor Day morning, Helen stepped out of the shower in the black-and-white-tiled bathroom, a beach towel wrapped around her expanding body. She inspected her appearance in the frameless mirror that was bolted to the wall over the sink, then shed her towel and began to apply cocoa butter to her stomach. Though she was only six and a half months pregnant, she looked nine, and her back ached constantly. She couldn't imagine making it to her late November due date.

Three years ago, Adele had arrived on time and with little fuss, weighing seven pounds, eight ounces. At Helen's obstetrician appointment last week, Dr. Russell had estimated that the twins were now about four pounds each. The sonograms had shown two different sacs, which added extra fluid, weight, and volume to Helen's pregnant belly. The doctor said the babies should gain about a pound a month from now on, and she wanted Helen to carry them as close to term as possible.

With her due date over ten weeks away, Helen had her doubts. If the babies did gain weight as the doctor said they should, by November she would be carrying thirteen pounds of baby inside of her. Luckily, her skin hadn't broken, probably because she'd been pregnant before. This pregnancy was much worse, though. She felt uncomfortable all the time. Her belly had seemed to stop protruding farther out in front, and had started expanding in width to make more room.

Adele was quietly playing in her bedroom this morning with some Barbies that Dawn had bought her, and Monty was at work. Apparently his Dutch employers didn't observe the American holiday; Monty said that they couldn't afford to take a day off as they raced with the clock to launch their product.

Helen still hadn't seen any pay stubs, but she had gotten tired of asking Monty for them and of wondering about his job. Her husband went somewhere every day, looked tired at night, and deposited over nineteen hundred dollars in their checking account every Friday. He still paid the bills, but Helen checked the account online and could see where the money went. He also did the grocery shopping on the weekends.

She was grateful that he did. She was sick of the stares she got when she went out in public. People frequently commented that she looked as if she were about to go into labor at any moment. More than once, she'd wished she was wearing a sign that read "Having Twins." Whenever she did tell someone that she was carrying two babies, they often told a twin story of their own: they either had twins, were related to twins, or they *were* a twin.

After she finished dressing, she went into the living room, sat on the sofa, and dialed her sister's number.

"Helen," said Dawn. "I'm glad you called."

"I hope I didn't wake you up on your day off. What are you and Frank doing today?"

"Getting together with some friends. The weather's going to be nice and warm. How about down there?"

"Hot," said Helen. "I'm staying in the air conditioning."

"Good. Hey, did I tell you that Frank has to go to New York next week?"

"No. For how long?"

"Just a few days. But he'll be there the same time Candace is going to be at Fashion Week. I read that they're moving it to Lincoln Center this year, from Bryant Park."

"You're so up on everything, Dawn."

Dawn laughed. "I don't get into it that much, but reading about the celebs who're going to be there is a lot more fun than talking to my clients."

"Who's going to be there?"

"You know, the usual. Actresses, models, people famous for being famous. I read that Candace is going to be showing a whole new line of swimsuits."

"Yeah, I heard that, too," said Helen. "I was surprised it was already out in the media ahead of time. I guess that's the way they do things."

"I don't know. Seems unusual. I thought they put out press releases on stuff like that during and after Fashion Week, not before. Anyway, how are you feeling?"

"Huge, and getting huger. I don't know how I'm going to make it all the way to Thanksgiving."

"Do you want me to come down? Like, in October? Or even sooner? I could take some time off and help you."

"Aren't you going to come down when the babies are born? That's when I'm going to need you."

"I can do both. You tell me. What would be best?"

Helen shifted on the sofa, trying to get comfortable. It was impossible. "I wish you could be with me from here on out. But maybe in a month or so? That way, if they come early, you'll already be here."

"Do you really think they'll come early?"

"I don't know, but I wouldn't mind if they did. Even though I'm supposed to do everything I can to make it to the due date. Dawn! I just don't know how I'm going to manage."

"I have Columbus Day off. That's in about a month. I can come down then and stay a few days—"

"That's the weekend Candace is getting married up in New York."

"You're not going, though, are you? Or is Monty going?"

"He's not planning to. It would be pretty awkward."

"How are things?" asked Dawn. "I mean—"

"They're okay. She's called me a couple of times since that day a few weeks ago when she called to correct me, after I sent her the thank-you email about giving us the house."

Dawn paused. "What about? I mean, since Monty's working now, you're pretty much out of the house deal, right?"

"Right. Everything is doable. She's been asking what I know about his job."

"What *do* you know?"

"Nothing. Except that he's getting paid, and making more money than I used to."

"Well, that's good, I guess. But don't you think you need to know more about it?"

"Yes. But at this point, well, I just—Dawn, I just don't want to deal with it, quite frankly."

"I'm sorry. I didn't mean to upset you."

"I'm not upset. Really."

"Let's just plan on me coming down that weekend in October, okay? I'll get a hotel room somewhere close by. I'll do things with Adele, and you'll be able to get some rest."

"Good. That'll be great," said Helen. Adele came toddling in the room and climbed up on the sofa next to her mother. "Hey,

Boo," Helen said while pulling her daughter close. "I guess I'd better hang up now, Dawn."

"Okay. Take it easy, all right? And let me know if you want me to come down there sooner."

"I will. Bye."

• • •

That morning, Candace woke up next to Rob in the Hamptons. She scooted closer to him, turned on her side, and rested a hand on his chest. Raising up on her other elbow, she looked steadily into his eyes. "How long have you been awake?"

He ran a finger up her arm and over her shoulder, then let it trail down in front. "Not long. How are you, darling?" He turned toward her and reached over her with his other arm, putting his hand on her lower back.

"Stay here." Candace pulled away and rose. "I'll be right back." Two minutes later, she walked out of the bathroom, still naked, and rejoined him in bed. He pulled her body to his and kissed her, his lips lingering on hers.

Several minutes later, his mouth ventured lower. She pulled his head in toward her. "This weekend has been wonderful," she whispered. His hands moved down her body and she felt an electric sense of desire. Whenever he touched her, she felt sexy and sought-after, never used or taken for granted, like she had felt years ago with Ted.

Almost an hour later, he lay beside her, his arm around her, her head resting on his shoulder. "I'm happy, Rob."

He smiled. "I am too, love. Would you like to join me in the shower?"

Candace turned and looked into his eyes. "I'll stay here for a few more minutes. You go ahead." She smiled and let out a deep breath.

Later, she stepped into the kitchen wearing nothing but a light cotton white robe, her hair wet. Rob had made coffee for the two of them in the French press. She poured a cup and added low-fat creamer, then joined him on the terrace. The midmorning sun shone on the sand and on the waves breaking in front of them. Candace breathed in the warm, salty air and closed her eyes.

"I'm so glad you talked me into coming out here this weekend," she said. "The next three days are going to be so busy. I'm excited about next week, but I'm also a bit anxious."

"Why, love? You're a veteran at Fashion Week. I'm sure everything will go as planned."

"That's just it. You know how much I don't like surprises. I'm still unnerved by the leak last month."

"Oh, pshaw. Your staff handled it very well and used it to your advantage. Everyone thinks you did the deed on purpose, even. Didn't you?" His eyes danced as he raised his eyebrows.

"Rob. You know me."

He laughed. "Like no one else. At least, that's what you've led me to believe."

She smiled and turned to look at the ocean. "Whatever people think, the deed *was* done, and I'm no closer to finding out who did it. Which *does* worry me. At least the actual designs didn't get leaked."

"Let it go, darling. You've some exciting moments ahead in the next ten days. Your new line will make quite a splash, pun intended." He grinned. "And afterward—"

"Stop. I can't think that far ahead right now."

"*I* can." He leaned back in his chair, eying her. "September will fly, then you have a wedding to attend. As the bride, no less."

"Are we really doing this?" she teased, smiling. "I mean, we could have just continued on—"

"Ah, but that's just it, *mon amour*." He reached his hand over the table and grabbed hers. "You know that we *couldn't* continue on that way. We need to be together. You're the love of my life."

"Rob, you're too romantic. No, you're just romantic enough. You're perfect." She picked up her coffee cup. "One more *tasse*, then I'm going for a run on the beach." She rose and stepped back in the kitchen, and then rejoined him with a fresh cup of coffee.

"So, since you brought up the wedding—" he started.

"*You* brought it up."

"Yes, well, since *I* brought it up, did I tell you that Julia found the ideal spot for us in Fiji for the honeymoon?"

"No, I don't think so. If you did, I was distracted." She took a sip of her coffee. "Tell me about it."

"It's private, luxurious, and incredible. The only downside is that it's not easy to get to."

"I suppose I'll have to get over that part. But I'm glad we decided to bag the Caribbean, close as it is."

"Right. There's just too much risk of a hurricane there. We can always hop over to Bermuda from the city when it's not hurricane season."

"Agreed," said Candace. "So what's the weather like in Fiji in October? And how difficult *is* it to get there?"

"Seventies. Ideal weather. Much like what we have here today. Let's look at the flights in a positive light: it will give us a chance to adjust to the time change. It's tomorrow there, you know."

"Flights? How many?"

"New York to LA. Then we go across the Pacific to Auckland, then just a jaunt over from there to our destination."

"My goodness. I suppose a private jet is out, then?"

"Not totally, but it's a lot more difficult to do than Europe. And if we're going to travel with a group anyway, first-class commercial will suit us, don't you think?"

She gave him another smile. "Whatever you say. Just take me there, and make me happy."

"I will." He smiled and rose to refill his coffee. "Now, how about a light breakfast on the terrace before you get ready to run?"

• • •

The next few weeks did fly by, and at the end of them, Monty put his plan in motion.

Fashion Week had come and gone without a hitch. But in the weeks preceding it, SlimZ had issued hastily written press releases about their new swimsuit line, thanks to him—actually, thanks to Jess. Candace had probably been in super-high gear worrying about whether more clues about the line would surface. But right about now, as orders began to come in from retail store buyers, she was probably feeling like everything was well under control. Which was exactly what he wanted her to feel.

This time she would regret having underestimated him. The damage that he was about to do to her precious company would get her attention, and then she would come around. If she didn't, he could do still more to hurt her, and do it quickly.

He sat down at the square kitchen table in the crumbling house—he called it the crap-house—and closed his laptop. It was eleven thirty on Friday night, September twenty-fourth, and his wife and daughter were asleep in bed. He had arrived here about forty minutes earlier after an evening spent with Rachel. He picked up his glass of vodka and drained it.

During the last few weeks, he had learned everything he needed to know about SlimZ. He'd accessed the IT system using basic SQL injection, something he learned back when he built up his coding knowledge, before pitching his personal assistant website idea. After just a few tries, he had guessed Candace's username—unimaginatively, she had selected her maiden name.

Discovering her password took some time, even though he had the benefit of Jess's hint. When he finally figured it out, he'd been furious: it was their mother's name spelled backward, plus the number 2.

When he saw the swimsuit designs in the system, he'd chosen not to leak them. Instead, he'd decided to do something else, something that would cause his sister not only embarrassment, but money.

The person at SlimZ tasked with production of the swimsuits was a bitch named Phoebe, and the one in charge of "fulfillment" and distribution was named Holly. Both of them reported to Ginger, the COO. Another bitch, Amanda, was in charge of sales and marketing. The sales team was already taking orders from the buyers. They would total up the orders and advise Phoebe's group of the numbers. Phoebe would then schedule production at the factory in Brooklyn. Several months later, if all went well, the stores would receive their orders.

But what if the numbers were changed in the system, after the sales team had placed its orders? As far as Monty could tell, the two areas—sales and production—didn't communicate with each other. He could easily alter the numbers in the orders placed by the sales team, adding or removing a zero or two. He could make this buyer's order larger and that one's smaller and keep the total the same, so as not to arouse suspicion. He could also change the amounts of the particular designs each retailer ordered. Then, after the wrong numbers and types of swimsuits were produced, shipped, and received, SlimZ would have to deal with a huge fuckup: angry retail buyers, bad PR, and maybe even a falling stock price. *That* should get Candace's attention.

He had already changed some of the numbers and was getting ready to change more. With a bunch of queen bees working there, he was sure that once problems were discovered, shit would fly, along with accusations and blame.

The fun part would be to sit back and see how long it took for chaos to ensue, and for Candace's company to implode. If it didn't happen quickly enough, he could do more damage, then watch the very fabric of SlimZ unravel around her.

18

Revelation

Wednesday, October sixth was a warm, sunny day: crisp in the morning but not too cool, with a hint of a breeze and a cloudless, dazzling blue sky above. Indian summer in Atlanta resembled the best kind of summer days up north, but it lasted longer. The heavy heat of the last few months had disappeared and the promise of a southern winter awaited—the kind when jackets are necessary but overcoats, boots, and gloves are rarely needed and usually worn only for fashion's sake. Fall colors were just beginning to appear in Georgia, but they were worth the wait: brilliant golds, oranges, and reds would soon adorn this city, built inside of a forest.

David Shepherd returned to his office from lunch and sat down at his desk. Several items awaited his attention and had to be addressed. One of them concerned Candace Morgan's property on Arcadia Lane. The house had gone on the market on Saturday and was listed with Charlotte Rivers, one of Atlanta's most successful realtors. Charlotte had a reputation for hard work and integrity, knew the market inside out, and was well connected with Atlanta's top-tier business community. If anyone could get Arcadia sold,

Charlotte could. She would get as high a price as possible, helping David minimize Candace's loss. Charlotte would also be aggressive in finding a buyer and skilled at closing the deal.

Charlotte expected any serious offer to be much lower than the $1,490,000 listing price Candace had decided upon, but had declared that the sale should top a million dollars. Candace's exposure in the deal was several hundred thousand over that figure. When David added in Ken's fee, the taxes and insurance, and the cost of Monty's movers and rent, Candace had just sunk another two hundred grand into the place, making her total investment over $1.7 million. Ken's team had taken five weeks longer than originally planned to get the house ready for the market, and David hadn't yet paid the invoice.

He was glad he hadn't. Late this morning, he had received a troubling message from Charlotte detailing several concerns. To name a few: the landscaping was unfinished, some of the doors were sticking, and several drawer pulls and cabinet knobs were missing. In short, although extra time had been allowed, the job was sloppy. Candace would be incensed if she found out that any of the work remained undone. David decided to give Ken a call and have him rectify the situation immediately, before any more showings took place.

The house needed to be perfect by Friday, in time for weekend appointments. Candace was getting married in New York on Saturday; by Monday, she and her new husband would be in Fiji, where they would stay for the next two weeks. David was looking forward to the respite from one of his most demanding clients.

• • •

On Friday morning, Candace woke up in Rob's bedroom—*their* bedroom—in Manhattan. She'd had all her things from her New York apartment moved over early last month, before the unveiling of the new line at Fashion Week at Lincoln Center. Despite the earlier leak to Woohoo, excitement about SwimZ had been high and buyers had loved the designs.

Rumors had buzzed about that Candace herself had decided to buck tradition and let the news out early, to get people talking. Whatever people believed, the unplanned strategy had worked—or at least, hadn't hurt—and Amanda's team had already taken orders from Neiman's, Saks, Nordstrom's, Bloomie's, and several specialty boutiques. Production had been launched with delivery scheduled to occur in late January, just in time for the spring break and cruise seasons.

After her coffee, Candace planned to go to the gym and then to return home and work from the apartment until late in the afternoon. Later that evening, she and Rob were hosting a dinner for twelve at one of Manhattan's newest restaurants, Slipaway. Their guests were Deirdre, Rob's mother; Myron Frisch, chairman of SlimZ's board, who would give Candace away; Charles Chadwick—the head of Rob's firm—and his wife, Nancy; Paula, SlimZ's head of design, and her husband Steve; CFO Courtney and her date Henry, an investment banker; and COO Ginger and her boyfriend, Mark.

Amanda planned to arrive tomorrow in time for the wedding, and Candace hadn't bothered to find out whether she was bringing someone. Jess would be arriving today with her boyfriend, Beau. They weren't attending the dinner—tonight was their own. Candace had instructed her to be up early tomorrow morning, however, and to be available to help as needed. Candace had a massage scheduled for ten o'clock and early afternoon hair and nail appointments at Carena's, a chic Manhattan *atelier de beauté* frequented by the city's super-wealthy. Photographs would be taken at half past four at the St. George Hotel, and the ceremony at Holy Cross was at six.

Then it was back to the St. George for the reception, a sit-down dinner for ninety-four people, and dancing until the wee hours.

Rob had left for the office an hour ago. He planned to put in a full day today before disappearing from the office for a fortnight, something he had never done. He would be home this evening around six, then the two of them would get ready for dinner. Candace dressed for the gym, dropped her iPhone in her bag, and left the apartment, locking the door behind her.

She finished her workout at ten thirty and entered the women's locker room to retrieve her bag, planning to walk the two blocks back home to shower and dress. She donned a light jacket—the weather was gorgeous today, if a bit on the cool side. Reaching in her bag, she pulled out her phone to check for messages. Eight new emails were waiting for her attention, one of them flagged as urgent. It was from Ginger. Candace sat down on a teak bench in the locker room and opened the message.

Ginger had forwarded an email from Phoebe, who was charged with scheduling production of the SwimZ orders. Candace read the message quickly and dialed Ginger, who picked up on the first ring.

"Did you call Phoebe?" asked Candace.

"Yes, but I haven't given her directions yet. Should we get her on a conference call?"

"Let's talk privately first. When did she notice the numbers?"

"This morning, just before nine o'clock. She said she spent the next hour trying to figure out what's going on."

"But she couldn't, and then she sent you this email."

"Correct," said Ginger. "She was panicking, with all of us up here in New York, and you about to be unreachable for two weeks."

"I won't be unreachable—at least, not all the time. But she was prudent to email you right away. Who does she have that can help her get to the bottom of this?"

"She has seven people under her. The best one is probably Wendy."

"Good. Let's do get Phoebe on the line with both of us in thirty minutes. In the meantime, tell her to have Wendy drop what she's doing and help her."

"Got it."

"You place the call. Phoebe can tell both of us what they've managed to learn. I'm leaving the gym and going back to the apartment to jump in the shower."

"Okay."

Candace hung up and placed the phone back in her bag. The situation was serious, and it was fortunate that Phoebe had caught the problem before Candace traveled to the other side of the world. Not that she needed something else to deal with today, of all days. She had planned to spend only a few hours this afternoon working, updating herself about the swimsuit line's orders from store buyers. Now she would have to channel everyone into dealing with a crisis.

She stepped outside and turned left to trot the two blocks over to the apartment. Ten minutes later, she stood under the shower jet in the marble bathroom, thinking through the problem.

The orders Phoebe had received were screwed up. One of the big department store buyers had asked for a very large number of a SwimZ design in red, in just the two smallest sizes. Another one had done the same in a different design in beige. Yet another order from a boutique called Water's Edge looked extremely large for that vendor. Given the situation, it looked suspect to Phoebe and it didn't make sense that the small boutique would order such a large inventory. Finally, a major department store buyer's order had come in with small but lopsided numbers: they had only ordered just five of the twelve SwimZ designs, but only in size fourteen, and only in three dark colors: black, eggplant, and chocolate.

If one of the vendors' orders had looked strange, the problem was likely in their purchasing system. Computerization had eliminated the routine tasks of many store buyers in recent years, but mistakes were still made from time to time. However, with several different orders coming in the way they had, it looked like an issue for SlimZ, not for the buyers. Was the problem in the SlimZ IT department, and if so, what else was wrong there? Or was it a problem on the sales side? What else was the sales team doing wrong? If any of the numbers were wrong when production was launched, mistakes would cost money—serious money.

A delay in production was not in the plan, and Candace couldn't allow it to happen, especially since she was about to leave the country. Production of the SwimZ line simply could not come to a standstill for half a month. This mess had to be handled, and it had to be done today. The company could not afford any damage to its reputation, and neither could Candace, to hers. Not only that—her career itself could be at stake, as well as the company's stock price. Everything she'd worked so hard for and everything she'd built could come crashing down if a solution wasn't found and implemented immediately.

She toweled off and combed her hair, then threw on a pair of black stretchy slacks and a blue rayon long-sleeved top. Ginger should be calling her soon to patch her into the conference call. She picked up her iPhone and set it on the vanity in the bathroom, making sure the volume was turned on. She sat down and pulled an attached magnifying mirror out and began to apply her makeup.

Two minutes later, her phone rang. She answered the call and put it on speaker.

"I'm on," she said. "Ginger? Who is on with us?"

"We've got Phoebe and Wendy here, Candace."

Both employees said hello. "Okay," said Candace, "tell me what you know, Phoebe."

"Well, you saw my email—"

"Right. What have you learned since you wrote that?"

"Not all that much. Not yet, anyway," said Phoebe.

No one spoke for a second. "Candace," said Ginger, "Wendy found another problem: no orders at all in the textured navy."

"That's *got* to be wrong," said Candace. "It's one of the most popular fabrics we have. Elena Masters loved the maillot and the one-shoulder design in it."

Elena was a twenty-eight-year-old up-and-coming actress who had grown up in Florida. After her breakout movie, she had been a regular celebrity at Fashion Week for the last four years. The textured fabric she had admired was a tightly woven lightweight in shades of dark blue, with a wavy look. It resembled a solid, but with its woven, uneven surface, hid flaws. Elena's photo regularly graced the cover of popular fashion magazines, and her approval of the fabric all but guaranteed a big order.

No one spoke for a moment. Then Candace continued, "Perhaps we need to get Amanda's people to contact all the buyers personally. She's not arriving here until tomorrow. Wendy, go get her so we can include her on this call."

"Um, I don't think she's in the office. I heard she was taking the day off," Wendy said.

"What?" asked Candace. "That's news to me. She's due to fly to New York in the morning."

"I don't know what she's doing," said Phoebe. "I haven't seen her."

"Okay, look," said Candace. "I'll give her a call myself, after we hang up. For now, I want to know what else you've found."

"Nothing, so far," said Phoebe.

"Keep looking," said Candace. "Ginger, I want you to manage this situation today, no matter how long it takes. And look into the replenishables from each buyer. If those are okay and we can eliminate everything except SwimZ orders, that would be helpful."

Replenishables were stock items that were automatically ordered by the buyers once their inventories reached a certain level. For most of SlimZ store buyers, they included several versions of the flagship product, the longer legging undergarments, the bras, and the shaping camisoles.

"Phoebe, you look for Amanda, in case I'm unable to connect with her," added Candace. "Get her involved in this immediately. I expect her to be there today until her side of these issues are investigated, and any problems she finds are resolved. Wedding or no wedding."

"Candace," said Ginger, "we'll get this handled, whether it's today or early next week. Your plans are set."

"We'll see," said Candace. "I'm getting off the line now. You three stay on together and go over every piece of this puzzle. Then get it solved."

"Got it," said Ginger.

Candace hung up. The situation was bad—very bad—and it could be devastating. If Amanda was playing hooky after she'd claimed not to be able to fly up to New York today—and in the midst of a crisis—Candace would express her displeasure in the clearest possible terms.

She dialed Amanda's number.

• • •

Jess opened the door to Beau's new black Camry and got in. Just as she buckled her seat belt, she heard her cell phone vibrate in her purse and retrieved it. "Damn," she said.

Beau glanced at his girlfriend before pulling onto Peachtree Road.

"Hello, Candace," Jess said sweetly. Beau smiled at her quick reverse.

"Where's Amanda?"

"Um, I don't know, exactly. Why?"

"Wendy told me she wasn't in the office today, and just now she didn't pick up when I called her cell," said Candace. "Have you heard from her?"

"No. Isn't she on her way up there?"

"She's supposed to come up tomorrow, but I need to reach her immediately. We've got a situation. I can't have her going dark."

"What's the situation?"

Candace took a breath. "It seems Phoebe's numbers on orders on the new line are wrong."

"That's not good," said Jess, throwing Beau a worried look.

"No. It's not good at all, and the timing isn't great, either. Are you still in the office?"

"No, I'm in the car with Beau, on the way to the airport. We just got on eighty-five."

"Well, you may have to turn around. I need you to track Amanda down."

"Should I call her at home?"

"Yes, do that," said Candace. "Then call her cell, and text her. I didn't leave her a voicemail, but she should see that I called. If you don't get her, leave her a message to call me right away."

"Got it. Should I say what it's about?"

"No. Just say that it's imperative that she call me immediately."

"What about my flight?"

"Keep driving to the airport. When you get there, text me and I'll let you know."

"Is the situation serious?"

"Yes," said Candace. "It's a colossal screwup, and Amanda's side is one of the pieces."

"Oh my God."

"Right. Talk to you in a bit."

Jess hung up and put the phone down. "What the fuck!"

"What is it?" asked Beau.

"Just a minute. I have to find Amanda's home number." She pulled up the WhitePages app on her phone and keyed in Amanda's name. "Orders are screwed up, and Candace has to talk to her, pronto."

"Or what?"

"Or I may not be going to New York. At least, not yet."

"Jesus, Jess. Can't someone else find her?"

"Apparently not. Wait. I think I found the number." She touched the screen, then put the phone to her ear. After several seconds, she spoke. "Amanda, this is Jess. Candace is trying to reach you. She called your cell and needs you to call her back right away. I'm going to call your cell, too. Candace wanted me to tell you that it's imperative that you call her immediately." Jess hung up, then dialed Amanda's cell.

Beau stared at the road ahead. "Good Lord."

Jess listened for Amanda to pick up, then left the same basic message. Then she sent her a text. Turning to Beau, she said, "I'm supposed to text Candace when we get to the airport."

"Why?"

"So she can let me know whether I'm going to get on this flight."

"Ahh! What are we supposed to do, get a later one?"

"Possibly. Don't freak out, though. If we have to, Candace will cover it."

"What about tonight?"

"We'll still go out." Jess placed her hand on his shoulder.

"It's just annoying."

"Welcome to *my* life."

A few minutes later, Beau took the exit for the airport and followed the signs to the South Terminal for Delta. "Why don't you text Candace now?"

"Okay," said Jess, her thumbs moving on the cell phone screen. "Done."

"So I guess we park, then wait?"

Jess gave him a look. "What else can we do?"

He exhaled. "Jess, I—"

"Hey, I just thought of something."

"What?"

"Candace's brother. He's kind of like a consultant for her, a behind-the-scenes guy."

"Really?"

"Yeah."

"So, what? Are you gonna call him?"

Jess paused, thinking. "No. She'll call him if she wants to talk to him. He's not gonna know where Amanda is, anyway."

Jess's phone vibrated, signaling a text message. "She wants me to call her."

Beau pulled into a parking space, stopped the car and listened.

"Hi, Candace," said Jess.

"I haven't heard from Amanda."

"What if something's wrong? Maybe she had an accident."

Candace puffed. "Well, I guess that's a possibility. Meanwhile, Ginger is on it from up here, and Phoebe is working on it in the office."

"What do you want me to do?"

"Nothing, I guess, at least not for now."

"Candace, have you talked to your brother about it?"

"*What?*"

"I just thought—"

"*What* did you think, Jess?"

Jess swallowed. "Nothing. I mean, I know this is a production thing, probably not something he helps with."

"What do you mean?"

"Doesn't he do consulting for you? I know that's not public knowledge, but—"

"Jess. No. My brother does not do *anything* to do with SlimZ. Why would you think that he does?"

Jess felt her shoulders stiffen. She looked over at Beau. "Because he *told* me he did."

Candace took a sudden breath and paused. "*When* did he tell you this?"

Jess felt the hairs rise on the back of her neck. She blinked, then looked down. "A few months ago. I ran into him at a bar and he introduced himself. He told me you and he were close, and that he worked for you behind the scenes, but that you keep it quiet. He said you talk to him about everything that's going on at the company."

"Fuck! Jess, he *lied* to you!"

"Oh my God, Candace. I didn't know. But—"

"Did you tell him about the new line?"

"He said he knew about it! At least, I think he did. I don't remember exactly. He acted like he already knew."

"He *didn't* know, Jess. He's got to be the person who leaked it to Woohoo."

"Oh my God, Candace, I'm so sorry," said Jess. Her eyes welled up with tears as fear overtook her body. Would she lose her job?

"What else did you tell him?"

"Candace, I had no idea he was—"

"I *don't* talk to him about the company, and he's not some kind of behind-the-scenes consultant!"

"I thought he was telling me the truth! He said—"

"I don't care *what* he said. I know this is a dumb question, but did you give him my password?"

Jess cringed. "No, but—"

"But what?"

"But—well, the subject of passwords came up. He joked about you. He said you weren't good with technology, and then I said something about—about how you liked to use a familiar word, spelled backwards."

"Shit! Did you tell him *what* word?"

"No!"

"But he may have figured it out. Listen to me: you are *never* to discuss what I do, or *anything* to do with the company. Never! Do you understand?"

"Yes. I just thought—"

"I don't care *what* you thought. Jess, I've trusted you with a lot of sensitive material—but obviously, I shouldn't have. I cannot have you going around idiotically giving out clues about confidential information! You made a serious mistake when you assumed you could do that. On top of that, if my brother were involved in the company, I would have told you! You should have known that! You should have realized that someone who's never even been to the office isn't to be trusted!"

"Oh, God!" Jess was crying now.

"Look, we'll discuss your employment when this is resolved. I've got to go. Sit tight and wait for my call." Candace hung up.

Jess dropped the phone and wiped away tears. "I may be getting fired." She looked over at Beau, whose face was white.

"No, baby. It's not gonna happen. She depends on you too much." He reached for her hand and held it, and with his other hand, gently brushed another tear away. "It's gonna work out, I just know it."

"Oh my God, Beau! I don't know what I'm gonna do!"

• • •

Candace read the text she had just received from Ginger and took a moment to think. Everything was beginning to make sense, maybe. She'd had a feeling that Monty had been responsible for the leak, and now she had reason to believe she was right. He must have figured out that Jess was her assistant and stalked her, then pounced when he found an opportunity. Jess had believed his story and had given him a gift, stupidly talking about the new swimsuits and her password habits.

Was that all that it had taken? If he could have accessed the SlimZ internal system right away, he would have done it. Apparently he hadn't been able to at first, and that was why the only thing Woohoo had reported was that the line was about to be unveiled. None of the designs had surfaced, nor any information about the colors and styles.

But now it seemed obvious that later, he had been able to access the system. He had probably guessed Candace's password and username and had figured out how to get in undetected. There may be no way to know yet, but it was a definite possibility, especially given his threat about causing her to lose tens of millions of dollars.

Feeling panicked, she dialed her COO's number.

"We found Amanda," said Ginger. "She was getting her hair colored—"

"Good. But listen. I've had a revelation, kind of. We still need Amanda, but I want to talk to IT."

"Amanda's on the way to the office. I brought her up to date. What's your revelation?"

Candace cleared her throat. "It's more of a hunch, and if it's true then I'm really worried."

"Erin's a whiz, Candace. I can't believe that she or her team are responsible for all the problems we've uncovered."

"I didn't say they were responsible. But I want to bring them into the loop. Or have you already called Erin?"

"No. Do you want to do another conference call?"

"Phoebe has identified the issues and done all she can, correct?"

"Correct."

"What about replenishables? Has she checked them?"

"She's working on it."

"Good. Get Erin on the line in twenty minutes, and dial me in."

"Fine."

"Ginger, if I'm right about this, it's bad. If I'm not—well, it's even worse. And I don't know how we're going to solve it."

19

Investigation

Helen was counting the hours until Dawn's arrival the next morning.

The last few weeks had dragged, and the one thing Helen had looked forward to was her sister's visit. Frank wasn't coming down, but he planned to come with his wife next month when the babies were born. They were going to help out with Adele while Helen was recovering in the hospital and getting used to taking care of twins.

Helen shifted on the sofa and tried to get comfortable while her daughter played on the carpet in front of her. She didn't feel like doing anything and she couldn't imagine when she ever would again. Soon enough, though, she'd be busy nonstop with two newborns and a three-year-old. She knew she should appreciate the quiet time she still had before the twins came, but she was anxious for the pregnancy to end. The babies kicked her all the time; when one moved, the other did, out of necessity. Helen felt they had almost run out of room.

She imagined her mother pregnant with Dawn and then later with her. Helen wondered why Diane had chosen to marry Tim when she was so young. Supposedly, she'd been very pretty and had had many admirers. Perhaps she hadn't had the confidence or the courage to wait for the right man, or she thought that getting married was her only option. From what Helen knew, her marriage to Tim had been volatile from the start and was complicated by her drinking.

Not that Helen thought Tim was a very nice guy. Neither Helen nor Dawn had ever been close to him. He moved far away when they were toddlers and had never pursued a relationship with them, nor tried to establish even the smallest bond. Now, Diane was about to reinvent herself in Hawaii without Rich, the man who had put up with her for the last thirty years. The little contact Helen had with her would probably decrease to almost nothing.

It was just as well. Strangely, now that Helen had forgiven her, the lack of communication with Diane seemed much less upsetting than it had in the past.

Helen had concerns of her own right now, the most immediate of which were giving birth to twins and taking care of them and Adele. Her next priority was finding another job after she recovered and could arrange child care. In the meantime, she needed to make sure Monty continued working and getting paid.

She also needed to demand that he earn her trust and make their marriage work. No matter what it took, she did not want to end up divorced with three small children to raise on her own. She didn't want to relive her mother's history or risk repeating her mistakes. And she wanted her children to know their father, flawed as he was. For their sake, she and Monty had to work out their problems and stay together.

Adele looked up and smiled sweetly. "Mommy, can we go to McDonald's for lunch?"

Helen gave a weak smile. "I don't know, Boo."

"Please, Mommy? I promise I'll be good!"

"Well, I have to drop off some clothes at the cleaners, so maybe we can go to McDonald's, too."

Adele bounced on the floor. "Yay!"

"First, I have to get them, and get ready." Helen stood slowly and waddled toward the bedroom that she and Monty shared.

His clothes for the cleaners were piled in a hamper in the corner. He had tossed his expensive black raincoat on the chair next to it after coming home late last night. Helen touched the still-damp raincoat. It was dirty and needed to go to the cleaners, too. Yesterday had been one of Atlanta's typical rainy days: a steady deluge beginning in the morning, continuing all day, and lasting into the evening hours. Days like those were a nuisance, but Helen wasn't depressed by them. She found them to be peaceful interludes, when the air was cleansed and the trees and streets were washed of dust and grime. Now the rain was gone and the sky was a clear blue.

She picked up the raincoat and dropped it in the hamper. Funny, the light coat felt a little heavy, though it was almost dry. She picked it up again and reached into the pockets, finding an object that felt like a cell phone in one of them. It was unlike Monty to forget his phone, and even less, not to miss it all morning. She pulled it out and then gasped.

It wasn't Monty's phone. Or, it *was* his, and he had gotten a new one without telling her. An iPhone. She picked up her own phone to dial his number, waiting for the iPhone to ring.

It didn't.

"What is it?" Monty asked on the other end of the line.

"Oh—nothing," Helen said while sitting down on the bed. "I just—you have your phone, then?"

"Of course I have my phone! What's wrong with you?"

"Um—oh, okay." Helen studied the iPhone, then swiped it at the bottom. Good—there was no passcode. The small screen lit up with apps. "Sorry I bothered you."

"Wait a minute. Why did you think I didn't have it?"

Helen thought quickly. "I *did* think you had it. I just wanted to be sure you had it with you and had the volume turned up. I had some contractions, but they've gone away now. False alarm. Sorry."

"Okay—"

"Bye." She hung up and put her own phone down, then pulled up the text messages on the iPhone.

There were several, all from someone identified as RB. The latest one, received a few hours ago, read: *Since her sister's coming this wknd, are you staying over at the condo w/me? What time tmrw?*

What condo? Who was RB? Helen sat very still, then felt a kick. She scrolled up the screen to read Monty's text conversations with RB.

As she did, she felt hot anger rising in her throat. RB was a woman, and Monty was screwing her. He went to her condo almost every day. Most of the texts were about timing and plans, but some were explicit references to sex and body parts: the shape and feel of RB's huge tits, the size of Monty's cock. In shock, Helen kept reading. She felt her mouth go dry and a pit of nausea form in her stomach. Tears welled in her eyes.

The audacity of Monty's unfaithfulness astounded her. How could she not have suspected it? She'd believed his lies for so long, had trusted him when intuition told her not to. Like an idiot, she'd never even considered he had a girlfriend. All those times when she had scratched her head wondering what he had done all day, why nothing had progressed over at the house—well, *now* she knew what he'd been doing: cheating on her.

She made herself stop reading after ten minutes. Thankfully, Adele was still engrossed in her television show and hadn't come to find her. She searched the short contact list on the iPhone, looking for more information. There was no Jeremy or Mack listed. There was an A. Langford, but the others were first names she didn't recognize.

Helen pulled up the iPhone settings and found the phone's number. Not thinking about covering her tracks, she called it and let it ring to hear the recorded voicemail greeting. There wasn't one—Monty hadn't replaced the default greeting with a personal one. She checked the mail setting. Monty had only one email account on this phone, a Gmail that she didn't know he had.

She clicked on the inbox and discovered several messages from rbenton@gmail.com. She opened them and scanned them, looking for a first name. Most were unsigned, but at last, she found one signed "Rach." Rachel? It had to be. Rachel Benton. Helen could look her up and possibly find the address of the condo. She checked the phone call history. There were tons of calls made to RB and received from her, at all hours of day and night. Gathering her wits and steeling herself, Helen went back to the text conversations and reread them in the order they were written, starting back as far as they went.

One of them, written by Monty several weeks ago, caught her attention—she didn't know how she had missed it earlier: *Need to transfer some $ first. Going to the bank.* Helen kept reading, looking for clues. There was little mention of money in the rest of his texts, but occasionally RB said she needed some.

Helen put the iPhone down and let out a deep breath. She stared into space, looking straight ahead, her eyes wide. What else did she not know about what Monty was doing?

"Mommy!" called Adele. She ran into the bedroom and over toward Helen, pulling on her leg. "When can we go?"

Helen rose, grabbed her purse, and dropped the iPhone in it. She'd have to think about whether Monty would still be allowed in Adele's life now. "We can go now, Boo. Let me get these clothes together to take. Do you have to go potty first?"

Adele nodded and skipped over to the bathroom. Helen followed, standing at the doorway while her daughter peed. Helen should probably go now, too, before they got in the car. When Adele stood to flush, Helen noticed the lid to the tank was awry. This toilet—the only one in the house—often ran. You had to take off the heavy tank lid and adjust the flapper inside, which was corroded and needed to be replaced. Whoever had messed with it last hadn't put the lid back on exactly right. The mechanism operated this time, and Helen went to the bathroom herself. After flushing again and making sure it worked, she moved the lid back to its proper place.

On the way to McDonald's, Helen did some thinking. Before long, Monty would miss having the iPhone, put two and two together, or both. She didn't have much time to figure out more about what he was doing. She didn't think he would come home to look for it, but it was good that she and Adele were going out, just in case.

She made sure that her own cell phone was set on vibrate—she didn't want to hear it ring if he called. She would take Adele to McDonald's and let her romp in the play area while she did more investigating using the iPhone. She could access the Internet via the free Wi-Fi and hopefully learn some things. She would clear the history after she did.

Then she would put the iPhone back in the raincoat pocket and drop everything off at the dry cleaner's drive-through window. They could find it and give it back to her when she picked up the clothing on Monday—or they could keep it. If Monty said anything about missing a phone, which she didn't think he would, she would claim ignorance.

At McDonald's, Adele ate her Happy Meal and started playing in the fenced PlayPlace. Helen pulled the iPhone from her purse and began searching for information.

• • •

Candace's phone buzzed.

"Charlotte?"

"Candace! I'm so glad I caught you!" said the realtor. "We have a problem—"

"Can it wait? I'm about to get on a conference call."

"Oh. Well, I'm not sure if it can. I've got four showings scheduled for this weekend with clients in from out of town, and the house isn't ready."

"What do you mean, not ready?"

"I got in from out of town myself late last night, and just had time to drive over there. The landscaping isn't complete. There are weeds and dead plants surrounding the front entry. The front door frame is rotting—"

"*What?*"

"That's not all, dear. Several closet doors are missing, and the other interior doors are hollow. Hollow doors are not appropriate in this price range—"

"Have you talked to David Shepherd? He's managing this. As I say, I'm waiting for a call right now. I don't have time to talk."

"I've called him. I left him a message, but I haven't heard back yet, and two of my showings are tomorrow morning. One of them is very interested, an architect—"

"Charlotte, I just can't deal with any of this right now. I'm in the midst of a crisis. I need for you to connect with David so that he can get the contractor out there to fix things."

"Well, that puts me in a tight spot. I really don't want to reschedule these weekend showings, but I may have to—and I'm not sure if that will even be possible. It's very difficult right now to find interested buyers in this segment, and if we get off to a bad start and then word gets out—"

"You can't let that happen. David must be on a plane—I'm up in New York, and he's probably on the way here. I'm certain he will return your call when he lands. Then you two can get this solved. David will just have to manage it with the contractor."

"What if he doesn't? What am I supposed to do in the meantime?"

Candace huffed. "Okay, look. I'll call David myself, as soon as I can."

"We've simply got to get the house in perfect condition, Candace. I cannot tell you how important that is. Homes in this price range have stayed on the market for months, despite cuts in the price. Word gets around if a home in this segment of the market is unkempt and unsellable. When you interrupted me earlier, I was about to say that the home is very dirty, too. It's dusty, there's trash in some of the rooms, and there's a mildewy smell."

Candace gritted her teeth. "This is unacceptable."

"Exactly," said Charlotte. "I knew you would realize this. You wouldn't be pleased if we showed the home in this condition. I'm a little suspicious about what else we may find that's not right, and what might turn up."

"So am I. All right, I'm jumping off now to get on my call, but you'll hear back from either David or myself, shortly."

Candace hung up. Thirty seconds later, Ginger called.

"I've got Erin here on the line, Candace."

"Good. Erin, what do you know?"

"The new IT system hasn't been compromised," Erin said. "Nothing you've uncovered in the old system is showing up in the new one."

"What does that mean?" asked Candace.

"Remember our decision to keep both systems in place through the launch, but to have the old one override the new if they conflict? The dual system approach?"

"Yes," said Ginger. "Erin, are you saying the issues are confined to the old system?"

"Both systems recorded the same production numbers initially. Then changes were made in the old system, but not in the new. However, since we have the old one overriding the new, Phoebe only saw the altered numbers—the ones you're saying don't look right. But she's accessing the old system, because we haven't changed over to the new one. Like I said, the old one overrides it—the new one isn't online yet."

Candace shut her eyes for a second, then let out a deep breath. "Do we have confidence that the new system's order numbers are correct?"

"Well, no changes have been made in it since Amanda's team sent their initial orders over. Replenishables weren't touched in either system."

"So whoever did this only hacked into the old system?"

"It looks that way."

"What do we have to do to be sure?"

"We'll have to look at both systems, carefully. At least, go through the new system's order numbers in detail, manually. That would be my advice."

"So, here's what we do," said Candace. "Amanda's team needs to confirm each order received and redo the totals. Then we start back at square one. She sends them over, but this time, I want you working alongside Phoebe, Erin. I want you to compare the numbers to what you say is currently being reflected in the new IT system. If they match up, I think we're okay—we can disregard the altered numbers. Erin, when Amanda gets in to the office, let me know. I'll speak directly with her about what to do."

"Will do," said Erin.

"What about security in the new system, Erin?" asked Ginger.

"It's tight. No issues. We have the agreed-upon procedures in place to prevent another hack."

"So, once we figure this thing out, we can trash the old one," said Candace.

"Right," said Erin. "But first, we should investigate further to see if any other security was breached in it, if anything else looks funny. I'd be interested in a full evaluation before getting rid of it."

"Why?" asked Candace.

"To make sure that our controls are adequate, that we aren't forgetting anything. Candace, you have a system-generated password in the new system. You know your passwords will be much more cryptic now and will be changed frequently, right?"

"Good," said Candace. "Just like everyone else?"

"Right. It's been company policy for some time."

"Well, I should never have exempted myself from that policy. Better late than never, I guess. Ginger, stay on this. I'll see you tonight, unless something happens."

"Got it," said Ginger. "Great job, Erin."

Candace hung up and leaned back in the brown leather chair in the apartment's living room and closed her eyes. Thank God for Erin. While Ginger should have remembered about the dual systems, Erin was on top of it. As COO, Ginger had a lot on her plate. She managed the highest number of SlimZ employees: thirty-five in the warehouse, under Holly, head of fulfillment; eight in production, reporting to Phoebe; five in IT under Erin; and four customer service people.

Candace called David and got his voicemail. "David, we've got some serious problems on Arcadia. Charlotte Rivers called me and said that she tried to reach you. I need you to call her as soon as you can, so you can get everything resolved today. Then call me back."

A text from Jess appeared. *At gate. Waiting for your call.*

Candace dialed her assistant's number.

"Candace? The plane is boarding," Jess said, her voice uneven. "Should I get on? I'm so sorry I screwed up. Everything is all my fault—"

"Calm down, Jess," said Candace, chiding herself a bit. She ought to be used to Monty's manipulation, but Jess had been unprepared for it, and Candace needed her tomorrow. "It's okay now, we think. Yes, I need you to get on the plane. I'll update you when you get here."

"So I'm not being fired?"

"No. Just get to New York, and get to the hotel. We'll talk when you get here."

"Okay. See you soon."

Five minutes later, Candace's phone buzzed again. It was Erin. *What now?*

"Erin?"

"I just wanted to alert you. We found something else that was altered in the old system."

"What is it?"

"Someone changed the ratio specifications for modulus, weight, and tolerances in the new line."

Modulus was the industry term for stretch, or elasticity. "Good God," said Candace.

"Right," said Erin. "The product would have been incorrectly produced. The ratios were way off from the ones recorded in the new system."

"Thanks for letting me know, Erin. Get Shelly to verify them with you, just as a precaution. We can't be too careful."

"Of course."

Candace hung up and shook her head. What an asshole Monty was. Thank God he hadn't figured out that a dual IT system was in use. She wouldn't let him know that the chaos he had tried to create was dissolving. Not yet.

• • •

Helen tucked Adele into bed for her afternoon nap. Lately, the little girl was on the verge of giving up her nap for good; she could probably push through the afternoon and go to bed early at night. But Helen was trying to keep her daughter to her nap schedule for the next few weeks. Today in particular, she needed some time to herself, even if it meant Adele would be up a little late tonight.

Helen walked into the kitchen, sat down, and looked at her notebook. She had written down everything that she had learned about Rachel Benton, and about Monty, before dropping off the clothes at the cleaners—the iPhone was back in the raincoat pocket where Monty had left it.

Rachel Benton lived in a condominium in Midtown. Helen had discovered the address, Rachel's age (twenty-five), and what she did for a living (interior designer). She looked up the condo's owner, purchase price, and date: Montgomery Carawan; $535,000; and October 15, 2009. Ten days earlier, his sister had cosigned the $500,000 home equity line of credit that he and Helen had secured on the house on Arcadia.

How could I have been so stupid? Evidently, Monty had diverted the loans Candace had already made to them and then drawn on the HELOC to buy the condo. He had probably also spent some of the loan funds to furnish and maintain it. The reason he hadn't paid the contractor's and vendors' invoices was because he was using the money to support a separate life. With Rachel.

The one thing Helen hadn't been able to figure out was whether Monty had a job. There were no emails, texts, or phone calls from a Jeremy or a Mack. If Monty was earning a paycheck, he was doing it at the condo, because that's where he went for most of the day, according to what Helen had learned so far. *If he wasn't working for some Dutch company, where was he getting the cash he was depositing in their account every Friday? Was he just transferring money from some other account, like the text implied?*

Monty hadn't set up his regular email address—the only one Helen had known about—on the iPhone. Maybe he *was* working, and he corresponded with Mack and Jeremy using that address, not the Gmail account on this phone. Helen could do more research on his laptop when she got a chance, later tonight.

20

Threats

Monty sat down at his desk in the condo, opened his laptop, and pulled up the SlimZ IT system.

He had worked out at the gym this morning and then met Chip for lunch. Chip was leaving town this afternoon to spend the long weekend at his lake house with the family and had invited Monty to join them and to bring his own family. But with Helen's condition, that was impossible. Since her sister was arriving tomorrow, Monty planned to spend tomorrow and Sunday here at the condo with Rachel. He'd tell Helen that his employers were having a company retreat in the north Georgia mountains, where there was no cell phone reception, and that he would be back Monday.

Her phone call earlier had unnerved him. He wasn't ready for a trip to the hospital yet, especially with Dawn in town. The twins weren't due for six or seven more weeks, and though Helen probably wouldn't make it that long, he couldn't deal with unnecessary distractions right now.

Candace was probably spending today up in New York getting ready for her wedding, and he doubted that she had an inkling of what he'd done in the company computer system. Even if she'd been in touch with the office today, there was no reason she would know about issues with the new swimsuit line. With the boss away on a Friday, the SlimZ bitches would likely all be taking advantage of it, going to get their nails or hair done.

When Candace got back from the Pacific two weeks from now, it would be too late for her to solve the production problems Monty had caused without it costing her a lot of money. He didn't want to wait that long to get what he deserved. He needed her to pay him now, before her stock price fell. Once she did, he would fix things, but if she didn't, what he had done so far was just the beginning. He had newspaper clippings from the accident that he wouldn't mind sharing with the press. If that didn't work, he knew where the warehouse was in Secaucus, New Jersey, and he wasn't opposed to committing arson.

It was only fair of her to share a small portion of her millions with him, to butt out of the house on Arcadia, and to put it in his name, free and clear.

He picked up the phone and dialed her number.

"What's up, Monty?"

"Nothing. Just wanted to wish you happy wedding."

"Thanks."

"Have you decided whether to accept my offer?"

There was a pause. "What offer?"

"You really don't know?"

"Monty, get to your point—"

"Candace, you're so impatient, and so forgetful. Don't you remember? You pay me ten million, give me the house on Arcadia, and pay off the bank, and you get your swimsuits produced. You don't, and you lose at least a hundred million, your image, and your reputation."

"How do *you* decide whether I get to have my swimsuits produced?"

"I guess you can't be bothered with what's going on over at the beehive. So let me be clear. You're leaving the country soon. While you're gone, production of your new line is going to implode."

"Bullshit."

"Go ahead, call my bluff."

"You're an idiot. You can't do anything to me. Forget about the house. I'm not giving it to you. When it sells, the bank will be paid, and then we'll talk about the rest. I'm not paying you ten million dollars. Trying to extort money from me is a crime."

"Fuck you, Candace. *You're* the criminal. You *killed* someone—right after you told her you wanted her dead."

"You're crazy."

"I was in the back seat that day, and I heard it all. I *heard* what you said to Mom: 'I hate you! I wish you were dead!' Then you swerved in front of a truck, hit a tree, and got your wish. You were jealous of my relationship with her and angry that she hated *you.* You killed her, and you ruined my life!"

"You need help."

"*You* should have died that day. If you had died instead of Mom, my whole life would have been different. Now you're going to make up for it. If you don't pay me—if you're so rich that you don't care about losing a fortune on your precious swimsuits—then I'll kill you myself."

"Stop threatening me."

"And then I'll inherit *all* of your money."

"You're not named in my will, and you never will be."

"But I should be, just like I should have gotten *all* of Dad's money. I'm your closest blood relative, and I'll contest it after you die. What's-his-fuck that you're about to marry has his own fortune."

"Listen to me. I don't *care* that you're related to me. Your life would have been different only if you weren't too lazy to work. If you had a job, you wouldn't need to make threats. *You've* made your life what it is, Monty. Stop blaming your problems on other people."

"I can prove what happened on that day, Candace. I have the documents, and they'll be valid in court. You're guilty of murder—"

"*You've* broken the law, not me. You hacked into my company's computer system—"

Monty huffed. "You have no proof of that."

"You've tried to extort money from me, and now you've threatened to kill me. I didn't murder Mom. There *are* no documents. The accident was long ago, and it was just that—an accident—no matter what my last words to her were."

"How do you live with yourself?"

"I'm hanging up, now, Monty. I'm calling Helen to tell her about our conversation, so she can protect herself. You've become unhinged, and I don't know what you're going to do next."

"Don't you dare call my wife."

"Helen needs to know who you are. I'm also calling my lawyer. You're not going to try to hurt me or my company ever again."

"If you call Helen and she goes into early labor, you'll be the one responsible. But then, you wouldn't get that, since you're not a real woman."

"Your feeble insults and accusations aren't working. If anyone's going to stress your wife physically, it'll be you, not me."

"Watch your back, Candace."

He hung up and slammed the laptop shut.

• • •

Candace took a deep breath. She had to call Helen. If she didn't tell her about Monty's threats, and if he took out his anger on her—it was just too frightening to imagine. Candace couldn't let anything happen to Helen or Adele; if something did, she would feel she was to blame.

She dialed Helen's number, then left a voicemail. "Helen, I just talked to Monty, and I need to speak with you right away. Please call me when you get this. I don't care what time it is."

Candace hung up and put a hand to her forehead. Here she was in Manhattan, about to host a dinner party the night before she and Rob were to get married, and then fly halfway around the world. Helen was in Atlanta, eight months pregnant with twins and married to a deranged man, the father of Candace's niece. Since he couldn't physically attack Candace, would he go harm his wife and daughter?

Candace couldn't take that chance. The situation was out of control. Even though he had done no permanent damage to the company, she knew that he was capable of violence.

Come on, Helen! Call me back!

Candace sent her a text message asking her to call. Then she called Rob, who didn't answer. She tried to push thoughts of her brother out of her mind, but it was no use.

Her phone rang.

"David. Have you talked to Charlotte?"

"Just got off the phone with her. I'm still in the airport."

"Have you called the contractor?"

"I've left him a message—"

"David, we can't have this. Charlotte told me she had a very interested client who wants to see the house tomorrow."

"I know. I talked to Ken Samuels on Wednesday, and he assured me that all would be finished by today. Some of the things Charlotte described on the phone were new, though."

"What do you mean, new?"

"The list of items she gave me the other day didn't include everything she just outlined to both you and me. But I'll chase Ken down and get him to handle it all. Whatever it takes."

"It better not take more money," said Candace. "These kinds of issues at this late date are inexcusable, David. You assured me we wouldn't have any problems with this guy, and here we are, down to the wire. I'm very upset."

David paused for a second. "Don't worry. I'll get it taken care of, even if it means I have to fly back to Atlanta and hunt him down. I'll direct him to get his team back out there today. Worst case, if they're still working during the showings, Charlotte can tell her clients they're just doing the final touches."

"I don't like it, but I see I'll have to accept it. This is not what I wanted to be dealing with the day before my wedding."

"Nor did I. As for the landscaping, though, we've had a lot of rain during the last few days—"

"So? That should have already been done, and not just in the last few days. Once you get through to Ken and know something, call me."

"Of course."

"That's all for now."

Candace hung up and put the phone down. A few minutes later, Rob called.

"I know it must be important, since we're to see each other so soon," he said.

"It is. Monty called me and threatened me again. Not just threats against the company. He said he was going to kill me."

"Good Lord."

"Rob, he's gone berserk. Our conversation deteriorated and then he hung up on me. I'm worried that he's going to do something to Helen or Adele, or both."

"Did he indicate that?"

"No, but he sounded—violent. He's a lunatic. He's desperate, and I don't know what he's going to do."

"Does Helen have anyone that she can go stay with?"

"I don't know. Maybe. I called and left her a message to call me. Wait. I think her sister is coming down from Chicago this weekend. She may already be there."

"Perhaps Helen has gone to the airport to collect her?"

"Oh, Rob. I have to calm down."

"You do. I'll be home soon. Let's talk about it then."

"One more thing. Monty brought up the accident. He accused me of wishing to kill my mother, and reminded me of the last thing I said to her—"

"Candace—"

"And he said that I should have been the one killed. That when Mom died, his life was ruined."

"That's not true. No matter how much she did for him when he was growing up, he always believed he was too smart to have go to work like other people do. It's who he is. Has he ever seen anything through to the end, start to finish?"

"Rob—no, he hasn't."

"I dare say that, had she lived, he would have caused your mother as much pain and disappointment as he's caused everyone else. You have to know this, Candace. His life was always going to be what it is."

"I—wait, Helen's calling."

"Yes, take it," said Rob. "I'll see you when I get home."

• • •

At just after eight o'clock, Helen got Adele down for the night. Then she sat on the sofa and picked up her notebook. She needed to outline her thoughts and decide what to do.

She'd still been in shock about Monty's betrayal when she talked to Candace this afternoon. At first, Helen had just listened, unsure of whether to divulge what she'd discovered. But after Candace recounted her conversation with Monty, Helen had decided to tell her everything she had learned.

She'd told her that she believed he was lying about having a job and that he was moving funds to pretend he was being paid. What Candace told her was more alarming, though: he'd hacked into her company's system, was trying to blackmail her, and had threatened to kill her if she didn't meet his demands.

Candace had pleaded with Helen to get out of the house and protect herself and Adele, or even call the police. But Helen had said she thought Monty had just lashed out at Candace in the moment, something she'd seen him do many times. She assured her that he would never follow through on his threat or do anything to hurt her or Adele. When it came down to it, she didn't think he had the courage.

She told Candace that instead of running, it was time for her to stop living in fear. She didn't know when she'd do it, but she felt she needed to confront him—maybe even tonight. She was angry, and she was tired of his lies. Things had to change before the babies came and her life got crazy. Monty needed come clean about everything and to end it with Rachel. He would have to prove to her that he was working—she would demand to meet his boss. He would have to sell the condo, pay Candace back, and forget about Arcadia. If he didn't, and then Candace took a hit on the property, she would be enabling Monty's lies and secret lifestyle.

Helen had just started writing when she heard his car in the driveway. Her pulse started to race and her hands began trembling. She took a deep breath, brushed her hand over her left shoulder, and closed her notebook.

She heard the kitchen door open and slam shut.

"Monty?"

There was no answer. Then he entered the living room, his eyes menacing. "Why aren't you in bed?"

"I wasn't tired. Monty, look—"

"No, you look. Don't hassle me, Helen. I'm tired, and I need a drink." He turned and walked back to the kitchen. A few minutes later, he reentered the living room and flipped on the television.

"Monty, we need to talk."

He glanced at her, then back at the TV. "Not now."

"Yes, now. Please turn that off."

He turned back and stared at Helen. "What the fuck are you worried about?"

"Please." She stared into his eyes, her face expressionless.

"Are you having more contractions?"

"No."

"Then what's the matter?"

Should she tell him? What was she waiting for? There would never be a good time, so it was now or never. "I found your iPhone."

Monty's jaw slackened. "So what? I have a work iPhone. Let me watch TV." He turned away and took a sip of his cocktail.

Before she knew what she was doing, she blurted it out. "I know who RB is."

He turned toward her again. "What the fuck are you talking about?"

"I read the text messages."

"You spied on me?"

Helen swallowed. She couldn't stop now. The words tumbled out faster than she intended. "I know about Rachel. Monty. I know she lives in a condo that you bought with money that was supposed to pay for the renovation. Money that we owe the bank, on the loan that Candace cosigned—"

"You're imagining things, Helen. You don't know what you're saying."

"Yes, I do. I know you're cheating on me with Rachel! That's Candace's money. You didn't pay the vendors for the work on

Arcadia. You kept the money. You go over to the condo when you say you're working."

"You can't prove any of this."

"Everything has to stop, now. We're about to have twin boys. You have to end it with your girlfriend and start being a good husband and father. We can't go on this way," said Helen. *Stay strong. Don't plead.* "Candace knows you stole the money—"

"What have you done, you bitch?"

"It's not what I've done, it's what you've done. You have to come clean about the money and sell the condo. You have to pay your sister back. We're legally liable to her and to the bank."

"Did you talk to Candace?" His face was white.

"She called me—"

He rose from his chair, came toward Helen, and stopped in front of her. He leaned over and grabbed her by the shoulders, yanking her up. "You fat cow!"

"Let go of me!"

"What is the matter with you? You don't tell me what to do, you fucking cunt!"

Don't back down, not a single inch. "Monty! Stop!" She pushed against him, trying to get away. "Stop trying to hurt me! It won't work anymore." Helen stared straight at him, fire in her eyes.

"You're such an idiot. Stay out of my business. It doesn't concern you."

"It does concern me. You're my husband and my children's father. You don't get to have a girlfriend, or another life. You're lucky I'm willing to give you another chance. You have to be faithful, and you have to provide for your family. You have to get a job."

"I have a job, bitch!"

"Prove it."

The next few seconds changed everything. Monty tightened his grip and slammed her against the wall. He pushed his body up against her pregnant belly. "Fuck you!" he shouted.

A sharp pain registered in her brain as a mixture of fear and anger rose in her throat. *Stay asleep, Adele—don't get up!* Helen felt a sudden, steady warm trickle down her legs and the babies inside of her readjust to a different reality.

She looked straight into Monty's eyes and spoke calmly. "My water just broke."

21

Worst Case

Monty left the hospital Saturday morning at eleven.

Dawn was due in from Chicago any minute. Her flight had landed almost an hour ago, and he didn't want to cross paths with her. Helen was in a private room, some drug being pumped into her to keep her from going into labor. The doctor said that the drug was just a temporary fix—once the water broke, the babies had to be born within a day or two. There was too much risk of an infection if they weren't.

Last night, Monty had woken Adele and taken her with them to the hospital. He had called Chip to ask if he could help out with her. Chip's wife, Kristin, had driven down from the lake and picked Adele up, saying they could keep her as long as Monty needed them to. The Duncan family would be back at their home in Atlanta on Sunday night.

Right now, Monty was beat. He hadn't been able to sleep at all last night, and he hadn't called Rachel. Apparently, his iPhone had been sent to the cleaners. He had contacted them about it, but the Asian owner acted as if he couldn't understand him. Monty would stop there first before going over to the condo to crash.

While he was up all night dealing with nurses, he'd had some time to consider his options. If the babies were born this weekend—and it seemed clear that they would be—he would pretend to agree with Helen's demands. He was not going to abandon his sons, and he wouldn't let her take them away from him. He would promise to be the model father. He would take his family home and let his wife deal with the kids, and he would say he was cutting it off with Rachel. He would tell Helen the condo was being put up for sale, and he would insist that he was working. Once the twins were born, she ought to be happy not to be so huge anymore and to be able to get her body back to normal.

Meanwhile, he would step things up with Candace.

Her disappearance for the next two weeks was ideal. He knew that she wouldn't cancel her trip because of the twins' birth, and he didn't want her to. She needed to have time for reality to sink in. She had never been as quick as he was, anyway. When she returned, he was certain that she would acquiesce and he would get the money he deserved and the house on Arcadia.

If she didn't, he would execute Plan B.

• • •

Dawn stepped off the elevator and approached the nurses' station.

"Hello," she said to a nurse sitting behind a computer screen. "I'm here to see Helen Carawan in room seven seventeen. I'm her sister, Dawn Mitchell."

The nurse smiled. "Hello, Ms. Mitchell. Ms. Carawan mentioned you'd be arriving this morning. Her room is down the corridor, last one on the left."

"Thank you." Dawn turned and hurried down the hall. When she reached room 717, she knocked on the door, which was slightly ajar.

"Come in," called Helen.

Dawn walked in and over to Helen's bedside. "How are you?" She leaned over and hugged her sister.

Helen gave a weak smile. "I'm hanging in there. I'm so glad to see you."

"How do you feel?"

"Not as bad as I thought I was going to. Whatever they're giving me is working."

"Good." Dawn set her purse beside a brown vinyl chair. "So what's going to happen? Are you going to be able to go home soon?"

"Not without the babies," said Helen. "Once the water breaks— the membranes rupture—they have to be born. The doctor is just trying to get me to go a little further, so they can be that much more developed."

"Isn't that dangerous? I mean—I'm sorry." Dawn sank down in the chair.

"No, it's okay. It *is* dangerous to keep them from being born for very long. They're big enough, but their lungs probably aren't ready yet."

Dawn took Helen's hand. "So—well, they'll be all right, though, won't they?"

"I hope so, Dawn." Helen's eyes brimmed with tears. "I don't know. Worst case, they'll have to stay in the hospital for a few days, or maybe a week or two, then come home."

"So you're not in labor?"

"No, the drugs are preventing that. I'm not sure what's going to happen—whether I will go into labor and have them vaginally, or have a caesarean. One way or the other, though, they're coming soon."

Dawn rested her other hand on her sister's forehead and caressed her cheek. "I'm not leaving you. Not unless you want me to."

Helen smiled. "Thanks. I'm so happy you're here."

"Where's Monty? And Adele?"

"He was here all night. He just left. Adele's with some friends. They're keeping her at their lake house until tomorrow night."

"Good," said Dawn. "Frank is coming in tonight. He'll get a room at a hotel. We can take care of Adele when she gets back from the lake. I'm staying here as long as you need me."

"Thank you so much." Uncomfortable on her back for so long, Helen shifted in bed.

"What can I do?"

"Nothing. Just talk to me. Stay with me, and help me get through this."

Dawn squeezed her sister's hand. "Of course I will."

• • •

That evening, at just after six p.m., Myron Frisch, chairman of the SlimZ board, walked Candace down the aisle of Holy Cross Episcopal Church in Manhattan.

Over ninety people stood in the sanctuary as Rob and the Episcopal priest waited for Candace, who was wearing an Oscar de La Renta embroidered ivory lace wedding gown. All the SlimZ invitees—including Amanda—were present, along with their significant others. Deirdre Chandler sat next to Charles and Nancy Chadwick. The remaining guests were colleagues of the bride and groom, friends of Deirdre, and an assortment of clients and celebrities.

A feeling of serenity flooded through Candace as she approached the man she loved. Robert Simon Chandler was the right partner for her, and she looked forward to their future together. Marriage with him would be worlds different from the one she had had in her youth with Ted Morgan, who had paid little attention to her needs and even less to her feelings. Her father had given her away the first time, of course, and she missed him at this moment. Before he did, he had gently kissed her cheek, then looked into her eyes for a few seconds, his own eyes brimming with unspoken love.

She willed herself to push thoughts of him away and tried to focus on the present and what she was about to do. Her company had become her family in recent years. Her team at SlimZ—from Myron at the top down to the lowest-paid intern—had replaced the family she'd grown up with. They were the people she could count on, the people who cared about her. Her father would be proud of her success and happy that she had found a second chance at love.

Her mind flashed to yesterday's conversation with Helen. She didn't know what her sister-in-law had decided, but she felt she didn't need to know. And she'd agreed with Helen that, for all his bluster, Monty just wasn't brave enough to hurt anyone. He was desperate and angry right now, but in reality he was just a coward. Rob had been right: Monty's life was always going to be what it was. Candace had no responsibility for it. It wasn't up to her to take care of him or to finance a lifestyle he desired but hadn't earned.

A fake lifestyle.

His victim mentality was part of who he was—no, it *was* who he was—just like her drive and ambition were part of her. He owned his choices about his attitudes and his behavior. She would not enable him anymore, nor would she allow herself to feel guilty about what she had achieved. She wouldn't take heed of his empty, desperate threats, nor would she worry about what he might do in the future. He couldn't touch her. Though it was unfortunate that this was the reality, it couldn't be helped.

She had done all she could, and she had probably done too much—way too much. David had gotten the contractor to finish the work on the house over the last twenty-four hours, and she couldn't worry about it anymore. When it sold, she would cut ties with Monty, and she wouldn't have to deal with him again. If the house didn't sell—no, it would eventually, for the right price.

Then she could forget about it and about the money she had lost. She wouldn't be subjected to his pleas anymore, and she would be immune to his guilt trips. The irony was priceless: Monty had used her money to buy a condo and to subsidize a girlfriend while she was agonizing that she hadn't been generous enough and should do more. The truth was, nothing she had done or could ever do would dispel his belief that he was a victim. Nothing would change who he really was: a liar and a thief.

Her lawyer would contact David about the money Monty had diverted and they would get as much of it back as they could. Life wasn't just about money, anyway—she had learned that from her father. No, it was about holding on to the people you loved. Love included forgiveness—and sometimes that meant forgiving yourself.

Would her life have been different if she hadn't been careless and distracted so long ago, the day her mother died? Would things have turned out differently if she hadn't failed to have the tires on the car replaced after she was told to do so? Would the present be altered if she hadn't argued with her mother or said horrible things to her just before the accident?

Would Monty's life have been any different?

Perhaps, in some small ways, but not in the big ones. He had always been the person he was now, and so had she. The anguish that had tormented her, the guilt that had lived and even flourished deep inside of her, melted away. Like the last vestiges of a hard frost disappearing in the warm sunshine, the icy barrier enclosing her heart softened and vanished. The shame and regret that had tortured her for so long, that had stayed frozen in some dark, cold place in her soul, was gone.

She was not to blame, and she would live the rest of her life unafraid to feel. She was ready to begin the next chapter in her life and to start a new journey with the man who knew her best in the world. He would be her family now.

After she and Rob exchanged their vows and listened as the priest blessed their union, her new husband kissed her with perfect tenderness. Her heart was full of love.

• • •

"Worst case" became even worse than Helen had allowed herself to consider.

Her body had stopped responding to the antilabor drugs around one o'clock in the afternoon. Dr. Russell had had her wear a fetal monitor as contractions began soon thereafter and rapidly became closer together. Two interns and three nurses hovered around Helen, who insisted on having Dawn at her side. Frank waited in the waiting room for news. The doctor called Monty and left him a message to hurry to the hospital, but he didn't arrive until very late.

When he did, everything was over.

Just before nine o'clock, Dr. Russell decided that, despite Helen's wish to avoid it, the best course was to take the babies by caesarean section. Indications were that one of the twins might have the umbilical cord wrapped around his neck, and both babies were in distress.

However, before Helen could be prepped for emergency surgery, she delivered one twin vaginally, and then, shortly afterward, the other. Neither was given to his mother to be held.

The first baby was stillborn, and the other wasn't breathing and was nonresponsive.

He died two minutes later.

• • •

Twenty-four hours after Dawn's arrival at the hospital, she sat beside Helen's hospital bed, trying to console her sister.

Both women were still in shock. Monty had come and gone last night, and Helen was relieved when he left. The person she needed most was here with her.

Dawn would help her with arrangements for the boys. They would have a private memorial service this week, and afterward Frank would travel back to Chicago. Dawn was going to stay for the next two weeks to help with Adele as Helen recovered.

Dawn heard Helen's cell phone vibrate where it sat on the small counter by the sink. She glanced at it and looked back at her sister. "It's Candace."

"I'll talk to her," said Helen.

"Are you sure?"

"Yes. Would you grab it?"

Dawn did as requested and handed the phone to her sister.

"Candace?"

"Oh, Helen, I'm so very sorry."

Helen felt tears forming again as her throat constricted. She took a second, then said, "Thank you."

"Rob and I are coming down today. We're canceling our trip."

"No, Candace. Don't do that. Really. It's not necessary."

"Helen—"

"You just got married yesterday. You've been planning this honeymoon trip, and I would much rather you go."

"We can go anytime," said Candace. "I can't imagine what you've gone through."

Helen glanced at Dawn as she responded. "I know. But it's okay now. My sister and her husband are here—"

"Oh, good."

"And she's going to stay with me for two weeks."

"What about—"

"We're going to have a small, private service. It's really not necessary that you come to it. I'd feel more comfortable with just my sister and her husband—and mine."

"Helen, you're in shock. You've got to be. You've been through this pregnancy, and now this—"

"Candace, it's okay. I promise. Yes, I'm in shock, but I have Dawn here. I want you to go ahead and go on your trip. Give me time with my sister, and time to grieve. When you get back, we'll talk then."

"What about our conversation earlier?" asked Candace. "About everything you found out the other day? I'm still worried about you and Adele."

"We'll be fine. I can't think about all that now. He knows that I know. That's enough for the moment. We're going to get through the next few days together, and then we're going to heal. Trust me to handle this."

"I feel so bad, leaving while you're dealing with everything."

"Don't," said Helen. "Go and enjoy. Let me have time to figure things out. I may even be going home tomorrow."

"How do you feel? Physically?"

"Not all that bad, considering. I'm glad I didn't have surgery after all. The doctor said that it wouldn't have mattered. Nothing could have been done." Helen sucked in a breath.

"You'll be in my prayers."

"Thank you. And congratulations. How was the wedding?" Helen wiped a tear and looked back at Dawn.

"Wonderful. I had no idea what was happening to you, though. I wish someone had called."

"Well, we couldn't find Monty. I was going to call you today, after the boys were born." Tears now began to fall freely. "Candace, I have to go. Thanks so much for calling."

Helen handed Dawn the phone and shut her eyes, hoping to rest.

• • •

Late Monday afternoon, Helen was discharged from the hospital.

Dawn and Frank had picked up Adele the night before and taken her with them to the hotel. Helen had spent most of today alone—Monty didn't arrive to pick her up until she called, when she received her discharge papers. They had barely spoken on the way home.

Helen was glad they hadn't. She needed more time to think, though she'd been doing a lot of that already. She'd gotten over the shock of losing the boys, and now all she felt was a deep sadness.

She hadn't told anyone about Monty's assault on her Friday night, or even that they'd had a fight. It wouldn't have changed anything if she had. Once her water broke, the course of events had been set. Who knew if the babies had died because of what happened? What would talking about it accomplish? Nothing could bring her babies back, and now she had to go on with life.

When they got home, she'd told him to go over to the condo—or wherever else he wanted to go—and to leave her alone for the night. She wasn't ready to be in the same house with him yet. They had a lot of talking to do and things to figure out, but she was too tired right now. All she wanted to do was rest, relax, and get clean. She had showered this morning at the hospital, but she planned to take a long hot bath this evening before she went to bed.

Candace had called again and talked to Dawn, then reluctantly agreed to go on with her travel plans. She was probably in Fiji right now, staying in an exclusive luxury resort with her new husband. Helen was relieved that she had gone. The last thing she needed was Candace in Atlanta, entering the picture as Helen tried to get through the memorial while recovering from the births—deaths— of her babies.

No episiotomy had been necessary, just like with Adele. Helen had delivered both twins even faster than she had her daughter, who came in record time after a short, easy labor. But Helen's bottom was sore and she was having strong cramps as her uterus contracted. Dr. Russell had given her medication to prevent her milk from coming in, thank goodness. At least her back didn't hurt anymore. The twins had weighed just over five pounds each, and the burden of carrying them was gone. But that physical feeling of relief was bitter, and quite opposite to the joy she had anticipated of holding two babies in her arms.

She poured a glass of water, drank half of it, and placed it on her nightstand. Then she changed into a loose gown and stretched out on the queen-sized bed. Thank God Dawn was here to help her. Together they would figure out what to do for the service. Dawn's presence in the coming days would be a huge source of comfort at a time when Helen needed her the most.

Five minutes later, she succumbed to a deep sleep.

• • •

Monty pulled up in front of the dry cleaners and parked.

He needed to get his iPhone back. When he stopped here on Saturday afternoon to make them find it, they wouldn't even look without his dry cleaning ticket. Annoyed, he had argued and cussed until they threatened to call the cops. Then he accused them of stealing it and left in a huff. Late that night he found the ticket in Helen's car and decided to come back today and apologize.

Ticket in hand, he got out of the car and walked up to the door. It was locked. *Damn!* He looked to the right and saw the Closed sign. What place of business, besides a bank, was closed on Columbus Day? It wasn't even a real holiday, like Thanksgiving or

Christmas. He muttered under his breath and turned around. He'd have to wait one more day for the phone, and if they didn't give it to him then, he'd report it as a theft.

He opened the car door, slipped behind the wheel, and put the key in the ignition. He reached over to the glove box, where he would stash the cleaner's ticket until tomorrow. He flipped the box open and noticed a card on top of his car owner's manual. It was the card he had saved, the last birthday card from his mother. The card he had found in the rubble back in April after the tree fell on the cottage.

He grabbed it and opened it, rereading his mother's handwritten prophecy about his future. But this time, her words didn't evoke sadness or sorrow. No, he felt betrayed. His heart was full of disappointment, bitterness, and hatred.

Susannah hadn't been there for him as she promised she would be. No one was there for him, and no one cared about him. He ripped the card in half, tore the halves into small pieces, and let the pieces fall to the floor.

He felt a profound sense of loneliness, a feeling of being forgotten and written off. He was supposed to have been the father of twin sons, but they had been taken away from him, dying before they could even live. He would never know them. He couldn't share his feelings of grief and loneliness with Rachel. His own sister disdained him and had abandoned him. For the first time, he believed she wouldn't cave in and give him what he wanted. She was too wrapped up in her own life to care about his.

His wife had trained his daughter not to care about him, either. Adele picked up on her mother's attitude and parroted her words of disrespect. And it was Helen who was responsible for the boys' deaths. If she hadn't spied on him and provoked him, he wouldn't have gotten angry at her. Now he was trapped with her and with a child who didn't love him, and he had no way to get the things that he deserved.

His life was a mess because of Helen, and she would have to pay.

• • •

Helen woke almost three hours later.

She still wasn't hungry, but she felt dirty and very sore. The doctor had said she could take a soaking bath, and that was exactly what she wanted to do. She brushed her teeth first, then turned on the tap.

She walked back to the kitchen and looked at the clock. It was after nine o'clock. She decided to get her notebook, look over what she had written on Friday night, and write a letter to Monty. She wasn't sure if she would give it to him; she'd probably tear it up. But she needed to express her thoughts and feelings on paper and to map out the conditions under which she would stay with him. Things were different now, and he had to change if he wanted to continue to be married to her and to see Adele.

She picked up her notebook and searched in her purse for her favorite pen. Finding it, she took both to the bathroom, set them on a small stool beside the tub, and took off her gown. The bathroom was a spacious one for a house this size. The small shower was in the corner and the claw-footed tub sat next to it, under the window. The toilet was on the other side of the pedestal sink. Helen sat down to pee and flush, then stood to inspect her body in the mirror.

Her skin was sagging, but her stomach looked better now than it did earlier. Her breasts seemed to have deflated a little. Her ugly scar was still there and always would be. But she wasn't going to let it bother her anymore. She had decided to take Dawn's advice and stop trying to hide it. If people didn't like it, if they stared at it or asked questions, so what? After what Helen had been through this year, did any of that matter anymore? She was sick of worrying about it. It was skin, that was all, and it wasn't who she was.

She had to take control of who she was, right now and from now on.

She stepped into the tub. The water felt wonderful as she eased herself in. She pulled her hair into a ponytail, poured a few drops of bath oil into the tub, and leaned back, relaxing. When the water level was just right, she turned off the tap and exhaled. After a moment she picked up her pen and started writing.

She wrote about her scar, her demons about it, and her decision to let them go. She didn't care what it looked like anymore, and she wouldn't let anyone—including Monty—make her. She wrote about her self-image—her looks and her acceptance of them. She was still young and she would recover from this pregnancy in a matter of weeks. She might not be the most beautiful woman in the world, but she was attractive. She would be confident in how she looked.

She wrote about her blessings. Even though her babies had died, she was alive. She was a mother. She had a beautiful little girl whom she treasured. She had lost her babies, but with their loss, her excuses for not standing up to Monty for so long had disappeared. Knowing that he had betrayed her made her feel even more determined. She would stop pretending that things between them would somehow get better on their own.

She wrote that she would no longer allow him to abuse her—not verbally, and not physically. She would not continue to play the victim or walk on eggshells around him, afraid to piss him off. He would have to accept the new, stronger her, and he would have to change.

Her pen flew across the page, strength and resolve flowing through it to the paper. She listed the conditions she would demand that her husband meet. First, he had to end it with Rachel immediately—Helen would have to see her in person and talk to her, to prove that he had. Monty was lucky that Helen hadn't decided to divorce him because of his infidelity; most women would. She had decided to give him another chance to be faithful, so that Adele could know her father.

Second, Rachel had to move out of the condo. Helen had to have proof of this, too. Then the condo had to be listed for sale. Just like for the house on Arcadia, Monty would have to let Candace decide the listing price. He would have to trust his sister to sell both properties for as much as the market would bear, even if it was much less that what he thought it would. When the condo sold, the funds would go to pay off the HELOC. When the house on Arcadia sold, the money would be applied to the rest of the debt.

Then, if Candace had to write anything off, Monty and Helen would sign a note to pay her back over time. They couldn't expect her to pay for their bad decisions by forgiving their debt. They would have to take responsibility.

Helen would have to meet Mack and Jeremy, Monty's so-called employers. She would have to know exactly what he was doing for them and how much he was being paid. If there were no such people—if Monty had been lying about it, which she suspected—then he would have to hit the pavement to look for a job. He would have to find work. He would report everything he did to her. There would be no secret cell phones, email addresses, or anything else.

Monty would have to cooperate in downsizing their lifestyle in the coming weeks and months. Helen would start looking for a new job as soon as she could, but in the meantime they would communicate about everything, especially money. They might have to sell their cars and buy cheaper ones. Anything nonessential would be dropped from their budget: entertainment, restaurants, cable TV, and coffee at Starbucks. They would rent this house until they had a big nest egg, and they wouldn't rush to buy anything. And they would never again take money from Candace, ask her to make them a loan, or ask her to cosign a loan for them.

After the tragedy that had just happened, Monty would have to earn back Helen's trust as a husband and a father. He would have to put her and Adele first. He would have to be loving, respectful, and protective towards them instead of mean and self-absorbed. If he wanted a relationship with his daughter, he had to stop ignoring her and start showing interest and involvement in her life. He had to begin helping Helen with her every day, whether they were to have any children in the future or not.

If he decided not to meet her conditions—if he decided to abandon her and Adele, the way Helen's father had abandoned his wife and kids—then she'd have no choice but to let it happen. She'd build a new life for herself and her daughter, and she wouldn't look back. She might keep the option open for him to know his daughter, but she wouldn't insist that he do. She wouldn't hide from Adele the truth of who he was.

Helen put the notebook on the stool and leaned back, closing her eyes, her pen still in her right hand. The hot water was so soothing, and her muscles were relaxed. She took a deep breath and felt at peace, almost in a slumber.

Then her eyes opened wide. Two hands were gripping her neck and strangling her, pushing her down. Monty's hands. He forced her head under the surface as water splashed on the floor and wall. She panicked, thrashing and kicking in the slippery tub and banging her elbows against the sides, her core muscles tender and weak. He pushed her farther down as she squirmed and flailed wildly.

Her head was completely underwater. The recurring dream she'd had since childhood flashed in her mind. She had to push him away from her and break his hold on her neck. His hands tightened. She couldn't breathe.

She pushed against the end of the tub with both feet, trying to force her head above the surface. Her feet slipped up and out and he forced her head and shoulders farther down. She pushed her arms and elbows against the sides of the tub, finally getting traction. As she pushed and squirmed, she felt his grip slip from her neck. She rose out of the water, clenched her right hand around her pen, swung it backwards, and felt it stop.

Then all at once, his hands fell away and she heard him scream. She felt the pen jerk out of her wet grip and she grabbed the side of the tub. She turned and sloshed, looking around frantically for her weapon. She got up and jumped out of the water, almost falling to the floor but righting herself, arms flailing in the air.

Full of terror, she stood naked on the checkered tile and faced him. Her pen stuck out of his eyeball. Blood spurted everywhere as she stared at him in horror. He staggered toward her, still screaming, his face red and his other eye wild and fixed on her. In that pulsating eye, she saw his madness. She backed away unsteadily toward the closed door.

He came at her, arms outstretched. Her back and head hit the door. She was trapped.

"My eye!" he screamed. "Oh my fucking God! You ugly fucking bitch! *I'm going to kill you!*"

Out of her peripheral vision she saw the toilet tank lid—it was sitting awry, as usual. She turned and grabbed it with both hands. Adrenaline soaring, she swung it hard as he lunged at her.

Blood oozed from his skull as he fell to the floor, writhing in pain. She staggered back, gasping and shaking. He lay on his side, his legs pulled in a fetal position. The lid was in shattered pieces on the floor, surrounded by a mixture of blood and fluid. She jumped over him, ran into the bedroom, grabbed her phone, and dialed 911.

"My husband attacked me and I hit him! He needs an ambulance!"

The paramedics arrived in four minutes, but it was too late. Monty was dead.

22

Beginning

Over eight months later, Helen stood at the door to her apartment and turned her key in the lock. After work, she had picked Adele up and driven her over to Dawn and Frank's house to spend the night. Helen was looking forward to her date this evening with John Caldwell, Frank's second cousin and the man she had been seeing since March. John would be here to pick her up at seven for dinner at Gabriella's, a posh new restaurant.

Helen had met him back in February, only a month after she and Adele moved in to this apartment and three weeks after her first day at Scopa Diboli, a Chicago graphic designer firm. John was a CPA with a major accounting firm; his wife of seven years had died of a brain aneurysm back in 2008.

Helen dropped her keys in her purse and set it on the kitchen counter. She pulled a glass from the cabinet and poured herself some water. Today was Friday, July 1, the start of the holiday weekend, and it had been a hot day, with temperatures rising to the upper eighties. A year-old memory flashed in her mind: Monty's joke about the two seasons of Chicago, "winter, and the fourth of July." She shuddered.

How different her life was now from what it had been last summer, and last fall.

That awful night in October, a night that she still couldn't forget, the paramedics had arrived to find her in shock. She had thrown on a robe and was pressing a towel against her dead husband's skull, blood flowing from it and tears streaming down her face. Her hair was wet and her throat was covered with purple bruises. Her pen was lodged in Monty's eye, and his finger marks bulged on her neck.

The police had arrived and had forced Helen to recount the chronology of events over and over. Her story of Monty's attack on her was more than plausible, as were her claims of his past abusive and violent behavior. Dr. Russell told police that Helen had experienced trauma to the uterus and echoed Dawn's suspicions that her ruptured membranes were caused by a domestic assault. Records showed that after Helen's first night in the hospital, Monty had been absent for much of her stay, including the delivery of her twins.

For Helen, the next few weeks had been hell—but a different kind of hell than what she had already experienced.

While the police were still gathering evidence, she recovered from childbirth and buried her twin babies. With Dawn's help, she organized a private memorial service at the same cemetery where the boys' paternal grandparents had been laid to rest—and where their father would also be interred.

Helen drained the water from her glass and set it in the sink. Grabbing her purse, she walked into her bedroom and pulled out her phone to check for messages—there were none. She put it on her dresser and opened the top drawer to search for her newest pair of SlimZ.

She planned to wear a clingy short black dress tonight and to take a thin cardigan along in her bag. Not to cover her shoulder, though—she was over that. The sweater would be needed just in case it got cool outside later tonight, as it often did here. Her dress had spaghetti straps and it flattered her figure, one that didn't look like she'd ever had a baby. She might not even wear the SlimZ underneath—she wasn't sure she needed to.

When she met John back in February, she'd been ten pounds heavier, but had lost almost all of her pregnancy weight. They'd gone out for coffee at first, then lunch, then to a concert. He hadn't wanted to rush things, and neither had she. He had adored Adele from the moment he met her. When he and Helen became physically intimate, which was a recent event, he didn't react when he saw her scar. He accepted it as part of who she was, something unique and uncommon, not imperfect.

She leaned toward the mirror over her dresser and examined it. Funny how the scar had once troubled her so much, had even defined her self-image. Now it didn't. It still branded her, but as no more of a mark than if she'd had red hair or freckles. She was happy to be who she was—*all* of who she was.

When the authorities delved deep into her private life after Monty's death, they had questioned her about it. Perhaps they had wondered if Monty had caused it, or if she would say he had. Of course, she'd told the truth: that it was the result of a childhood accident. The only physical marks that Monty had left on her were much more recent.

Everything became more intense a few days later, when the police recovered Monty's iPhone. The cleaners found it, and after a call to Rachel Benton, identified its owner and turned it in to law enforcement. The information it provided to police pointed to a possible motive for murder: Monty was cheating on his wife and was hiding funds.

The nightmare that had followed felt unreal. At the time, Helen was afraid it would never end. But she had lived through it and had survived. She studied her face in the mirror, then stood up straight and stretched her arms back behind her. She'd had a long day and a long week at the office working on multiple projects. Her upper back and shoulders were a little achy from spending hours at the computer. It was just after six p.m. and she was looking forward to that first glass of wine.

Thank God others had confirmed her account of her life with Monty and had accurately described how malicious and depraved he was. Dawn, Candace, Rob, and David had all come forward to the police with details of Monty's behavior and had provided emails he had written. The tangle of lies he had told his wife and his sister about the house on Arcadia Lane began to unravel. Rachel Benton didn't defend her lover and wanted nothing to do with his family. By Thanksgiving, all the evidence indicated that Helen killed her husband purely in self-defense as he attempted to strangle her in the bathtub. To murder her.

She and Adele had driven up north that weekend and had never looked back. The little girl had missed her father at first, but as time passed, she had accepted his absence.

They had stayed with Dawn and Frank for the next six weeks until Helen found this apartment. During that time, Arcadia sold for slightly under a million one, and Monty's condominium sold for over six hundred thousand. The Carawans' debts to Candace and to the bank were paid in full, and Candace didn't have to write off a loss. Helen had felt bad that she couldn't repay the amounts Candace had gifted the family, but her sister-in-law assured her that gifts were gifts, no strings attached and no repayment necessary.

She heard her phone buzz, turned, and picked it up.

"John?"

"Hey. I know we said seven, but if you're almost ready, I can come now. If that's okay?"

"Well—"

"I just—I can't wait to see you." He sounded breathless.

Helen smiled. "Then come on. We can have a drink here first if you like."

"I'm almost there. See you in a few."

• • •

Candace Chandler entered her Manhattan apartment and began to rifle through the day's mail lying on a table.

"Hello, love," Rob called from the kitchen. "How was your day?"

"Delightful," said Candace, not looking up. "My goodness. Did you see this invitation from Jess?"

Rob walked into the room and stopped next to his wife. "Yes, I believe so."

Candace turned and looked up at him, her eyebrows raised. "An August wedding in Atlanta! It's going to be so hot and humid then. What were they thinking?"

"Perhaps that it would be easier for relatives with school-age children to attend."

"I suppose so. Though early June would have been much nicer. And I could have had a drink."

Rob smiled. "It's just for nine months. Or eight, now."

Candace gave a weak smile. "I hope I can do this mothering thing. I certainly have my doubts."

"You'll not just do it, darling, you'll excel at it. Have no fear." He reached an arm around her and pulled her to him, kissing her. "We'll be wonderful parents, I'm certain of it."

After a second, Candace pushed back and placed her hands on his upper arms. "I hope you're right, Rob. I mean, I know we made the right decision. And even though I'm glad our baby is on the way, I'm apprehensive."

"That's natural. I feel somewhat the same."

"Do you?"

Rob reached around and pulled his wife closer. "Of course. But you'll see. Life is a wonderful thing, and as you said, we'd both regret it if we had decided not to take the plunge."

She gave him a tender look and slid her hands up on his shoulders. "You are so good for me."

"And you, for me."

She stroked his cheek, then stepped back and out of his arms. "But, practically speaking now. We have a lot of planning to do for the baby, and things are busy as ever right now. I'm so glad I found Lydia."

"So she's working out well?"

Candace cocked her head. "Very well. She's everything Jess was, and then some."

"Older, wiser, more mature?"

Candace laughed, turned, and slipped off her high heels. "Definitely more mature. Only three years older, but much savvier."

Rob turned, picked up the pieces of mail, and placed them in a stack on the table. "How's Jess doing in design?"

"Swimmingly," said Candace, throwing him a look. "Paula says she's eager to please."

"Well, that's a happy ending then. Or, beginning."

"Yes," said Candace. She stepped toward the kitchen. "She'll learn a lot working under Lucy on the new maternity SwimZ line."

"Good. If it's half as successful as the rest—"

"It will be, at least. I'm convinced of it."

Rob looked over at her. "Your confidence has always been alluring. Even sexy, I dare say."

"Well," Candace said while turning around, her eyes dancing. "SwimZ made a huge splash in the stores last winter and spring, just in time for the season. Despite all the issues of the fall."

"And your stock price has been soaring ever since. You absolutely murdered your competition. Sorry. Bad choice of words. Forgive me."

"Pshaw, Rob. I mean, let's don't deny it—Monty *did* try to kill Helen. He was guilty of attempted murder. But I never thought she was responsible for his death. If anyone was, it was me. I should have gotten her to get a restraining order or something."

"I doubt you could have done that. Until that night, he hadn't committed a crime."

"Yes, well, he was dangerous, and I knew it. Perhaps—"

"My love," said Rob as he walked toward her. "It's tragic that he's gone, but you're not to blame. Neither you nor Helen was responsible for what happened to him. He was. I'm just glad that Helen protected herself that night, and that she and Adele are doing well now."

"Yes. The thing is, there's a part of me that's—well, that's relieved he's gone. That's so terrible to say, or even to think."

"No, it's not. You're allowed to feel that way. Look at what he put you through. What he put his wife and child through."

"I know. I can't help but wonder, though, if it could all have been prevented, if I had just given him what he wanted. Which I could have done."

"I don't think it would have, not in the end, anyway. It might only have prolonged Helen's agony, and yours, too."

"But—"

"If you'd given him the house on Arcadia Lane, even—let's say, back in the beginning. If you'd just outright gifted it to him, do you think he would have stopped there?"

"Well—no. I don't."

"Right. And if you'd done exactly what you did in the beginning, but *then* done what he demanded of you last year—paid off the bank, given him the house and ten million—"

"Rob, I know where you're going. No, he never would have stopped coming to me for money. The more success I had financially, the more demanding he would have become. He would have never left me alone."

"Exactly. And during all that time, his wife would have had to deal with him. He'd probably still be lying to her, and of course he would have continued having affairs. And he would have been dangerous, or at least abusive—that, we know."

Candace leaned back against a counter. "Though it feels like we're rationalizing, I think you're right. In any case, what happened, happened. I can't change any of it now. Though Helen and I will never be close, we're more connected through all of this—through tragedy and heartache. That little girl is my niece, Rob. I love her, and I want her to know our child. We need to stay in touch and be supportive, especially after the dark times we've survived."

Rob approached his wife. "Of course, darling. We will. Now, what about your plans for the rest of the maternity lines? Are you doing several?"

"Not that many. We're just putting our toes in the water, not jumping in the pool."

"Speaking of water, how about a drink before we go out to dinner? Hard for me, soft for you? Then we'll continue this conversation."

"I do need to stay hydrated. Let me take a quick shower, and I'll join you in a few minutes."

Rob gave her a look. "Hmm. Perhaps we should forget the drinks and conversation, and *I'll* join *you*, right now."

Candace smiled. *"Bonne idée, mon amour."*

Acknowledgments

I am thankful to the many people who assisted me in the writing of this book. Elen Christopher helped me with many of the details of Candace's lifestyle, gave me several key suggestions, and offered her unceasing support. Kathy Fowler and Becky Dannenfelser supplied me with important elements about the world of retail and women's apparel companies. Special thanks to advance readers Elen, Lucille (Lucy) Spann, and Dennis McDermott for their opinions, comments, and advice that helped make *Underwater* a much stronger, better novel.

I am grateful to the Writers Circle Critique Group for their feedback and encouragement, especially co-leaders Gelia Dolcimascolo and Beth Horton, and members Mona Haddad, Bill Hines, Jim Huskins, Jaya Kamlani, Freddie McGee, Ron Saint, and June Smith. I owe a debt of gratitude to Gelia and Beth for their continual support and amazing suggestions, and to Beth for reviewing all the sections she missed. Thanks to Jim for his constant encouragement, friendship, and ability to make me laugh; to Freddie for teaching me about pacing and plot; to Jaya for inspiring me to continue and to believe in myself; to Ron, Mona, and June for their spot-on observations and comments; and to Bill for finding my extra *had*s, and for helping me to "get it right."

I am also thankful to Bill for connecting me with my wonderful and thorough editor, fellow Tar Heel Laura Ownbey. Laura worked diligently on the first edition of *Underwater*, and her commitment was outstanding. She cheerfully listened to me, and pushed me to dig deep into each character's motivations and emotions.

For this second, current edition, I am grateful to Anh Schluep, my editor at Thomas & Mercer, and to the entire editing and proofreading team, for their professional focus, direction, and hard work to improve, polish, and sharpen the novel.

I thank my author friends Peter Morlon-McKenzie, Ernie Pick, and Don Reichardt for their friendship and much-needed words of encouragement as I worked on *Underwater*. I am also grateful to my wonderful cover artist, Michael Faron (and to Peter for referring him), for his hard work, patience, and creative focus on the first edition cover. I thank Thomas & Mercer cover artist Scott Barrie for his work to revamp, enhance, and refine the original image into a powerful and updated second edition cover.

Special thanks to my mother, Sally Cooper; my daughter, Annette; my son, Jack; and my mother-in-law, Mary McDermott, for encouraging me and believing in me. As always, I'm grateful to my husband, Dennis, for his unending love and support.

About the Author

 Julia McDermott was born in Dallas, Texas; grew up in Atlanta, Georgia; and earned a degree in economics from the University of North Carolina at Chapel Hill. She also studied French and spent her junior year in the south of France. She and her husband were underwater on their first house in Texas (before being underwater was cool).

She loves reading, watching football, cheering on the UNC Tar Heels, France, and all things French. The mother of four, she resides in Atlanta with her husband and family.